THE
THIEF-TAKER'S
APPRENTICE

Also by Stephen Deas from Gollancz:

THE ADAMANTINE PALACE
THE KING OF THE CRAGS

THE
THIEF-TAKER'S
APPRENTICE

STEPHEN DEAS

GOLLANCZ
LONDON

Copyright © Stephen Deas 2010
All rights reserved

The right of Stephen Deas to be identified as the author
of this work has been asserted by him in accordance with
the Copyright, Designs and Patents Act 1988.

First published in Great Britain in 2010 by Gollancz
An imprint of the Orion Publishing Group
Orion House, 5 Upper St Martin's Lane,
London WC2H 9EA
An Hachette UK Company

A CIP catalogue record for this book
is available from the British Library

ISBN 978 0 575 09447 5 (Cased)
ISBN 978 0 575 09448 2 (Export Trade Paperback)

1 3 5 7 9 10 8 6 4 2

Typeset by Deltatype Ltd, Birkenhead, Merseyside

Printed in Great Britain by Clays Ltd, St Ives plc

The Orion Publishing Group's policy is to use papers
that are natural, renewable and recyclable products and
made from wood grown in sustainable forests. The logging
and manufacturing processes are expected to conform to
the environmental regulations of the country of origin.

www.stephendeas.com
www.orionbooks.co.uk

This one is for Christopher and Evan and Lily.
Because I can.

Be all that you can be.

Same goes for the rest of you.

PART ONE

THE THIEF-TAKER

1

BERREN

The crowd had come to watch three men die. Most of them had no idea who the three men were. Nor did they particularly care. They'd come into Four Winds Square for the spectacle, for a bit of blood, for a Sun-day afternoon of entertainment. They'd come for the jugglers and the fire-breathers, the pies and the pastry-sellers, the singers and the speakers. They'd come for everything the city had to offer, and that's what they got.

The thief ran through them with practised ease. The crowd barely noticed he was there. He slipped between the larger bodies around him like an eel between a fisherman's fingers, finding space where none seemed to exist. If anyone had asked him how old he was, he might have said twelve or he might have said sixteen, depending on who was doing the asking. The truth probably lay somewhere in between. The truth was that he didn't know and he didn't much care. He was small for a boy who might nearly have been a man, and his name was Berren.

He'd come for the executions like everyone else, but he'd come for the crowd too. A watcher, perched on one of the rooftops around the square and taking an interest in his progress, would have seen him pause now and then amid all his motion. Each pause marked the crowd as a fraction poorer and Berren as a token richer. The same watcher, if he stared for long enough, would have seen that Berren was

3

slowly meandering his way towards the front of the crowd. When the executioner and his charges finally emerged, Berren had every intention of watching from as close as he could get.

After a time the crowd began to hush. At one end of the square stood a wooden platform, built especially for the occasion. For the last few hours a succession of dancers and jugglers and other petty entertainers had paid for the privilege of using it. The crowd had largely ignored them, talking amongst themselves. The coming of quiet meant something worth watching was about to happen. Berren began to worm his way further forwards. He was a head shorter than most of the people around him, and navigated by the simple expedient of watching where everyone else was looking, and then heading that way. From time to time he caught a fleeting glimpse of the platform. A man in yellow robes was standing there now, making slow gestures with his hands. Even Berren knew enough to know that the yellow made him a priest.

As he reached the front of the crowd, his progress slowed. He changed direction and edged sideways until he reached the corner of the square. Four Winds Square was in the centre of the Courts District of Deephaven city. The buildings around it were high and made of stone, with tall doors of heavy wood and dark wobbly glass in their windows. Each of the doors had a stone lintel protruding a good six inches from the wall. Boys smaller than him filled them, jostling for space, squeezed up precariously close to the ends but never quite falling off. Berren spotted a gap on the corner of one of them. He scaled the wall and made it his own. It was too narrow to be properly comfortable, but from up there he could see everything. That more than made up for having to constantly push himself against the stone and the grumbling boys next to him.

The priest was gone. The executioner had ascended the

platform now, a big brawny man standing with his legs braced apart, holding an axe that was almost as tall as he was. Behind the executioner stood the three who'd been sentenced to die, chained and surrounded by guards. Beside them, someone bald and dressed in fine clothes was making another speech of some sort. The crowd wasn't very interested. They hadn't come for speeches and they were talking restlessly again, so that Berren could barely hear anything that was said. Snatches reached him, the occasional two or three words, not enough to make any sense. He didn't care any more than the rest of the crowd. Executions were a rarity. He was here to see people have their heads cut off, not to listen to boring speeches. The crowd agreed. It was late spring, the month of Floods, and the stifling afternoons of humid summer heat were arriving early this year.

Berren wondered briefly what the three men had done. He knew a thing or two about how the city punished thieves. Boys like him caught cutting purses usually got a beating and that was that. Berren had had plenty of those. If the watch knew your face and you got unlucky then you got a branding or maybe had a finger cut off. He shuddered to think about that sort of thing. Losing a finger, that was ... well, something he didn't want to think about. Just as well Master Hatchet kept things sweet with the watch around his piece of the city. Master Hatchet was a bear in a man's body, but that wasn't his secret. His boys, when they weren't thieving, kept the streets around Shipwrights and the south end of the Fishing Quarter clear of animal filth. Most particularly, they kept Reeper Hill clear of animal filth. Every morning and every evening and all through the night, Hatchet would have someone up there with a dung-cart. Keeping sweet with the ladies on Reeper Hill mattered more to Master Hatchet than anything else. Their favour was what gave him clout.

People lost their whole hands sometimes. He'd heard of

it but he'd never seen it happen. Mostly, if the city decided it couldn't stand to put up with you any more, you got loaded onto a barge and shipped off up the river to the imperial mines. The mines were somewhere in the north, hundreds and thousands of miles away where it was always raining and cold and no one ever came back. Berren didn't know what you had to do to have your head cut off, though. Every now and then the city just decided to put on a show and that was that. They didn't do it very often, which was why today there was such a crowd come out to watch.

The boy on the lintel next to him nudged him. ''Scuse me. You ever seen one of these before?'

Berren looked at him with all the scorn he could muster. The boy must have been eight. ''Course I have,' he lied. 'Lots.' He snorted and shook his head as though it was the stupidest question in the world, but the boy didn't give up.

'What happens, then?'

'Wait and see.'

'Is there lots of blood? I hope there's lots.'

'Did you know that the heads, after they get chopped off, they can still move their eyes and wrinkle their nose and talk and things like that for hours before they die?' Hatchet himself had told him that.

The boy's eyes grew wide and his jaw dropped. 'No! Really? Can you go and talk to them afterwards?'

Berren shrugged. 'I suppose. If you want to. If they don't take them away.' Then the man on the platform did something that got Berren's full attention. He stopped talking and held up a purse. The crowd's murmuring subsided, enough that Berren caught a few words of what he said next. Something about a reward. Something about ten gold emperors. *Ten* gold emperors.

A new man came forward from behind the executioner. The one who'd caught the men about to be killed. The thief-taker. From what Berren could see, there was nothing special about him. He didn't have particularly rich clothes. He didn't have a fancy sword or anything like that. If Berren had seen him in the street, he would have thought him a shopkeeper, or maybe a foreman from the docks. But now ...

Now he had a purse, given to him by the man with the fine clothes. Now Berren would think of him as a man who had ten emperors in his pocket ...

'What's happening?' asked the boy beside him, craning his neck and squinting to see. Berren cuffed him silent. Ten emperors! His eyes went wide even thinking about it. He felt himself wobble and almost tumbled off the lintel. He'd never heard of such a fortune!

The man who now had this fortune stepped back while the executioner came forward again. The prisoners were dragged to the front of the platform so that everyone could see. The executioner made a big show of his axe, holding it high so everyone could see that too. He spun and twirled it, the axe head tracing wild arcs in the air, until he brought it down on a thick lump of wood and split it. Splinters showered all around. The crowd roared. The three prisoners were forced down into the three blocks that waited for them. Berren barely noticed. He was watching the man with the ten emperors, lurking in the shadows at the back of the platform.

Suddenly the executioner brought down his axe again. The boy beside him let out a soft whistle of awe. Berren's heart leapt. One of the prisoners had been beheaded and he hadn't even seen it! The body was still there but the head was gone. He noted the dark spattered streaks across the planks and the stain where the head had fallen. The executioner was holding it up in the air now, gripping its hair, making sure everyone got a good look at his handiwork.

Berren's eyes began to dart back and forth, from the man in the shadows to the executioner and back again, back and forth, back and forth. He didn't dare lose track of the man with ten emperors in his pocket but he wanted to see the head, too. He squinted, trying to see if it was still moving. A waning trickle of blood still dripped from its neck; he couldn't see it, but he could see the dark stains, spattering across the pale wood around the headsman's feet.

Abruptly the executioner turned and tossed the head away into a large basket lined with straw that was on the platform behind him. He stood beside his second victim and raised his axe. The man in the shadows hadn't moved. Berren held his breath and let his eyes settle on the axe. He watched it start to fall, slowly it seemed. His own heart thumped in his chest, slow and hard, and he felt a thrilling tightness inside him. As the axe struck flesh, he gasped with glee. Skin and bone parted. Blood sprayed further than Berren could spit. He was almost rigid with exhilaration.

One of the dead man's legs twitched with such force that it almost twisted the body off its block. The executioner shied away in surprise. One foot slipped in the pool of blood. When he caught his balance, he gave the severed head a hefty kick. The head rolled away and fell down somewhere under the platform. The crowd laughed, but by then Berren was already searching again for the man in the shadows.

The man still hadn't moved. Berren sighed with relief.

For the last execution, he allowed himself to relax and take in everything the executioner did. He appreciated the careful preparation, the cleaning of the axe head, the touch of a sharpening stone. When it fell, he watched and grinned. The last one was every bit as good as the first. Not as much blood as he'd hoped, but still quite a bit. When the executioner picked up the last head and held it up for the crowd to view, Berren strained his eyes to see whether anything was still moving. He squinted. He was sure he saw the dead head blink.

He turned to the boy beside him, overflowing with excitement. 'Did you see that? He blinked! Did you see it?'

The younger boy's goggling eyes stayed riveted to the head. 'Yeh yeh, it did, yeh.'

Berren stared intently at the head again, peering in case there was more. Finally, when the executioner turned to go, Berren sent his gaze back in search of the man in the shadows.

He was gone.

2
TEN EMPERORS IN AN ALLEY

Patience didn't come easily to Berren. He shifted back and forth on his lintel until the crowds had dispersed and the square was almost empty. Then he dropped to the ground and crept from shadow to shadow, eyeing the building where the man with the small fortune had gone. He wasn't entirely sure what he was doing. He was already late. Even if he ran all the way back to Shipwrights, he'd still get a cuffing from Master Hatchet. Didn't like his boys out too late, did the master. At least not unless it was his errands they were on. Berren had a decent enough take, too. Enough that he could give it over and keep a few pennies to himself without Hatchet getting too suspicious. That was the unspoken deal. The more you handed over, the less likely you were to get searched. Gods help you if you got searched and Hatchet found something. Boys who did that once learned not to do it again. Boys who made a habit of it wound up face-down in the bay.

Ten gold emperors, though. That was something else. Hatchet's eyes would likely pop right out of his head. Or he could keep it. Keep it and run away so far that even Hatchet couldn't reach him. Then live like a king. That's how much ten emperors was, wasn't it?

So he didn't go home and he paid no mind to the restless worries that told him to leave a man such as this thief-taker well alone. He'd been cutting purses and picking pockets for more than half his years and that was enough to be considered an expert in any other trade. No, he didn't go home; instead he watched and he waited, slinking from one corner of the square to another, trying not to arouse the suspicions of the soldiers who stood on watch there. They weren't the sorts of soldiers he was used to either. In the rest of the city, the various district militias wore whatever they could get their hands on, and carried clubs and sticks, or maybe knives if they were lucky or happened to spend their days as a butcher. The soldiers here were different. They wore uniforms and carried swords. They had mail shirts and shiny steel helmets and on the arms of their surcoats were flaming birds, bright red on a black field. They were the emperor's soldiers, and no one Berren knew had a nice word to say for those who wore the colours of the emperor.

Maybe they thought he was too far beneath them; although they watched him, they left him alone, and eventually Berren saw what he was waiting for. The man from the platform, the thief-taker with ten gold emperors in his pocket. He came out of the front door of the courthouse and walked straight across the square, in plain view, bold as brass. He still didn't look like much. If anything he was a bit short, a bit skinny. His boots were battered and worn and most of him was wrapped up in a stained leather overcoat that had clearly seen better days. The coat hid most of the rest of him. It was much too hot for the thick humid air of a Deephaven spring and made him almost impossible to miss.

He was also on his own. Berren felt a new anxiety surge inside him. The man was a thief-taker, and good enough at it to bring in men worth hanging. Surely he wasn't so daft as to walk through the streets of the city with all that money and no bodyguard. But as Berren was wondering about that, his legs were already moving. As far as the rest of him was concerned, he had to get in quick. He'd seen three or four others while he'd been waiting. Men lurking around the fringes of the square. Big men with sticks. Probably there were more, and they looked like the sort who'd take a runt like Berren and break him over their knee just because they could. One way or another the man with the fortune was in for a mugging. Best, then, if Berren got to the gold first. He jammed his hand into his pocket and fingered the tiny knife he kept there, the blade only as long as his finger but sharp as a razor. His purse-cutting knife. Secretly, because he'd heard that all good swords got given names, he called it Stealer. Not that he'd ever dare admit something like that in front of Master Hatchet or the other boys.

He followed the thief-taker out of the square. To his horror, almost the first thing the man did was to turn off the main road and walk into a narrow alley. Berren could only stand and watch as two other men followed suit. A third suddenly sprinted away, probably dashing for the far end. For a second, Berren hesitated. The man with the fortune was about to get his throat cut. The men who'd be doing that for him were the sort that even Berren went out of his way to avoid. Almost every instinct told him to turn and go, cut and run, take his beating for being late and be glad to still be alive. You didn't mess with cut-throats. About the only instinct that disagreed was a new one that had started to rear its head in the last few months. One that said that he didn't have to listen to *anyone* any more, not even himself. *Ten emperors*, it kept saying to him. *The emperor's face, stamped on gold. Ten of them!*

The air had grown still and heavy, like a warm, damp blanket. Berren took a deep breath and dived in.

The sun was sinking low by now and the buildings on either side of the alley were tall in this part of the city. The air was gloomy and dank and smelled stale, of sweat and piss as well as the ever-present stink of rotting fish. Berren found the deepest shadows and darted from one to the next, hiding in doorways. He could see the two men in front of him and he could see the knives cupped in their hands. The man with the small fortune was a little way ahead. He seemed unaware that he was being followed. Berren crept closer.

The first fat splats of the evening rains began to hit the cobbles. A moment later, sheets of it were hissing down, soaking everything. The thief-taker had almost reached the end of the alley. As he drew close, the third man, flushed and out of breath, entered in front of him. Through the blurring roar of the rain, he held one hand cupped loosely at his side. Like the others. Berren pressed himself into a doorway and froze. He knew how this played out. The first man would stick his knife into his victim's guts as they passed and walk on as if nothing had happened. The other two would jump in from behind and force him to the ground. When they'd got what they wanted, they'd either slit his throat or simply leave him to bleed to death. And then they'd run. All Berren had to do was watch through the rain as carefully as he could. He had to make sure he knew exactly which one of them made off with the purse. That was all. Didn't have to do anything else. Just had to use his eyes and not be fooled.

And then what? He didn't know. Follow the fortune in gold, probably. He didn't have time to think about that. It was happening. He held his breath, as the man with the money and the man with the knife came together ...

... And then something happened that Berren couldn't quite explain. The rains cascaded down. Rivulets of water were already running through the crevices of the alley. Fat drops ran into Berren's eyes. He blinked, and the man with the knife doubled up and crumpled to the ground. Berren hadn't even seen the thief-taker move, yet now he was suddenly facing back the way he'd come. He held a short and stubby sword that glittered wetly all the way to its hilt, bloody rainwater dripping off it. The two men who'd followed him faltered. They seemed paralysed as the thief-taker leapt between them. The sword blurred in several arcs. Blood and rain sprayed all across the alley. The men fell over. It was done in a blink, so quick that the two throat-cutters had barely even moved. Berren stared, frozen in awe ...

The thief-taker walked straight at him, grabbed him by the arm and pulled him out of his shelter and into the twilight and the rain. Close up, there was something odd-looking about the man. Something exotic. Not someone who'd been born to this city, that was for sure. Didn't look right. Didn't smell right either.

'Are you with them, boy?' Through the hammering of the rain, the voice sounded refined and educated. There was another hint of something foreign there, too.

Berren shook his head. The man with the sword let him go.

'I'm not going to kill you, boy. So if you weren't with them, what is it? Keeping an eye on me for someone else? Or were you thinking of having a go at my gold yourself?'

Berren said nothing. His mouth wouldn't move. The man crouched down in front of him.

'You're not old enough to be working someone like me on your own. Who sent you, boy? Who looks after you? You tell me who he is and where I can find him, and there's a crown in it for you.' The man put his sword away some-where under his coat and pulled out a silver coin. Berren stared hungrily at it.

'Master Hatchet, sir ...' His voice sounded feeble.

'Speak up, boy!'

'Master Hatchet, sir. That's who gives me shelter.' He had to shout to make himself heard over the roar of the rain. Master Hatchet would never send one of his boys to do something like this. Safe and soft, that was Hatchet's motto.

'And where might I find your Master Hatchet?'

'Please, sir, he'll kill me if I tell.'

'Maybe I'll kill you if you won't.' The man moved closer. His coat opened. Berren caught a glimpse of the sword again. And something else. He lifted his face and looked the man in the eye.

'Please, sir. Please don't hurt me. He lives in the Fishing Quarter.'

The man sneered. 'I can tell that from the smell of you.' He gave an exaggerated sniff. 'That's not the only thing I smell on you. *Where* in the Fishing Quarter?'

Berren backed away. The man followed, until Berren was pressed against a wall.

'Where?'

'Shipwrights. Behind the toolmaker on Loom Street. There's an alley there. That's where. Near to where all the ...' He hated himself for hesitating. The younger boys laughed and giggled about the brothel next door. They made up all sorts of names for the women who worked there. The older ones, they just called it what it was and got on with things. 'Near to the brothel,' he said firmly, jutting out his chin.

'Ah. I know it.' The man smiled nastily. 'Hatchet, is it? Yes, the dung collector. In the one alley in this rotten city that stinks of something more than fish. I went into that brothel once to take a man. It had been raining. The cobbles were slick with shit.' He frowned. 'You look a bit like someone. Anyone ever tell you that?' He straightened himself and stared at Berren. He stared hard, and behind his eyes his mind seemed to wander. For a moment he seemed to relax. Berren lashed out with both arms at once. One to punch the man between the legs. The other to take what

15

he'd seen beneath the coat. And then he ran, skittering on the wet stones. He didn't stop or look back until he was out of the alley and half a dozen streets away. When he did, and when he was sure that the man with the sword was nowhere in sight, he found a place to shelter from the rain and opened his hand. In it he held a purse. He let himself feel the weight of it, listen to the coins jingling. He didn't dare stop for long enough to look inside. He didn't need to. He *knew* what was there.

Much later, when his curiosity finally got the better of him, he opened it.

All that was in the purse were a few coppers and some rusty iron.

3

MASTER HATCHET

In the days that followed, Berren tried to forget those few moments in the alley. Watching three men have their heads cut off from a comfortable perch several dozen yards away had been a fine thing. Watching three men killed right in front of him, fearing he'd be next, had been quite another. But worst of all had been opening the purse, sure he was rich beyond his wildest dreams, and finding nothing but junk. When he'd finally returned home, he'd taken a beating from Master Hatchet for being away too long. By then he was so numb with disappointment that he'd barely noticed. He hadn't even remembered to stash away a couple of pennies for himself. Hatchet could have searched him and found nothing.

He'd been one of Hatchet's favoured boys before the execution. Not any more. Now he lay awake in Master Hatchet's attic in the middle of the night, listening to the muted breathing of the other boys, straining his ears for sounds from downstairs. Hatchet had a visitor. An unwelcome one, from the sounds of things. It had started with the crash of a door being kicked in. Hatchet was a big man, a barrel of fat and muscle, built of beef and beer, with hands like hams and arms as strong as a ship's mast. Berren had seen Hatchet batter a man nearly to death over a few pennies, and he certainly wasn't the sort who'd take kindly to having his door staved in. Instead of a fight, though, all Berren could hear was a tense exchange of words.

'Who the bloody Khrozus is there?' Hatchet shouted. Then: 'Who the bloody Khrozus are *you*? I'll make you a bloody cripple ...' That had been followed by a heavy crash, the sound of wood splintering and then nothing.

There was a long silence. When Hatchet spoke again, his voice was quiet and strained. 'What do you want?'

Dim candlelight flickered through the cracks between the floorboards. Berren shuffled sideways, and pressed his ear to the floor, but whoever the intruder was, they spoke too softly for him to hear.

'I don't know nothing about it,' said Hatchet.

Some murmuring followed before Hatchet raised his voice loud enough for Berren to hear again. 'Him? What do you want *him* for?'

Pause. Hatchet's voice took on a sly tone.

'What's he worth.'

Silence.

'A crown? A bleeding crown? What's that to me? Nothing! You think you can ...' The words stopped abruptly. For almost a minute, Berren heard nothing. Then the narrow stairs up to the attic began to creak. Berren counted the steps. He knew the tread. Hatchet was coming up and that was never good. He didn't know how many of the other boys were awake. You could smell the fear in the air, though. Tasted sharp.

The door burst open. Hatchet stood there, lit up by a candle held out into the room.

'Berren!'

Berren rubbed his eyes. Hatchet pushed his way into the attic.

'Berren, get your worthless soul out here.' He grabbed an arm and hauled Berren towards the door and down the steps. 'You're in trouble, boy. Been stealing. Thieving!

Horrible! Never thought to have a thief in my house. After all the things I've given you.' The words were clearly meant for the stranger waiting downstairs. At the bottom, a single candle lit the rooms. Hatchet hurled him into the pool of light. 'This the one?'

'Yes.' The words came out of the shadows. Berren strained to see who it was. The voice sounded refined and educated, with a twang of something foreign to it and there was that smell again, the hint of something ...

The man from the alley.

Berren froze. His heart skipped a beat and then began to race. He had to run!

The man from the alley stepped out of the shadows and took hold of his arm. The grip was strong. Not painful, but firm enough that Berren knew he'd not easily tear himself away.

Hatchet was shaking his head. 'I'm very sorry, sir, that this thief here has caused you such trouble. Whatever his punishment is, I'm sure he deserves it.' He turned on Berren and hissed at him. 'Ungrateful boy! Food and shelter I gave you, and how do you repay my kindness? With this!'

'Here's your crown,' sneered the man from the alley. 'Now let us both hope that our paths never cross again.' He pulled Berren away, backing towards the door and into the cool night air. Berren watched as the door slammed closed. Behind it he heard Hatchet shouting. Probably one of the other boys had crept out of the attic to better hear what was happening. Whoever it was, Berren winced on their behalf. Most likely, the mother of all beatings was about to rain down.

The hand on his arm grew tighter, a reminder of his own predicament.

'Someone stole something from me once, years ago,' said the man from the alley. 'Something very important and very precious. Something I couldn't really do without.

19

As a consequence I'm not so fond of thieves. I'm also very good at catching them. I've made it my business. Would it surprise you to know that you're the only person who's ever stolen from me since? In all that time, not one thief has managed to take my purse. Can you imagine that?'

Berren made a play at being mute. The sky was clear and a near-full moon hung brightly in the sky right above them, but the man's face was hidden in shadows. Berren couldn't see his eyes.

The hand on his arm shook him and began to hurt. 'No, sir,' he mumbled.

'Speak up!'

'No, sir!'

'Do you know who I am?'

Berren shook his head.

'I'm a thief-taker. Do you know what that is?'

Berren knew exactly. Someone who hunted down thieves for the bounty on them. He nodded.

'Where I come from, people often have lots of names. We acquire them the way you Arians acquire gold. They just fall out of the air and land on us. Some of those who know me call me the Undertaker when they think I can't hear.' The man laughed. 'Do you understand?'

Berren nodded. 'Because you kill people,' he blurted.

The thief-taker shook his head. 'No, boy, it's a play on words. Because I *undertake* to do things and I always hold my promises. And yes, because sometimes I kill people as I do it. The sort of men who pay me like to have their little jokes.' He snorted. 'But unlike others, when I *undertake* to do something, it gets done. I swore an oath that no one would ever steal from me again without being hunted down and punished. So I've come to punish you for stealing from me. Had to. I'm not going to hurt you, not unless I have to. No, but you and I have some business to attend to.' He pulled Berren around, so they were staring eye to eye, just as they had when they first met in the alley. 'That man back there. Hatchet. I might hurt *him*, though. Would you like me to? If you want me to, I will. I'm sure the city would be a better place without him.'

Berren stared at him. Without doubt the man meant every word.

'I'm sure he beats you.'

Berren nodded.

'He sold you to me for a silver crown. That's all. So. Do you want me to hurt him? Just ask. That's all you have to do. Or nod. We can say nodding if you're finding it difficult to talk.'

Berren said nothing. He could feel his eyes burning.

'What if I were to say that I'd let you go? I'd have to. Couldn't hold on to you while I was crippling your master, now could I? You could get away. If you think I wouldn't find you.'

Berren could feel the tears ready to burst out of his eyes. He pulled his arm as hard as he could, trying to get away, but the thief-taker's grip was like a shackle. The man shook him.

'Answer me, boy.'

Berren shook his head. The tears were out now, rolling down his cheeks.

'Good.' The thief-taker nodded. 'At least now we know you have something to work with in there. Remorse or shame or a bit of both, either will do. Gods know I have enough of both to drown.' He stared at Berren again, the same half-not-there stare he'd given in the alley, except this time his grip didn't slip. 'By the Sun, there really is a bit of him in you.'

Then the thief-taker shook his head, as if in amazement, and he marched Berren away.

4
THE THIEF-TAKER

The man from the alley, whatever names he had, dragged Berren through the streets of Deephaven. They left Shipwrights, crossed Reeper Hill and skirted the edge of the sea-docks. Out in the deep bay that had given the city its name, dozens of tall ships lay at anchor in the night, silhouettes in the moonlight. Their creaks and groans echoed across the still waters like the calls of restless souls. Berren's neck prickled at the sound. Sometimes voices rang out, the distant and ghostly shouts of men calling news from ship to ship. They walked past bawdy houses and Moongrass dens, the drinking shops and the gambling holes. Men with hunched shoulders hurried by, hiding their faces. Women strutted on corners, idly flashing their pale skin at anyone who passed. Then the thief-taker turned and led the way up the Avenue of Emperors, the broad straight road that led up from the sea-docks to Four Winds Square and down to the river again on the other side of the city. Even at this hour, a steady stream of carts and wagons rumbled up from the sea. Halfway towards the top, the man stopped. He turned around, dragging Berren with him. Berren would have done anything to get away, but the hand on his arm never relented.

'You see those ships, boy? Those ships can take you anywhere in the world. Eight years ago I came here on one of those. I know this city better than I know my home now.

Watch out for the ones with the black flags. Those are the slave-ships of the Taiytakei and they'll take you places even further than I've been, whether you like it or not. But that's not what I want from you, lad. When I'm done with you, you'll come here every day and you'll look at the flags. You'll tell me if you ever see four white ships on a red field. That's one thing you can do for me. If ever you do, there's an emperor in it for you.'

They crossed over the Avenue of Emperors and climbed to The Peak, the top of the low flat hill that overlooked the bay, and the richest part of the city. At the top of The Peak sat Deephaven Square, an enormous paved expanse of marble. One end of the square was fully occupied by the magnificent solar temple, the even more magnificent Guild Hall, and behind them both sat the looming bulk of the Overlord's Palace. At the other end of the square were the infamous city moneylenders. Along either side, the houses of Aria's richest merchant-lords competed for attention. In sunlight, gaudy colours and murals and statues of bronze and marble and even gold fought with each other, blended into a confusion of glittering opulence. Now, under the moon, they were muted and dull. Berren looked around, twitching and jittery. Old instincts had him. This wasn't a place where someone like him was supposed to be. Boys like him disappeared up here.

The grip on his arm tightened. 'You like gold, lad? Here are the gold-kings of your city. There's a mile, maybe a bit more between the river-docks and the sea. The men here make more money every day buying and selling across that mile than you will ever see. Money is the blood of this city. The rest of it, the flesh and bones where everyone else lives: that sprawls inland, that's the stuff you know. But here is its heart. Ships and money, lad.'

Berren gawped and nodded as if all that made any sense. The thief-taker tugged him sharply away and headed inland again. Down Lime Street and then along Stonecutter's Way, leaving Berren to wonder what he should make of all this. They crossed Four Winds Square again and walked into the Courts District, but before they'd gone a dozen yards the other side, the thief-taker turned sharply to his left, almost pulling Berren's arm out of its socket. They plunged into the shadows of a narrow street where the darkness was so thick that Berren might as well have been blind. Then down an alley and into a yard. The thief-taker stopped, fumbling at the wall with his fingers. He reached under his coat and pulled out a key. He gave it to Berren.

'Open the lock,' he said, propelling Berren to a tiny iron door set into one wall of the yard and barely visible in the gloom. Berren did as he was told. He offered the key back and it disappeared under the thief-taker's coat.

'In you go, boy.' The thief-taker almost threw Berren inside and then quickly followed. He lit a lantern and sat down. Berren looked around. He wasn't sure what he'd expected, but certainly not this. The house – what he could see of it – was tiny, even smaller than master Hatchet's. The furniture was old and battered. There was nothing here worth more than a few copper bits, except what the thief-taker carried. For a moment, Berren was more bewildered than scared.

'Did you think I was rich, boy?'

Berren said nothing. He nodded.

'You saw the Secretary to the Courts give me a purse and say that it was filled with gold. It's true; I was well rewarded for hunting down those men and bringing them back. I was well rewarded for others before them and will be rewarded again. But I rarely receive much gold. My rewards are what you see here. This house, in this yard. Other things like that. Goods and services and favours.' He laughed. 'I suppose you would have much preferred the shiny golden emperors.'

Berren nodded.

'And what use is gold, lad? Not good for much except what you can buy with it, and favours are much less easily stolen than gold. How much money does it cost to stay at an inn for a night? A few pennies, perhaps, but my tastes run a little finer than some sailors' flophouse. Ten emperors must sound like a ransom for a king, but how long, do you suppose, could you live on so much gold?' The thief-taker shook his head. 'Why am I asking you? To you, it probably seems like enough to last forever. I promise you, boy, that gold would barely last someone like me a year. So I take things like this house instead.'

Berren frowned, though he still didn't dare speak.

'You saw the purse, is that what you're thinking? But you never saw what was in it. Not until too late, at least.' He laughed again. All of a sudden he was talking easily, as though they were friends. Sometimes, when Hatchet sent Berren to collect a debt or to deliver a warning, men would speak to him like this. Usually he took it as a sign that they were terrified of Hatchet. Usually they were sweating. With this man he didn't know what to think.

The thief-taker seemed to read his thoughts. His demeanour changed again, grew hard and distant. He looked at Berren for a long time before he spoke again.

'I came to this city years ago, looking for something. I had almost nothing. I took what work I could get, for what money I was offered. As you've seen, I have a sword, and I know how to use it. Finding honest work was hard. Finding dishonest work was easy. I've known plenty of men like your Master Hatchet. I've killed for them. I know what they're like.' He grinned, showing his teeth. 'Then I learned more about how this city works. I betrayed the men I worked for, betrayed them for a few crowns. Ever since, I've hunted thieves for the money put on their heads. The rewards can be pleasant enough, as you've seen.' He shook his head. 'Certainly better than picking pockets and lurking in alleys. That way leads you to the mines, boy. There or to your ancestors.'

Berren listened, feigning interest. When he'd been hauled away from Hatchet he'd assumed it was for one of the usual punishments – a beating, to be shackled in public and have abuse, rotten fish and the occasional stone thrown at him. He didn't much fear those. Worse was the prospect of being sold to one of the work-yards. Boys caught thieving were often sent to the yards and they were said to be dreadful places. But if the man was going to send him to the yards, why all this?

'Sir?'

The thief-taker looked at him in surprise. 'You have a question?'

'Yes, sir. I'm very sorry I stole your purse, sir. I promise it'll never happen again.' It was a practised speech, one that Hatchet had taught them all. He'd used it a few times, too. Usually there was more, about how he was an orphan caring for his little sisters and trying to keep them from starving. That sort of thing. Usually it didn't work, but the times it did were enough to make it worth a try.

The thief-taker spat. 'I'd be a piss-poor thief-taker if I fell for that. Try again, lad. A bit harder this time.'

'Sir, what do you mean to do with me?'

The man gave him another long look. 'Better. What's your name, boy?'

'Berren, sir.'

'Well then, Berren, I mean to keep you, that's what I mean to do with you. Until you have worked off your debt to me. I have need of someone to keep my possessions, such as they are, in order. Someone to run errands and buy goods. Someone to keep an eye on what ships are in the sea-docks. A boot-cleaner, knife-sharpener, water-carrier and flag-watcher.'

To Berren this sounded a lot like being a slave. In fact it sounded a lot like being with Master Hatchet except with a much better prospect of an easy and early escape, possibly with some of the thief-taker's goods or money. So he said nothing.

'Rich men have house-boys who are slaves, is that what you're thinking?' His new master bared his teeth with disdain. 'They're for decoration, and that's certainly not what I have in mind for you! No, you'll work, boy, and work hard. You stole from me. For that you must absolve yourself.'

Again Berren kept his silence. A few days. Then the man would let his guard down and Berren would be away.

The thief-taker stared through him. 'I'm thinking I might take an apprentice,' he said slowly. 'Someone to learn what I know.'

Berren blinked. He suddenly saw the fight in the alley again, as clear and vivid as if he was right back there, drenched in the rain. He saw the thief-taker with his sword, powerful and deadly, cutting down his assailants. 'Does that mean you'd teach me swords?' he blurted.

'If I were to decide you were worth taking on as an apprentice?' The thief-taker grimaced. 'Yes, lad. In time and if you proved yourself then I suppose I'd teach you the beginnings of how to use a sword.'

In his head, Berren still thought he'd run away after a few days. But something warm and bright was building inside his stomach. 'Sir? May I ask something? You said a thief once stole something precious from you. What happened to him?'

The man's laugher died and a bitterness entered his voice. 'Nothing, lad. Absolutely nothing at all.'

5

THE SEAMSTRESS'S DAUGHTER

He was propelled up a precipitous flight of stairs and pushed into a room. The door closed behind him and he heard the click of a key in a lock. Moonlight filtered in through an open window that looked out onto the yard. The floor was bare boards. Not even a bed. He was halfway through the window when he heard the key in the lock again. The door opened and there was the thief-taker, now with a bundle of blankets under his arm. He looked long and hard at the window and then at Berren.

'Going somewhere?'

'No, sir!' Berren stared at his feet, eyes already half screwed up, waiting for Master Hatchet's ham of a hand to slap him sideways.

The thief-taker didn't move. 'Don't lie to me, lad. I can smell a lie and you'd best remember that. It's a long way down and the ground's hard out there. You owe me a few days' hard work, boy. After that I'm not going to stop you from running away if that's still what you want. But you might think first on where you'd go.' The thief-taker threw down the blankets and looked at them. Then he looked at Berren, looked at the window, shrugged and left. 'Night rains are almost here,' he said as he closed the door. 'It's late. Get some sleep in the dry, lad. Be a long hard day for you tomorrow. With a bit of luck you might learn a thing or two.' The door closed. The lock clicked for a final time. Berren heard the thief-taker's footsteps creak outside. Heard another door opening into the second upstairs room next door. Two paces inside, door closed, another two paces. The creak of a bed. The grunt and sigh of boots coming off. More bed noise. Then silence for a while and finally snores. Berren stayed very still when he heard the snores, listening to them for a long time. Even then he wasn't sure he should trust them. He was still listening when he heard a rustle of wind from outside. The pit-pat of raindrops began, turning quickly into a steady hiss.

Berren reached his hand out of the window. He let the rain fall on his skin for a while and then pulled it back inside, closing the shutters behind him. Very quietly, he spread the thief-taker's blankets across the floor and lay down on them, flat on his back, staring at the ceiling. He listened to the drumming of water on the roof, the spatter of a dozen tiny waterfalls pouring into the yard below.

He had a room. A room of his own. That deserved some thought. He'd never in all his life had a room of his own. In the orphanage they'd slept almost on top of each other, dozens of them in a long, thin stone room with tiny slits for windows that faced the wrong way to let in any sunlight. When Master Hatchet had bought him for two shiny new pennies – the going rate for a boy just about old enough to push a hand-cart – he'd been put in the attic with all Hatchet's other boys. The windows had been bigger but they'd still been sleeping on top of each other.

And now he had a room. His own space. So small that he could touch all four walls with his hands and feet if he lay across it from corner to corner, but still ... It smelled of old wood and smoke, the unfinished plaster walls were dry and crumbled when he picked at them, but it was his. All his.

It terrified him. The silence behind the rustle of rain. The aloneness. He lay there, the thief-taker's last words running through his head, chasing themselves in circles, looking for a way out and not finding any. *I'm not going to stop you from running away if that's what you want. But you might think first on where you'd go.* He could go whenever he wanted. It couldn't be that far down to the ground, could it?

'Boy!' Berren jerked. The sound of the rain had stopped. Daylight stabbed through the gaps in the shutters. Gods! He'd fallen asleep and now it was morning and light already! A hot flush ran through him and he scrabbled to his feet. The shout came again. 'Boy! Get down here, lad!' Footsteps creaking on the stairs. In the House of Hatchet, that was never good. Berren ran for the door, clawing at the handle. It wasn't locked. He fumbled it open in time to meet the thief-taker eye to eye, three quarters of the way up the steps.

'Lazy.' The man shook his head. Berren sniffed. He could smell air, fresh outside air on a tiny breeze wafting past his face, and another smell. A people smell. The sort of sickly perfume smell he was used to from the whores next door, only not as strong. Woman smell.

The thief-taker was looking at him. 'Good, lad. Yes, we have a visitor. You'd best come and meet her.'

Berren hesitated, but the thief-taker had his arm before he could even think. He pulled Berren out of his room. 'Lazy *and* rude, eh? I won't tolerate either in this house, lad. Best you get used to that.'

Tonight. Tonight I'm gone. As long as it doesn't rain. Night rains. That was the summer coming, that was. Balmy evenings and steamy mornings; night rains, afternoon downpours and sultry days. Thieving season. Gingerly he tiptoed down the steps into the largest room of the house. There was a table and a couple of chairs and a hearth and nothing else. Nothing even to steal.

There was a girl, too, probably about his age. She was

looking at him with her lips pressed tightly together, as though trying not to laugh. She was sitting at the table, half turned towards him with a plate and a crust of bread in front of her smothered in dripping. Her face was plain apart from being covered in freckles. She wore a loose shirt belted tightly at the waist. It showed off curves that demanded attention. Despite himself, Berren realised he was staring.

A cuff around the head put a quick stop to that. 'Rudeness, lad. I told you I won't tolerate it. This here is Lilissa. She breaks bread with us some mornings. Lilissa, this is Berren. No ...' He held out a hand as she started to rise. 'You stay there. This lad here is my apprentice and barely worthy of your notice. Berren, bow to the lady.'

Berren blinked. 'What?' That got him another cuff round the head, hard enough to make him stagger.

'Bow, lad. That's what a gentleman does when he meets a lady.'

Feeling stupid, Berren gave a clumsy bow and earned himself yet another cuff.

'No no no. From the waist. Keep your back straight.' Berren started to try again, but now the thief-taker's hands were all over him. 'Back straight. That means not bent in the middle. No, not like that, no, you have to ...' The thief-taker sighed as Berren stumbled across the room. 'Try again. No no no, eyes up, eyes *up*! When you bow to someone you look at them, not at the floor. Don't look her in the eye though lad, that's rude. And not *there*, either.' Another cuff almost knocked him over. Berren jumped round.

'What's that for?'

'Watch your eyes, boy. Maybe where you come from you think you can look at a lady how you please, but that will change. Parts of this city are full of bravos with swords who like to show off how dangerous they think they are. Look

31

at the lady on their arm like that when you bow and you'll find yourself on the wrong end of one of them. And since they have names that matter and families with money and you don't, no one will care either.' The thief-taker's face wrinkled up in disdain. Lilissa just looked frightened.

'But she's not a lady,' Berren blurted.

The thief-taker's face went cold and flat. 'Really? And how do you know that, boy? Because she doesn't dress up in fine clothes?'

Berren sniffed. 'Well. Yeh, I suppose.'

'From now on, boy, for as long as you live under this roof and until I say otherwise, every person you meet is either a lady or a gentleman to you. If I see you treat anyone otherwise, there will be punishment. Do you understand?'

'But …'

'Do you understand?' The thief-taker didn't even raise his voice but the words were edged with steel. Berren took a long deep breath and nodded.

'Yes, sir.' *Yes. For as long as I live under this roof. Exactly that long.* He was thinking of the window again.

'Good. Now we shall do this until you get it at least crudely right, and then, perhaps, over the next month we might even find some grace and elegance in you. You may practice while we eat. Lilissa, please pay no attention to my apprentice for however long he chooses to remain here. Once we've broken our fast, Berren will be carrying out your usual chores, so we'll have more time for your lessons today.'

6
MOON STREET

'Water, air, earth and fire, sun-heart shields from dark one's ire
Fire, earth, air and water, moon-pride brings us naught but
  slaughter
Air and water, fire and earth, dead god lifts forgotten curse
Earth and water, fire and air, star-song rends what must
  repair
Black moon comes, round and round
Black moon comes, all fall down.'

After the song came the muffled sound of giggling from
outside. Berren groaned and rolled over. Light filtered in
through the window.

'Oi!' The shout rang through the whole house. Every
noise did. Four tiny rooms, walls so thin that a good kick
would bring them down, old timbers that creaked and
groaned in the wind. Wherever you were, you heard everything. But next to Hatchet's place, the quiet was deafening.
More than the singing and the laughing and the shouting,
it was the quiet that came after that roused Berren from his
torpor. He wasn't used to waking up on his own. When he
opened the shutters and looked out into the yard, a gang of
ragged dirty children were dancing around, shouting and
pointing up at his window.

'Thief-taker man, thief-taker man

Is he hungry, is he thirsty?
If he is he'll do you dirty
Thief-taker man, thief-taker man
Run while you can from the thief-taker man.'

They stood there, jumping up and down, shrieking and laughing. As soon as the thief-taker opened his door they ran, skittering helter-skelter out of the yard and away.

The thief-taker's name was Syannis, Sy to his friends, Master Sy to Berren, and being his apprentice proved to be a lot of work. Boring, tedious, repetitive and frequently pointless work. It seemed to Berren that he spent most of his time fetching, cleaning, carrying and polishing while Master Sy sat in his comfortable chair and contemplated the world. Running away was never far from his thoughts. It would have been easy. Compared to Master Hatchet, Master Sy was blind and deaf. He left the door to the yard ajar as often as not, and frequently paid no attention at all to what Berren was doing. In fact, how easy it would be to leave was probably what kept him there for those first few days. That and the promise that one day he'd learn about swords.

And Lilissa. She came to the house most mornings with fresh bread for their breakfast. Each time she did, Master Sy made Berren practice bowing. At first that was the part he hated most about the day, having to scrape and crawl to some girl who was as much a nothing as he was. But then, after the first two days, he caught her looking back at him, trying not to smile. The next morning he tried as hard as he could to get it right and caught her smiling back at him a second time. Then Master Sy had her curtseying too and they were both at it, trying to outdo each other. By the time they were done, even Master Sy was grinning. Berren never got a chance to talk much to her, though. She came in the morning, broke bread with them, stayed for an hour while

Berren did his chores and then was gone. While she was there, mostly what she did was read aloud, while Master Sy closed his eyes and listened and occasionally corrected her or helped when she stumbled with one of the words.

'Who is she?' Berren asked one day.

'Who is who?'

'Lilissa.'

Master Sy snorted. 'Not someone you should be thinking about, lad.' The thief-taker wrinkled his nose. 'Her mother was kind to me once, bless her soul. She died of the pox last year. Now I repay her favours by helping Lilissa to better herself. Get her out of your head, boy.' And that was all he ever got. *Get her out of your head.*

On the twelfth day, after Lilissa had gone and they were alone again, Master Sy folded his arms and gave Berren a long hard look.

'You're still here,' he said, as if that was somehow a surprise. Berren shrugged. He'd learned to keep his mouth closed unless Master Sy told him to open it. The thief-taker was still looking at him, slowly nodding. 'I suppose you've worked well enough. Enough to work off your debt.' He opened the door to the yard and gestured outside. 'You're free, lad. Off you go.'

Berren didn't move.

'Come on, lad. You can go back to your Master Hatchet now if you want.' There was a long pause. '*If* that's what you want. Is it?'

Back to the dormitory. Back to the bigger boys who bullied him, the smaller boys he bullied in turn. Hatchet himself who bullied them all. He took a deep breath. This was something he'd been thinking about for days. Living with Master Hatchet meant beatings and always being on the lookout. On the other hand, living with the Hatchet meant he had the run of half the city as long as he was careful what he did. In the complex network of gangs and

35

territories, the dung collectors were allowed to go almost anywhere as long as they kept to collecting dung. That was a freedom other boys his age didn't get, one he wouldn't get here either. And Hatchet always let him keep a few pennies of whatever he took. Hatchet gave him freedom, and then there were the women across the street.

He bit his lip. All the boys had their favourites and he was no different. He'd gone over there one night, pockets full of copper pennies, nervous as anything, heart fluttering. He knew which one he wanted, knew her face even if he didn't know her name. He'd emptied his pockets. She'd opened her shirt and the smell of her had poured over him, heavy with musk; but as he'd reached out to touch her, she'd slapped his hand away.

'They cost more than you've got.'

She'd taken everything he had and he'd gone with a lot more than mere touching in mind, but he knew better than to argue. He'd stood there, mute, while she'd buttoned up her shirt.

'Do I have to call for Jin?' she'd asked when she'd finished and he was still there. Club-Headed Jin dealt with visitors who got out of hand. Berren had turned and fled, cheeks burning with humiliation. It had been all around the other boys the next day. For months afterwards, even now, he still dreamed of somehow being rich, of going back and flaunting his money. Let her see what it was like to look but not touch.

He nodded and then bowed. Still a clumsy bow, but better than he could have managed a few days before. 'I want to stay, master.' He could always change his mind, but did he really want to collect horse shit off the city streets for the rest of his life?

The thief-taker ran his tongue over his teeth in exaggerated thought. 'If that's really what you want, lad. Roof over your head and meals on the table, I can promise you that.

Don't know if you'll learn anything. That's up to you. You'll work, though. Work or I send you back to Shipwrights. Do you understand me, lad?'

Berren nodded vigorously. The thief-taker nodded back and then set about sharpening his sword, something he did most mornings while he watched Berren work. He didn't say anything more as the rest of the day went by, but late in the afternoon he went out and left Berren alone in the house. He wasn't gone for long, but it was time enough. If he'd wanted, Berren could have run upstairs, stolen whatever took his fancy and vanished back to Shipwrights. When Master Sy came back and saw Berren still hard at work, he nodded, and maybe there was a slight smile, half hidden by a hand and quickly wiped away.

The next morning there was no sign of Lilissa. After breakfast, instead of his usual chores, Berren found himself being handed a scruffy pair of boots.

'For you. Lot of walking in this job.' They were old and falling apart, but that still made them the best pair of boots Berren had ever had. Wooden clogs, that was what he was used to, that or nothing at all. He stared at them in amazement.

'Mine?'

The thief-taker snorted. 'Well they won't fit me. Right then. Come on. If you're going to be a thief-taker, you'll need to learn your letters.' The thief-taker turned and walked out the door. Berren gawped for a second, then hurried after. 'Come on lad, jump to it! Get the door!' Master Sy called over his shoulder without looking back, and then he strode off, through the yard and down the alley. At the end he turned left, away from the Court District, out of the shadows and into the harsh sunlight and the noise and bustle of Weaver's Row where the morning market was already in full swing. Tables crowded against the walls, piled high with white sheets and nothing else. Men and women, old and young, shouted at each other to be heard, haggling over pennies. The air smelled of sweat and the sour milk they used to bleach the cotton white. Berren darted sideways as a matron took a step back into the street to shake open a sheet and almost knocked him flat. The thief-taker was only a few paces ahead, but half the time Berren couldn't even see him through the press of people. He caught up on the edge of a small crowd wedged into the street so tightly that none of them were moving. The shouting was a lot louder here, and angry. Someone with a cart had had the stupid idea of trying to come up from the Godsway to Market Square, had made it as far as the end of Moon Street and now they were stuck.

And everywhere, purses. Pouches on strings, dangling in invitation from belts. Purses held tightly in hands. Purses in pockets. Girdle purses, shoulder purses ... Berren's eyes flicked from one to the next, sizing them up. Instinct, that was. Instinct from years on the street where stealing a few pennies every day was how a boy stayed alive. He glanced over his shoulder, checking his route. There was a man with a pouch in his hand, clutching it like it was his own mother's life. Those were the sort Berren had learned to look for. Ones with money that mattered to them always gave themselves away. The ones who held it tight in their hands. Then you just had to be patient, following them for as long as it took, for that one instant that always came when they put it down for a moment while they picked up something else. You never had long, a second, perhaps, so you had to be ready. Snatch and run ...

The thief-taker was suddenly in front of him, looking down at him, a quizzical expression on his face. Then he shook his head slightly, took Berren's arm and dragged him through the crowd, forcing his way past the stuck cart to where Weaver's Row turned into Moon Street, out of the Moon-day market hubbub and into the relative quiet near

Godsway. He stopped at a wide flight of steps and hauled Berren up to an enormous arched door. The door was made of black wood and studded with bolts of silvery white metal. It was firmly closed, but set into it was a second, much smaller door. The thief-taker pushed the small door open and pulled Berren inside, into a huge round vaulted room with a ring of tiny windows in the roof. Berren winced, half expecting a beating, as if the thief-taker had been reading his mind back in the street. Master Sy let go of him, though, and just stopped and looked around as if taken by surprise at where he was. When he spoke, he spoke in a whisper.

'Where I come from, lad, this would have been a palace for a king. In fact, where I come from, it would have been the envy of most kings. Here in Deephaven, though ...' He took a deep breath and stared up at the windows in the roof. Berren looked around as his eyes adjusted to the sudden gloom. The hall was mostly empty. The floor was laid with worn flagstones. At the far end, he could make out the shape of something in the shadows. In the centre, lit by the light from above, stood a cylinder of black stone half wrapped in strips of silver. The stone must have been ten feet across and was as tall as Berren. As he stared at it, the silver metal bands seemed to shift, never quite holding still. He started towards them, mesmerised, but came up short with the thief-taker's hand on his shoulder.

'You know where this is, don't you, lad?'

Berren shook his head. He sniffed the air. It tasted old and rich and carried the hint of some scent he couldn't quite place.

'It's Moon-day, lad. This is a temple to the Moon.' Master Sy looked bemused. 'Have you never been to one before?'

Berren shrugged. 'Gods is for rich folk.' Master Hatchet had never had much time for gods and had never seen why anyone else should either.

The thief-taker chuckled. 'Gods are for rich folk, lad?

Do you think that's true? Does the sun shine only on rich people? Does the moon? When it rains, does it only rain on the rich man's field? Laws – now *they* might not be for all folk. But not gods. What do you smell?' The thief-taker spoke softly, but the bare stone walls and floor picked up his words and carried them, made them unnaturally loud. Berren flinched.

'I don't know,' he whispered. The smell was a strange one. It was the smell of rich people, mingled up with something else that he didn't recognise.

The thief-taker's lips curled with disdain, but his eyes glittered with desire. Berren backed away. This was a new Master Sy, one that he hadn't seen while he'd been practising his bows and cleaning the floors. 'Money. Power. Magic. They all flow through this city. Learn how and you'll be the master and I'll be the apprentice. That's your first lesson, boy. Money, magic and power. They're always behind everything.' Then he chuckled. 'On a Sun-day I'll take you to the solar temple in Deephaven Square for the dawn prayers. Then you'll see.'

There was a shuffling noise from the back end of the temple, and then a pointed cough. Master Sy's head snapped round to look, as a disembodied voice spoke. 'Well, well. Syannis the thief-taker prince.'

7

DEEPHAVEN

A man emerged slowly out of the shadows. Berren couldn't make out his face, but he moved like a grandfather. *Like an ancient*, Master Hatchet would have said. 'Syannis, Syannis.' The old man started nodding. 'Yes, yes, well. I haven't seen you here for a while. And then you come in the middle of the morning when we should be sleeping. But no, you didn't wake me up. I don't sleep all that much these days anyway.' He seemed to notice Berren for the first time. 'Oh. You brought a friend. Sorry, son. Path of the Moon, you see. Makes us more night people than most.'

'Teacher Garrent.' Master Sy, Berren realised, was now staring at his own feet. His fingers were steepled together. Almost in a gesture of prayer. *A devout who's a thief-taker?* Berren grinned. *Who'd have thought?* 'The rude oik I have the shame to have brought before you is my apprentice.' Master Sy still didn't look up. Berren quickly bowed his head and tried to look cowed. The old priest shuffled over. Despite the din of Moon Street right outside the door, the only other sound Berren could hear was his own breathing.

The priest came and stood in front of him. He could feel the man's wheezy breath on his hair. It smelled of fruit. Sweet fruit.

'What's your name, son?'

Berren knew better than to answer. 'His name's Berren, but "boy" is more than good enough for that one, Teacher,' said Master Sy. The priest didn't move. Berren could feel the old man's eyes staring at the top of his head, as if he was trying to look inside. 'I apologise for him. I'm surprised he's even aware that the two paths exist. It's not his fault, so please don't be hard on him.'

'There are four paths, Syannis, not two. You know that perfectly well.'

'Two that deserve the name.'

The old priest gently put his hand on Berren's head. Berren tensed, but the hand didn't withdraw. 'Berren, is it? Just Berren? No titles? Don't worry. I'm not going to put a curse on you. Your master would have taken you to one of his many other friends for that. So, have you ever been into a moon temple before?'

Berren shook his head. *Never have, never want to again.* But for some reason that made the old priest smile. He took his hand away.

'Can't say I blame you. Who'd want to, eh? Nothing for you here I'm sure. Still, if you're never coming back then I'd better get on and show you something while you're here. Don't be afraid, it has nothing to do with gods. It's just a nice view, that's all.'

Master Sy let out a slight groan. The priest snorted.

'Oh, don't pretend you brought him here for the sake of his spirit, Syannis. You just wanted to take him up the tower, didn't you?'

'I brought him here to further his education, Teacher. In all ways.'

'Well we'll start with the tower. It's probably the best part of being here. Never mind all this other nonsense, eh, Berren? We have the tallest tower in the city outside The Peak and we're quite proud of it. Come on!'

For an ancient, he moved with sudden speed and

purpose, and Berren found himself hurrying along in the wake of the priest's silver robes. Through the gloom he saw other shapes at the side of the temple but that's all they were; then the priest was through another tiny door and heading up stairs that spiralled up a dim circular tower. Turn after turn, until Berren's legs started to burn with the effort of climbing. The further he went, the more windows there were and the lighter it became. They were the sort of windows he was used to. No glass, no shutters. Simple open holes in the wall, narrow slits that let in the breeze and the city-smell of dead fish. They didn't even have a curtain to pull across them. Then another half turn and light flooded the tower. Teacher Garrent was standing in a doorway which had no door, leaning against its arch of stones. Berren could see the roofs of the city beyond. The climb up the stairs had been long enough that even Master Sy was breathing harder than usual, yet the old man didn't seem the least bit troubled. As Berren climbed the last step, the priest moved aside.

'Have a care, young one.'

Berren stepped through the door. He was standing on a wooden balcony that ran around all four sides of the tower. It was about three feet wide and there was no fence, no rail, nothing at the edge except a long drop to the ground. He took a bold step into the sunlight and then looked down. The Godsway was perhaps a hundred feet below, straight down to a steady stream of carts and wagons that moved back and forth along it.

'Not much fear in that one, Master Syannis,' Berren heard.

'No indeed, Teacher Garrent.'

'A worry, don't you think, in your line of work?'

'There's not much fear in this one either, Teacher, yet here I am.'

'Yes, here you are. But I don't remember you walking

43

straight up to the edge and standing there, steady as a rock. Even you showed the odd errant sign of caution.'

Berren felt the wooden boards under his feet shifting up and down, telling him in their own jumbled whispers that the priest was coming up behind him. He couldn't move though. The view of the city had him transfixed. He could see everything, everywhere. Right to the river docks and the estuary beyond. To the top of The Peak and the huge palaces up there with their towers, even taller than this one. Over the dome of the moon temple and across Craftsmen's to the Sea Docks, to Shipwrights and Master Hatchet, to all the ships out at anchor with their forest of masts. Inland, where the city seemed to stretch on forever, slowly mingling with fields and streams and even clumps of trees until it finally gave up and shrunk down into two long lines of villages, one beside the river and the other beside the sea, both vanishing into the distance.

But most of all, he was looking down on it all. This, he knew, was where he wanted to be. Looking down on the world.

The old priest came and sat down beside him on the edge of the balcony, his spindly legs dangling in the soft breeze coming down from the river. 'It's not the highest place in the city by a long way. That's over there.' He pointed up towards The Peak. 'The Overlord's Palace and the solar temple both have towers that are exactly the same height. Did you know that? Because neither could stand to see the other have the tallest. After the war I sat here and watched them both build tower after tower, each one trying to be bigger than the other. As soon as one was finished, they'd start on something even grander. That was after Khrozus took the Sapphire Throne and called himself emperor, and he and the old Autarch down in Torpreah would have gone to war with each other all over again if they could. Well then The Butcher died and His Imperial Majesty took the throne and things got a bit easier for all of us. Now the Sunherald and the Overlord have towers that are exactly as tall as each other and they're not allowed to build any more. And of course no one else is allowed to build one that's taller.'

He felt the boards move again as Master Sy came to crouch behind them. 'That's this city, Berren. Tension and compromise. Show him the parts of the city he thinks he knows, Teacher.'

The priest laughed. 'You'd be surprised what I see from up here, both of you. Now look the other way, son.'

Reluctantly Berren wrenched his eyes away from the jagged gleaming of The Peak.

'We're in the Craftsmen's Quarter here. Follow my finger. See that straight road?' Berren saw a long, dark gash between the mass of houses that sprawled away from the temple.

'What? The really narrow one?'

'Devil's Row.' The priest nodded. 'Now follow it. Goes out across the Market District. Do you see where it stops? Do you see the wall? That's the old city wall, that is. Can you see the line of it?'

Berren squinted. He thought maybe he could see something. A scar across the city, maybe. He tried to see where it went, but lost it somewhere behind the temples and towers of Market Square.

'It's hard, isn't it? You can see it from up here, though. On the ground you'd hardly know it's there, but it is. That's the wall, young Berren. That's what held Emperor Talsin back for the best part of six months. That wall and the Grand Canal on the other side. Changed the world, that wall did.' He chuckled to himself. 'Have you ever been to the Grand Canal?'

This time Berren nodded. He knew the name, although what he'd seen had been a foetid stinking mass of standing water close to the Great North Road and Pelean's Gate. The south end of it ran off into the ground somewhere, he knew that. The north end just stopped. You could tell the people who lived next to it from their smell, even worse than the rest of the city. He wrinkled his nose at the memory.

'Yes. Doesn't seem much now, but I remember it choked with bodies. It used to go all the way from Pelean's Gate down to the river.' The priest laughed again. 'You won't remember that. Got covered with so many bridges during the siege that afterwards people just built on top of it. Canal's still there though, underneath the streets and alleys. They say that if you have a good enough nose, you can follow its course from the smell.' The priest winked. 'Others might say that the smell is how you know you're in the Canal District in the first place. The rest of the city past that? Talsin's Forest? That's what was really there. A whole forest chopped down and turned to mud by Talsin's army. Look at it now ...' The old priest chuckled and shook his head. 'What do you care, eh? You're young. You don't remember any of this. You come from up there, though. Somewhere up there. Somewhere down the wrong end of Reeper Hill and Shipwrights, I'm guessing.'

For a moment, Berren looked up, startled. *How does he know?* But that was easy. Master Sy could have told him days ago. He sighed and stifled a yawn.

'Well, can't see much of that from here. Pelean's Gate and a bit of the hill behind it. Look the other way though. Down to the river and the Rich Docks. See where the gulls are circling right by the River Gate?'

Berren nodded. Right at the end of the docks, it must have been.

The priest's voice dropped and his tone darkened. 'Watch out for that house, young master Berren. A dark thing lives there and he knows your master. Keep away if you can.' He grunted, and then gestured out across the

river. 'Now see the houses over there on the other bank?'
Berren peered in the direction the priest was pointing, over
the top of the Rich Docks to the far side of the estuary.
He could see something there, perhaps. A line on the other
side of the water. If he was honest, his mind was still set on
the towers and which was the tallest. He nodded, not sure
what he was looking at or why he should care.

'The waters of the Arr are deep on this side of the river
and that's why we have the Rich Docks where we do. On
the south side it's a different matter. There are miles of
mudflats and that's where the mudlarks live in wooden
shacks built on stilts in the mud. The city would like to
be rid of them. They tried once.' He gave Berren a long
hard look. 'I imagine that would have been a couple of
years before you were born. Didn't work, but the trying
changed the world too. Now the city puts up with them.
Just about.'

Berren tried to keep looking at the river and the dull
expanse of flat nothing that the priest was talking about.
His eyes kept darting back up towards The Peak, though.
For a moment, Berren felt immensely stupid. A couple of
weeks ago, he'd gone to an execution and seen Master Sy
given a purse of ten golden emperors and he'd been in awe.
He was in the wrong place. *That* was where he wanted to
be. In among those towers, up there on The Peak ...

'Am I boring you, son?'

Berren started, wrenched back to the mundane world
of an old priest and a thief-taker. From where he was, it
was hard to see which tower was the tallest. As soon as he
thought he could get away with it, he turned to look at
them properly.

'Which one is the Overlord's tower?'

The old priest gave a long sigh. 'Here I am, trying to tell
you about the people who are the poorest in our little world
so you might pity them and help them, and all you care for

is who are the richest and the most powerful so that you can envy and resent them.' He gently shook his head. 'I suppose I shouldn't be surprised. Your master came here to me eight years ago, almost fresh off his ship. No money, no nothing except a belly full of rage, a head full of ambition and a heart full of ...' He frowned and then he looked at Syannis. 'Yes. Well. He came to the temple and I brought him up here and he sat on the edge with me, just like you, and he asked me the exact same thing. All that ambition.' He glanced back over his shoulder towards Master Sy. 'Hasn't really gone away, has it? And what about the rage?'

The thief-taker didn't flinch. 'Don't lecture me, old man. You know what I'd lost when I came here. And when I said I brought the boy here to have an education, history was not foremost in my mind.' Berren couldn't help but think of the alley and the men he'd seen the thief-taker kill there. The memory made his heart trip along faster for a few beats.

'Do you still go down to the sea-docks every day?'

Syannis didn't answer, but the priest obviously saw something in his face. 'Still looking in case he comes?' He shook his head. 'Then you're going to teach this one all the wrong things.' The priest looked sad. 'You have a young man here to guide. Let it go. If you don't, you'll spoil him.'

'I'll be the judge of that.'

Old men talking about the past. Berren had heard plenty of that in his few years. 'So which one is the Overlord's tower?' he asked again, loudly. Master Sy glared at him but the priest laughed.

'Do you see the one capped with gold? That's the solar temple up on The Peak. The Overlord's Palace is next to it. His tower is the one that looks like it has wings.'

From where Berren was sitting some of the other towers looked taller. There were a lot of them, all clustered together on The Peak. The Overlord's didn't seem that special at all.

He stuck out his bottom lip. 'I like the gold one better.'

The priest chuckled. 'Well don't say that to the Overlord.'

'Real gold on the top of that tower,' murmured the thief-taker. He took a deep breath and put on a heavy frown. 'Teacher, I brought the boy here because I was thinking that he should learn his letters.'

'Does he want to?'

'I think he should.'

The priest turned to Berren. 'Do you *want* to learn to read and write?'

Berren shrugged. *Not really* was the honest answer, but obviously not the right one. 'I want to learn to fight,' he said. He was staring at the towers again.

'Oh, well, you've already got the right man for that.' The old priest shook his head at Master Sy. 'If he doesn't want to learn, I won't try to teach him. Bring him back when it's something he wants.'

There were a lot of towers, all clustered together, too many to count. They were magnificent gleaming things that sucked him in with their grandeur. Towers topped with ramparts, towers topped with golden domes, with giant carved crowns; or with dragons or other beasts that Berren couldn't name. Whenever he stopped paying attention to the priest and Master Sy, there they were, calling him.

Master Sy's frown grew deeper. 'Teacher ...'

'No point in trying to teach a boy who's nearly a man something he doesn't want to learn. Show him why he should want it.' The priest clapped Berren on the shoulder and rose unsteadily. 'Look at you. I can see where your mind is right enough. You come back when you're ready.'

Berren sighed. He'd been away from Master Hatchet for two weeks. And now he was standing on the top of the city, dreaming of things he could never have, of things he'd never even dreamt he could have back when he'd spent his days picking dung off the streets. The men who built and lived in those towers probably each had enough gold to sink a ship. None of them had started as an orphan boy from Shipwrights.

'Ach!' The thief-taker leaned forward and spat over the edge of the balcony. 'Boy, you could pick any of those towers on The Peak. Pick the one you want. Whichever it is, the person who ordered it built knew their letters.'

The priest grumbled under his breath and wagged a finger at the thief-taker. 'Urlik the Grim has a place up on The Peak and he certainly didn't know how to read and write when he got it. Doubt that's changed.'

'The Grim was no better than a pirate in the war and I doubt that's changed either.' Lines of anger filled the thief-taker's face. He jerked his head towards the doorway. 'Come on, boy. Time we were going.'

Berren got up. He followed the priest and the thief-taker down the stairs; with Master Sy wrapped up in a cloud of anger strong enough to crack stones, Berren kept his distance. They emerged into the back of the temple next to another enormous door. On the other side stood a smaller door, like the one into the tower. The old priest stopped. He followed Berren's eyes. 'That one goes down,' he said. 'There's nothing there you'd want to see.' With a deep sigh he turned and ambled around the side of the temple. Berren hesitated, but Master Sy shooed him on. Beyond the black and silver altar in the centre, Berren passed a row of five black and silver columns, each reaching up to the roof.

'The five are for the five faces of the moon,' said the old priest without looking round. 'Teachers, Guardians, Seekers, Savants and Wanderers, if you care to remember them. Syannis here is on the road of the waning moon. Seekers of truth and unravellers of secrets. Obvious as though it was written on his face. You, though ...' The priest went to the column in the middle. He touched it and murmured something. The air crackled. 'You I can't read at all.' He frowned and shook his head. 'I can give you a blessing if you want it,' he said. 'You might need it.'

Berren shied away. Master Sy growled something. He'd walked straight past the columns. Set into the black wall beyond were three altars. Master Sy went to the nearest one, a golden sun set into the stone of the temple wall. He touched the sun with his fingers and then dropped to one knee for a moment. A little past the sun was a slab of black stone flecked with tiny white spots that seemed to glow in the dark. The third altar looked as though it was broken, a slab of granite half hanging out of the wall, cracked and split with pieces missing. Berren wondered what he should do, whether he should bow before one of them as well. Without really thinking he drifted towards the furthest one, the broken one. Then Master Sy was suddenly on his feet again with a hand on Berren's shoulder.

'Not that one, lad.' He turned to follow the footsteps of the priest. Garrent was heading for the door through which they'd entered.

'It looks broken.'

'It is. There were four gods once. Something happened to one of them.'

That was too much. 'Broken?' he scoffed. Always there. That was the *point* of gods. The sun and the moon and the earth and the stars and the wind and the rain and the sea. Stuff like that. That was what the thief-taker had said, wasn't it, up on the top of the tower? Broken gods? Fool's talk!

'Something funny, boy?'

Berren quickly bowed his head. 'I didn't think gods could be broken, that's all,' he said, as contritely as he could.

'Really?' Master Sy pushed Berren towards the way out. 'And how would you know that, lad? Did I make a mistake and take a priest's boy? Because I thought I took a little thief off the streets who had wandering fingers and a head full of nothing. Expert on gods, are you? Eh?'

Berren kept walking. He glared at the floor and didn't say anything.

'No, didn't think so. Come on, out. We've got more places you need to see and we didn't come here to talk about gods. Garrent here can tell you all about how the world got broken and the earth god with it on some other day. It was the moon-folk who did it, after all, so he should know.' He pushed open the door. The light and the noise of Moon Street gushed over them. For a moment, Berren thought he meant the priests in Deephaven. He stopped, too shocked to move, and turned back to the thief-taker, mouth agape in wonder.

'The priests …?'

'Not Teacher Garrent, you dolt!' Master Sy roared with laughter. 'For pity's sake, lad, did no one tell you any stories when you were growing up?'

Berren just stared at him. He remembered stories aplenty. Stories about how he'd better do what he was told or he'd be beaten black and blue, that was the gist of them. Mixed in with a healthy smattering of stories about how he was going to die in all sorts of colourful and gruesome ways. The idea that he might receive a story as a pleasure was a new one and he didn't quite know what to say. Slowly he shook his head.

The thief-taker looked shocked. The laughter went away. 'No, I suppose perhaps they didn't. Well that's all it is, lad. Just stories. Stuff from long before the first men blew in from across the seas. I suppose gods fight just like men do.' He sucked in a deep breath between his teeth. 'They say the first sun-king rose up from the ruins, long long ago. Fey stories, boy. Dusty old legends. Nothing that matters any more. Keep walking.'

Berren shook his head and turned his mind back to the

world outside. After the quiet of the temple, stepping out into Moon Street felt like stepping out into a war. Even though the steps were shallow and wide, he took them carefully. His head was spinning.

'When you've learned to be civil, I'll take you to one of the solar temples. They'll tell you all the stories you want, if you have the courtesy to open your ears.'

Another voice rang down from the top of the stairs. Teacher Garrent, standing at the door behind them. 'But if Syannis ever tries to teach you anything about the gods and the four paths himself, you'd best know now that he's probably wrong about almost everything, young Berren! You should always listen attentively to your master, mind, but come back here afterwards and I'll tell it to you properly.' The priest smiled and closed his mouth and waved farewell, but Berren heard him whispering in his ear. *And remember what I told you, young man. Beware the house on the docks.*

Further up the hill beside the market, the cart that had been blocking the street was gone.

8

WHERE THIEVES FEAR TO TREAD

'Come on boy, don't dawdle!' Master Sy marched away from the temple in big swinging strides, forcing Berren to run to keep up. The thief-taker was positively steaming. 'If you ever have any trouble, boy, go to Teacher Garrent. He's kind and he's safe and he'll look after you. If you ever want any actual *help*, though, then you might want to consider looking somewhere else.' He cut sharply right off Moon Street and wove between the alleys into the traffic of the Godsway. The road here was every bit as busy as Weaver's Row, but it was a different kind of busy. This was a steady, orderly procession of carts, rolling up and down the hill between Four Winds Square and the river docks. No, the *Rich* Docks, that's what the priest had called them. Berren wondered why.

At the top of the hill in the huge open space of Four Winds Square, the carts scattered. Master Sy ignored them. He marched straight across the middle towards the city courthouse on the other side, the place where the execution scaffolds had been. As Berren walked beneath where they'd stood, the hairs on the back of his neck prickled. He stopped to peer at the ground and look for traces of blood; but before he could find any, Master Sy was yelling at him to keep up and he had to run again.

The thief-taker passed the courthouse. He went down a narrow street that ran alongside it and arrived at a much smaller square that opened out along the back. On the far side of this square, the smell of beer and a loud rumble of talk washed out of a low house wrapped in ivy. In the middle, a small fountain in the shape of an octopus bubbled and gurgled. Berren stared. He'd never seen anything like it.

'Oh come on, lad. Have you never seen a fountain?'

Berren shook his head. He reached out to touch the water with his hand and then drank a few drops. It tasted clean. 'Where does it come from?'

Master Sy shook his head impatiently. He pointed up to the roof of the courthouse. 'Rain. They catch the rain in great big buckets the size of houses.' He pulled Berren gently away. 'Come on. They use it to make beer, too. I'll get you one. Proper beer, lad. Not like the rat-piss they sell in Shipwrights.'

As they ducked under the ivy and in through the wide-open door of the drinking house, the conversation died away. People looked up and stared. They stared at *him*, Berren realised, not at Master Sy. Then their heads dropped, one by one, and the chatter resumed.

'This is the Eight Pillars of Smoke, or the Eight as most of us call it,' murmured Master Sy. 'As I said, if you need looking after, go to Teacher Garrent. If you need some actual help, come here.' He made a gesture at the barkeeper and wandered in among the low tables and the squat stools that surrounded them. The air, Berren thought, was unusually fresh and he could even feel a wind. Then he looked up and saw that the house had no roof. Just a criss-cross of beams thickly wrapped in ivy. The thief-taker picked his way to a far corner where three grim men sat together. Life had taught Berren a great deal about reading faces, but these three were impossible. They were blank. He didn't like blank. Blank made his skin crawl. Whatever they were talking about, they stopped long before Berren could overhear anything. They looked up, waiting patiently as Master Sy approached them. They obviously knew him. Berren found himself nervously scanning for a clear path to the door, for a fast way out, but the floor was too cluttered, the tables and the stools too closely packed. From table to table, over the top. That was the only way to do it ...

The nearest of the men got up. He was taller and heavier than Master Sy, with thick curly black hair and a thick curly black beard. The man's eyes narrowed. He bared his teeth and clenched his fists, and then he leapt at Master Sy, wrapped his arms around the thief-taker and crushed him. Berren jumped a yard backwards. He almost bolted.

'Syannis! Where have you been?'

The black-haired man had arms like posts, but if anything, Master Sy only looked slightly embarrassed.

'Mardan.' The thief-taker smiled weakly. The black-haired man let him go and glared down at Berren instead.

'And who's this tiger?'

'This is my apprentice, Berren. Berren, this is Master Mardan. Another thief-taker. If you ever have need of aid and I can't help you, come to him. You'll find him here much more often than you should.'

Mardan threw back his head and laughed. 'That's so true. Teaching your boy a few lessons, are you? Send him to me, Syannis. I can give him a few of my own.'

'Oh I'm sure he can learn drunkenness without any help. But either way he can wait until I'm done with him.'

Mardan wagged a finger in front of Master Sy's nose. 'It's an art to do it well and then win a fight, though. As you well know, my bloody-nosed friend.' The black haired thief-taker laughed. 'I suppose you're here to see Kol, eh? Well we're done with our business. Sharing a cup or two for the pleasure of it, we were, but I don't suppose you'd wish to join us.' He chuckled to himself again. 'Come on, little imp, let's be going.' He picked up a bulging bag from the floor and threw it easily across his shoulder. The second of the three men rose from the table. This one was smaller, slighter, much more like Master Sy. He wore a hood that cast most of his face in shadow, except for the sharp point of his nose. He almost seemed to float across the floor as he left.

'That other man was Teacher Orimel,' said Master Sy after they were gone. 'He's a witch-breaker. Don't be fooled. Mardan is taking his coin, not the other way around.' The thief-taker pulled up one of the now vacant stools and sat down. Berren fidgeted from one foot to the other. The last man wore clothes that spoke of money, but he was bald, his lips were thin and bloodless and his eyes were the eyes of a killer. He looked like a snuffer and he made Berren scared.

'Sit, lad.' Master Sy patted the other empty stool. Berren did as he was told. He sat, stiff and straight, still ready to flee. The bald man raised an eyebrow and pretended to smile.

'Hello, Syannis.'

The thief-taker gave a solemn nod. 'Justicar. This boy here is my apprentice. His name is Berren. I brought him here so you would know him.'

Watery eyes looked Berren up and down from the inside out. 'He reminds me of you,' said the bald man. 'Well then, Berren, good day to you. I am Justicar Kol. I am charged with keeping the peace in this city.'

Berren's jaw dropped. He *knew* this man. This was the bald man he'd seen at the execution! The man on the platform! The one who'd come out with the executioner. The man who'd ...

The bald man blinked. 'Does my name mean something to you?'

'You were at the execution!' he blurted. 'It was you who gave Master Sy that purse. Ten golden emperors, that's what you said. And it was all rubbish!'

For a moment, the table fell silent. Then Master Sy rolled his eyes. 'He waited until I came out and then he snatched the purse.' He sighed. Justicar Kol's lips quivered.

'He stole your purse?' He was smiling for real now. '*Your* purse. This boy stole *your* purse?'

The thief-taker shrugged. 'I was somewhat distracted.'

'Yes, you told me.' Justicar Kol was chuckling now. 'I heard all about you gutting three cut-throats down in Speakslate Alley. I don't remember hearing the bit where some boy snatched your purse in the middle of it all.' He looked at Berren and shook his head. 'Boy, you must have balls of steel.' He laughed again as the barkeeper wound his way among the tables and plonked three full foaming tankards down in front of them. 'Syannis, when I'd heard you'd taken on some boy, I have to admit that I wondered what in the name of Kelm's Teeth you were up to. Now I think I have a much better idea.' He took hold of his tankard and raised it at Berren. 'To you, young man. I was a thief-taker once. *No one* steals a thief-taker's purse. Really. No one does. It's a bit like walking up to the Overlord and spitting at him. Dim as a donkey's arse.'

'Or telling him that you like the Sun Tower better than his,' muttered Master Sy.

The bald man laughed some more. 'Yes, or that. Much the same really.' He shook his head again. 'I hope you know what you're doing, Syannis. So why are you really here? Have you found my pirates yet?'

The thief-taker pursed his lips. He hesitated and glanced at Berren.

Kol's face grew sour. 'He's either with you or he's not, Syannis. If he's not, you should never have brought him here. People have seen his face now. So have you found them?'

'It's not as simple as that, Kol. I know parts of it. I could bring you a few faces you might recognise, but that wouldn't stop it for long.'

'Then go and get them. Syannis, my privates are on the block here and if mine are then so are yours. Stopped for a bit is better than not stopped at all.'

Berren couldn't stop himself. 'Pirates?'

9

PIRATES

'Pirates.' Master Sy glared.

The bald man clucked his tongue. 'Pirates, young Berren.' He cocked his head at the thief-taker. 'Well, Syannis? Is there something you should be telling the boy?' When Master Sy didn't answer, the bald man smiled thinly. 'Well, if you won't then I will. Once upon a time, the folk from the fishing villages a little further up the coast used to row down at night whenever the moon was full. They'd come around the Wrecking Point and into the harbour and they'd try to climb up the mooring ropes onto the ships anchored there. Now, the people on the ships weren't stupid, mind; they used to set guards on watch to stop that sort of thing. Most nights the folk in the little boats came away bloodied and empty-handed, if they came away at all. It was a trip for the desperate and the starving.'

'People like your Master Hatchet might send boys like you,' muttered the thief-taker.

'But every now and then they'd manage to take a whole ship. Then they'd gut it. They used to throw the crew overboard and then steal everything they could carry. First we'd know about it was when the bodies started to wash up in the harbour. It used to be a real problem back in *my* thief-taking days, but that was before your time. The merchant-lords, when they came back after the civil war, took the opportunity to hire a company of sell-swords.

While no one was paying any attention, they put an end to any piracy from the fishermen once and for all. Never mind what they did or how, but you can be sure it wasn't pretty.' The Justicar barked out a laugh. 'After Marshall Kyra crucified Talsin's son on Pelean's Gate during the siege, a lot of things weren't pretty in these parts. Anyway, there's been little to speak of since I've been Justicar here, and that's how I like it. At least until now. Now it seems that they have taken up their old ways again.'

Master Sy was shaking his head. 'It's not fishermen.' He took what looked like a short wooden knife and drew it across the top of his tankard, decapitating the foam growing out of the top. He flicked the head onto the floor and did the same for Berren. 'Try it. Go easy though. This isn't like the beer you know from Shipwrights.'

Berren picked up his drink and sipped. Then his eyebrows furrowed in amazement and he took a long slow swig. 'Wow!' It was like drinking bitter honey. Master Sy was right, it wasn't like the weak watery beer in the taverns around Loom Street. Nothing was like the beer in the taverns around Loom Street. *That* tasted like the dirty water that used to drip out of the bottom of Berren's dung-cart when it was raining.

Justicar Kol drummed his fingers impatiently. 'Well *someone's* coming round the Point. Who else would it be?'

'That's where you're wrong. I don't think anyone *is* coming round Wrecking Point. And that means it could be anyone. My gut tells me Siltside.'

'Oh, well, yes all right, that *is* who else it would be. Just a little awkward matter of how they're getting right across from one side of the city to the other without anyone happening to notice.' Justicar Kol screwed up his face. 'Mudlarks. Has he told you about the mudlarks, young Berren?'

Berren nodded vigorously. He took another gulp of beer and swilled it around in his mouth. He couldn't remember ever tasting anything as good as this. And it was going straight to his head, too. He could already feel a warm buzzing behind his eyes.

'Nasty folk. Thieves, the lot of them. If it was down to me I'd sail across the river with a boatload of militia gangs and be rid of them. Gods! The Overlord would be happy to pay for someone to do it, too, and if not him then the merchant houses would. What do you think, young man? Should we sail across and put an end to them?'

Berren thought fast. *Yes* was the answer the bald man was waiting for. But the bald man had the look of someone who liked laying traps. So he asked: 'Why don't you?' instead.

Justicar Kol threw him a wry smile. 'There's those iron balls again,' he purred. 'You might have made a good choice here, Syannis. If he doesn't stab you in the back when he's done with you.' The Justicar chuckled at himself, then looked Berren in the eye. 'Because, believe it or not, I'm not allowed to, young man. They're not in my jurisdiction. The river marks a border. The city itself lies under Imperial administration, and that means me. Over there?' He stuck out his bottom lip and shrugged. 'Strictly, if they pay any taxes at all, then it's to the Borolans in Tarantor. One of Aria's great noble houses. One with a rather strained relationship with the throne in Varr, too. I'm afraid Lord Mellith is far more concerned about who his errant cousin chooses for his friends than he is with us and our trivial little pirate problems. So they endure.'

'But couldn't you just ...' Berren stopped himself. He knew he shouldn't be asking questions of someone like the Justicar, but the beer was making him bold.

'Couldn't we just what? Sail over there and burn the place down?'

Berren looked sheepish. That was pretty much what he'd been thinking, but when the Justicar said it out loud, it didn't sound half as clever as it had seemed. Kol looked

Berren over and sniffed. 'You're one of Khrozus' boys, aren't you? One of the thousands of bastards that Khrozus' army gifted us before they left. You can probably thank the mudlarks you were born, boy.' He sniffed. 'Yes, we had a go at the mudlarks once. There are a lot of people in this city who remember that. They remember the civil war that came a year later as well, and they can't shake an uneasy suspicion that the two were somehow related. The city nearly died in the siege. I was here and it was hell. We ate the dead, boy. And when we didn't have any of them left, we started on the sick. You don't see it on the surface now, but underneath it's there. People remember. Those big weevils you can buy down by the docks, roasted and spiced? They call that a delicacy now, but no one ever used to eat weevils. Not until they had to. So the mudlarks stay. Sheltering under a confusion of authority and bureaucracy and a reluctance to do anything. Some people even think of them as the city's lucky charm. It's true that now and then a few of them will try to sneak in among the boats and barges at the river docks to steal whatever they can find, but so what? Keep me out of it. Keep all of us out of it.' He raised his tankard. 'A toast! To the mudlarks!' He took a deep draft. Berren raised his tankard too. The sudden movement made him sway sideways, so much so that he almost fell off his stool.

'Good, eh?' The bald man lunged and pulled Berren towards him. He hissed in Berren's ear. 'Your master is looking for thieves and pirates. There are plenty of them over there across the river. Make it stop and there's gold in it for both of you.'

A hand shot across the table and grabbed the Justicar's arm. He let go.

'Been here a while have you, Kol?' Master Sy withdrew his hand and sipped his beer. The Justicar's face twisted into a thin and mirthless grin.

'You'd be just right, Syannis. I've got a bag of gold for you. Go and find yourself a company of sell-swords and help yourself. You can be a king at last. King of Siltside.' He chuckled mirthlessly to himself. Berren flinched. He didn't quite understand, but the cold fury around Master Sy was strong enough to freeze the whole room.

'Mercenaries are more my little brother's line,' said the thief-taker crisply. 'I'll write and see if he's interested, but I rather doubt you could afford him.'

The bald man smirked. 'Maybe I should write to him myself. One crappy little kingdom is as good as another, right? Or perhaps he'd like to be a thief-taker too. I've always got room for more. So. My pirates. When are you going to get rid of them?'

'Someone in the harbour-master's office is up to his neck in it.'

The Justicar's face changed again. He looked hungry now. The sort of face a leopard might make as it circled its prey. Berren slouched back on his stool, sipped at his beer, which was still delicious, and listened. His head was humming nicely now. This was probably the best place he'd ever been. Certainly the best he'd been to with Master Sy.

'Can you prove that?'

The thief-taker shook his head angrily. 'Not yet. But I will.'

'You do it soon, Syannis. I have the guild on my back. They'll take matters into their own hands if things get much worse.' His eyes narrowed. 'And you're not the only thief-taker who's after my gold. Who knows? Maybe one of the others will get there first.'

Master Sy shrugged, unconcerned. 'I'll tell you what I know and you can share it with whoever you like. I've spent nights out on Pirates' Point and they don't come around into Fisherman's Bay. I'm certain they row out from the inside of Wrecking Point but I've searched and I can't find their boats. So far the goods they steal haven't found their way back into the city. I'm guessing they go south, out through Siltside, but I don't know that for sure and I don't know how they get there.'

Justicar Kol wrinkled his nose. 'And what's this about the harbour-masters?'

Master Sy snorted. 'Hiding boats somewhere in Deep-haven Bay? Someone in the docks knows who and where.'

Berren's head was starting to feel thick and fuzzy on the inside. He grinned. 'Master Hatchet. He knows lots. Lots and lots.'

The two men stopped talking and looked at him. 'He thinks he does,' said Master Sy.

'I think you'd better get your apprentice home. First time for proper beer, young Master Berren?' Berren leered back. Amazing to think that he'd found Justicar Kol so frighten-ing at first, when he was just a small old man with creases in his face and no hair on his head.

'It's the best!' Berren smiled. He looked in his tankard and was surprised to find it was empty. He stood up, swayed. For some reason, it seemed like a good idea to bow to some-one important like bald Justicar Kol. And he knew how. He was really good at bowing now. Really, really good.

He bowed, stumbled, banged his head on the edge of the table and sprawled across the floor. For a minute or so he lay there, too apathetic to move. Then he giggled. There was a puddle on the floor and beer was dripping from somewhere.

'Nice, Syannis,' said a faraway voice. 'I've met him now. Don't bring the boy back here again.'

Arms reached under his shoulders and hauled him up into the sky. He was in a room full of lots of people and they were slowly spinning around him. He closed his eyes, but the spinning didn't seem to want to stop. He was start-ing to feel a bit sick.

'Boy, you're going to hate the world this evening.'

'Are we going to fight pirates now?' he slurred. His tongue was suddenly too big for his mouth and none of his words came out properly.

'No, boy. You're going to bed. You're going to be sick and then you're going to clean it up. And then in the morning, we're going to start you on learning your letters. When you've done that, you can fight as many pirates as you like.'

10

LETTERS

They marched in sullen silence away from the Eight Pillars of Smoke. Berren staggered in the thief-taker's wake, occasionally pausing to retch. His stomach was empty before they even reached the other side of Four Winds Square, and yet just when he was sure there was absolutely nothing left, the next wave of nausea would hit him. They barged through Weaver's Row and back into the thief-taker's yard. Someone from a neighbouring window leaned out, shouted a warning without bothering to look and then emptied a chamber pot as they passed, spattering the thief-taker's boots. He didn't flinch, but when they got back he tore them off and threw them at Berren.

'Sit outside and make them clean, boy!'

Berren had already polished Master Sy's boots once that day. First thing before breakfast, one of his daily chores, and yet here they were, covered in mud again. Mud and worse. Master Sy disappeared into his room and came out wearing a second pair. 'Spotless,' he growled, and then he stormed away back into the city, leaving Berren sitting on the doorstep on his own. He hardly dared to move. Alone in the thief-taker's house for a second time, left to look and pry as he pleased. Left to take whatever caught his fancy and run away ... except this time he felt so sick that he couldn't bring himself to move. Hands trembling, he picked up the thief-taker's dirty boots. The smell of sewage wafted over him and his stomach began to heave again. He turned away, took a deep breath and then stayed exactly where he was, cleaning and polishing until the thief-taker's boots gleamed like the golden towers on The Peak. When he was done, he crawled back inside and stumbled into his room and lay down. He thought he might doze for a few minutes and then sneak a peek into the thief-taker's room, but he must have fallen fast asleep. The next thing he knew, Master Sy was back, stomping on the floor, tearing off his second pair of boots and throwing them across the house.

'Those too,' he snapped as Berren emerged, hollow-eyed, peering down from the doorway of his room. The thief-taker didn't even look at the first pair. Instead, he threw down a stack of pieces of paper, most of them torn and all of them written on. Then he took out a pot of ink, fumbled, and spilt half of it over the floor. He let out a violent curse, threw Berren a grimace of unfettered rage; then he took a deep breath and stormed out into the yard in his stockings.

Berren crept down the stairs, wincing at every creak from every step. He still felt like he was going to be sick at any moment and now his head had joined in too. Some slave-galley drum-master was thumping away on the inside of his skull. Even his eyes had largely given up. He stumbled to the outside door and peered into the yard. Master Sy was leaning against the wall a few feet away, pulling furiously on a pipe. Without a word, Berren cleaned up the ink, slowly and painfully. Then the thief-taker came back inside, and that was when the real horror started. The horror of Master Sy trying to teach letters. He stuffed a quill into Berren's shaking hand and told him to write his name. Berren hadn't the first idea how. Master Sy snatched the pen off him and wrote on the paper, in a perfect script that would have made a scribe weep: *Berren*.

'Like that.' He handed back the quill. Berren dipped

it in the ink pot and dripped ink all over the paper. He tried to ignore how Master Sy clenched his jaw and how the veins stood out on his temple. He did his absolute best to copy what Master Sy had done. The result was such a blotted mess that neither of them had any idea how well he might have done.

'Again.'

Berren tried again. Second time around was, if anything, slightly worse. So was the pounding in his head.

'Again.'

This time Berren made absolutely certain that he didn't take too much ink. The result was that he didn't take nearly enough and kept running out halfway through each stroke. Still, he thought he'd done quite well. You could see some of the letters were almost the same as some of the letters Master Sy had drawn. Admittedly it looked as though someone had cut his name up into lots of different pieces and then put them back together in slightly the wrong order, but at least there were lines this time, instead of just blobs.

Master Sy closed his eyes and swallowed.

'Again.'

Berren tried again. Too much ink again. By now his hand was trembling too much to draw a straight line.

'Are you doing this deliberately, boy? Are you trying to make a fool of me? Because children learn to do this. And if children can master a quill and ink, I fail to see why a young man who has such a high opinion of himself as you do should have any trouble at all.'

'I ...' *I'm sick,* he wanted to say, but the thief-taker's face left him in no doubt that saying anything at all would be bad. Flustered, he tried again. This time his hand was shaking even more. He took far too much ink and dripped all over the paper again.

The thief-taker clenched his fists. He closed his eyes and

took three long breaths. 'You will stay here until you get it right,' he said finally. And that was what Berren spent the rest of the evening doing. Writing his name. Badly, and with a splitting hangover. He was writing well into the evening, by candlelight with his stomach rumbling loud enough to set the walls to shaking before the thief-taker finally relented. With a scornful sweep of his arm, he swept all the paper off the table and thumped down a plate with a slightly stale half loaf of bread and a mug of gruel that had gone cold enough to grow a crust of fat on the top. Berren gobbled it down. Master Sy watched. He was frowning so much that his eyebrows met in the middle.

'More tomorrow, boy,' he said curtly as soon as Berren had finished. 'And we'll work on you manners too. To your room now.'

The next morning, the table was covered in paper again. He'd almost come to look forward to practising bowing to Lilissa, but just like yesterday, she didn't come. There was no sign of breakfast. Maybe that was a mercy. He felt rotten and in no mood for either.

What there was, was Master Sy standing by the table, one hand on his hip, the other pointing a pen at Berren as though it was a sword.

'Write, boy.'

By the end of that day, Berren was starting to think he had the hang of it. By the end of the next he was feeling better again and was copying any word that Master Sy showed him. Not well, but well enough that you could see it was the same. Now and then he still took too much ink and ended up with an illegible smudge and a clip round the ear, but on the whole, he thought he wasn't doing too badly. On the next day he was even allowed a break; Master Sy took him out in the afternoon, out towards the Courts District this time and then down the Avenue of Emperors that ran right up from the river to Four Winds Square and down the other side to the sea in one dead straight line. There weren't any trees but there were a lot of statues. Master Sy started to tell Berren all about them, but after the third one, when it was obvious that Berren wasn't listening, he stopped.

'History doesn't interest you eh, lad? Well it's not my history. I suppose I shan't be offended.' He led the way down to the sea-docks in silence and then bought them each pickled fish in a bun. He stared out to the sea and Berren could see his eyes flitting from ship to ship, mast to mast, flag to flag. Looking for something and not finding it. After a while he shrugged and turned away. Berren took a hungry mouthful of raw fish and vinegar. The taste was strong and good. He ate it slowly, savouring each mouthful, the tang of it. A breeze was blowing in off the sea, taking the edge off the sultry afternoon heat. The air smelled of salt and waves. Master Sy, for a moment, looked quite content.

'Who is she?' Berren asked and then held his breath.

'Who is who?'

'Lilissa.' The same ritual they went through every time Berren asked. *Get her out of your head, lad*, the thief-taker would say, and that would be that until the next time.

Except this time master Sy grinned. He pushed the last piece of bread into his mouth and swallowed. 'Like her, do you, lad?'

Berren nodded. He was beginning to understand that when the thief-taker called him 'lad', he was safe. If the thief-taker called him 'boy' then he'd best keep his mouth shut and his head down.

'Yes, I thought you might. She's her mother all over. Easy on the eye, eh?'

Berren nodded again and then bit his lip. This wasn't quite what he'd expected.

'Well, all right. Since you're my apprentice now. She's a seamstress. She lives a few streets away, just off Weaver's

Row. Her mother did me a very great favour once. After she passed over to the Sun, I took it upon myself to look after Lilissa.' He shrugged. 'Really she's old enough to look after herself. I just watch out for her. And if you don't keep your hands to yourself with her then I'll cut them off and dump them in the sea and the rest of you with them. Got that?' His mouth was smiling but his eyes weren't. Berren had the uncomfortable idea that Master Sy meant absolutely every word of what he'd said.

'She's nice,' he said, fumbling for something to say and silently cursing himself for not doing any better.

'Yes, she is.'

'Is she going to come back?' There, *that* was what he wanted to say.

The thief-taker chuckled again. 'You're as bad as each other. When you've learned your letters, lad. When you can bow to her as though you're a gentleman and speak to her like she's a lady, and have found at least a *few* table manners, then yes, maybe I'll have some time for her lessons too. Kelm's Teeth! When you can do all that, you might even start to be useful.' He walked over to the edge of the docks and sat on the harbour wall, beckoning Berren to sit beside him. Their legs dangled in the air above the lapping waters. Now and then the wind blew spots of salt water into Berren's face. The ships out in the harbour were all facing the same way, sterns towards him, bows to the wind, swaying on their anchors. The thief-taker looked up at the sky.

'Reckon the wind's going to spare us the rain this afternoon?'

Berren nodded. 'Night rains later, that's all.'

'Be heavy, though. Some nervous sailors out there tonight.' The thief-taker grinned. 'Start pulling their anchors and they'll drift right into the shore. That's the trouble with this harbour. Nice and safe except for two things. Sea-wind and pirates. Tell me, lad, if you were a pirate, which of those ships would you pick?'

Berren licked the last pieces of fish and bread off his teeth and belched. The ships all looked much the same. They had different flags, none of them ones that he knew. A lot of them had no flags at all. Some of them were bigger than others. Apart from that ... 'The biggest one, I suppose?'

'Oh? The one with the most sailors on guard?'

'The smallest?'

'The smallest?' The thief-taker laughed. 'Don't lie to me, lad. You wouldn't chose the smallest. Come on, think. You want the ship with something easy. Nothing too big, nothing too heavy, nothing *too* valuable but something worth having. Something you could sell in the city nice and quick. Or small, so you could get it out without anyone seeing. That's what you want. How do you know where to find it? How do you know which ship carries what you want? Oh, and while you're thinking about that, even if you knew which ship was worth taking on, how would you know which one was which in the dark?'

'They all look different, don't they?'

'Not in the dark, lad.' The thief-taker sighed and stretched and stood up again. 'You think about that and tell me when you come up with anything useful. Now back. Letters.'

Berren walked back up the Avenue of Emperors in the fading sunlight, the heavy warm sea-wind blowing him up the hill. He looked at the faces carved into the white marbled stone. Strong faces, all of them. He had no idea who they were, whether they'd been good men or bad men, but he wasn't sure if that was how emperors should be measured. Strong kings fought wars and won them. Weak ones lost their crowns. Somewhere along here was the Emperor Talsin, who'd lost his throne a few months before Berren had been born. Somewhere else was Khrozus the Butcher, who'd taken it.

'Which one is Khrozus?' he asked. Master Sy actually smiled. It sat awkwardly on his face, as though happiness was something that didn't come to visit often.

'Up the top, of course. Right slap in the middle of Four Winds Square, riding his horse. He's up on Deephaven Square at the top of The Peak too, outside the Overlord's palace. Khrozus on one side, his son Ashahn on the other. We'll go to visit them one day, but not today. They don't let people like us so close to the Overlord's palace except on festival days.'

A drop of something wet slapped Berren on the nose. He looked up, and heavy drops spattered his face. They'd both been wrong about the rains. As the daily downpour began, he laughed and started to run.

That night Berren went to sleep with a smile on his face. It was a little over a twelvenight since the thief-taker had ripped him away from everything he knew, and for the first time he went to sleep without thinking that tomorrow might be the day he would run away.

It wasn't. He lasted three more weeks.

11
WELCOME HOME

Copying the words Master Sy showed him was one thing. Reading them was another; and when it came to taking thoughts in his head and writing them on to paper, he didn't have the first idea where to start. It took a few days for Berren to realise that he was never, ever going to be able to do what Master Sy wanted him to do, but the thief-taker was relentless. For three weeks, the horror unfolded. Each day, Berren was left in the house to practice his letters while Master Sy went about his business. Each day, he was supposed to copy out a section of some old book with half its pages missing that Master Sy had found. Each day, he was supposed to read back what he'd written. And each day, he couldn't. Yes, he could copy what was in front of him well enough, possibly even had a knack for it. But when it came to knowing what the words actually meant, he hadn't the first idea. Couldn't even begin. Every day the thief-taker came back, tense and frustrated, the afternoon rains dripping from his hat and coat, already anticipating Berren's failure. He would listen to Berren stumble and make up a few words, and then he'd rage and swear and tear at his hair. Each day got worse and worse.

On the second Mage-Day in the month of Lightning, Berren had a stick in his hand. He was jumping back and forth around the room, lunging and slashing as though it was a sword, shouting curses at imaginary enemies, something he often did to pass the time when he was on his own. Papers lay strewn on the table. The afternoon rains were hammering down outside and the thief-taker never came home until after the rain had stopped.

Berren didn't even hear the door, only a change in the sound of the rain. When he looked round, Master Sy stood in the doorway. Berren stood frozen, the wooden sword in his outstretched hand, caught in mid-lunge. The thief-taker didn't even wait for Berren to speak. He took one look at the papers on the table and scattered them across the floor with a sweep of his hand.

'Boy!' he roared, lips tight with rage. 'So this is why you never learn anything! Stupid boy! Do you think this is all for fun?'

Berren skittered around the table, keeping it between them. The look on the thief-taker's face made him want to run. It was the sort of look that spoke of broken bones and worse. Weeks of frustration welled up inside him. He snatched up the ink pot. 'It's not fair!' he shouted. 'I can't do it and I don't want to do it! None of it makes any sense and I don't want to learn your stupid letters!'

Master Sy snarled at him, trembling. 'Boy, sit!'

'No!' Berren was holding the ink pot to throw it, but then a mad impulse seized him. Very deliberately he emptied it over the papers littered across the floor. The thief-taker's eyes bulged. His knuckles clenched white. For a moment he stood rigidly still and then he lunged. Berren dodged him, round the other side of the table. He dropped the ink pot and ran out the door into the rain. 'I don't want to learn letters!' he shouted. 'Letters are stupid! I want to learn swords and you never show me anything that I want!'

The thief-taker picked up the ink pot and threw it at Berren as hard as he could. It missed his head by inches and smashed on the wall behind him. 'Get back here, boy!'

He strode to the door. As he did, he picked up a belt. 'Get back here now!'

Berren backed away, trembling. He'd felt the rush of air past his head when the ink pot had missed. Now the look on the thief-taker's face was murderous and terrible. Master Sy strode out into the yard and kept on coming, belt in hand. Berren ran. He shot out of the yard, slipping on the wet stone. Through the alley and out into Weaver's Row, quiet in the afternoon rain. A sharp turn into Button Lane got him into a part of the city he knew well. He glanced over his shoulder. Master Sy wasn't chasing him. He slowed down to a trot through Craftsmen's and then zigged and zagged through The Maze, the warren of narrow streets and alleys that separated the Market District from the sea-docks. The rain meant there weren't many people about. The city was quiet at this time of day. Most folks were in their homes, done with their work for the day, pulling off their boots if they had any and getting ready to take their supper. Then there were the ones who came out after the rains, the ones whose trade were more suited to the evening. They'd be watching the skies, waiting by their doors to rush out as soon as the cloud began to break. As for the ones who came out after dark – well, it wasn't dark yet.

The Maze slowly merged into the back of the sea-docks. Berren stopped. He stood, bent almost double, hands on his knees to hold the rest of him up, gasping for breath. Once he was quite sure the thief-taker hadn't followed him, he sat down heavily in a doorway and held his head in his hands.

Master Sy could have killed him with that ink pot. He told himself that again, partly in disbelief, partly to *make* himself believe. And now he'd run away. Whatever else, that meant he couldn't go back. Not to someone like that.

So he was never going to see Lilissa again. And he was never going to learn swords after all, or be rich and important and powerful and tell people what to do. It was all a big lie. He bit his lip. Crying never got you anything but jeering and a beating from the older boys, but his eyes burned all the same. Right there and then, he hated the thief-taker more than anyone in the world for showing him so much and then taking it all away again.

The rains slowly relented. The evening sun broke through the cloud and glittered across the bay, already fiery red. It would be dark soon. Reluctantly Berren got up. Wandering the back alleys of the sea-docks at night was no place to be if you were small and on your own, even if you didn't really have anything worth stealing. There were gangs about who were interested in things other than money. Berren had never run into them, but that was because he was careful. He'd certainly heard the stories. Gangs of men who took boys and dragged them off to sea. Gangs of men who took boys for other reasons. Right now, going out to sea on a ship and never coming back didn't seem like such a bad thing, but Berren wasn't sure how you could tell those gangs apart from the other ones.

And anyway, there was always Master Hatchet. It wasn't as if he didn't have a place to go. He took a deep breath. Shipwrights was a part of the fishing quarter and the fishing quarter was a huge place, but Loom Street was close enough to the docks. With a bit of luck he could get there before the streets got really dark. He set off again at a run. That was the thing. Never stop anywhere that wasn't out in the open. Never stop in the shadows. Never stop if someone shouted at you or if a hand grabbed at you. Never stop at all if you could help it. Not here in the back alleys of the sea-docks. He didn't stop when he reached the harbour and the waterfront either. There was less to fear among the crowds of sailors and the teamsters. Some of them were drunk, but most were still hard at work. The work on the docks never stopped. There were always people there at all hours of the night, hauling bales and crates to and from the boats at the edge of the sea.

He slowed down again once he passed through the Sea Gate and reached Reeper Hill. Every house on the street here was a brothel, from the crumbling ramshackle town-houses at the bottom by the docks to the almost-mansions at the top and back to the squalid shanty-town of huts down the other side on the edge of the fishing quarter. Everyone came to Reeper Hill. Sailors and dockers mostly but princes and priests too; you'd find them all if you knew where to look. No one wanted any trouble on Reeper Hill. Although he'd learned the hard way not to stop and stare for too long at any of the ladies out by their doors.

Near the top of the hill on the fishing quarter side there was a small road that led out around the north side of the sea-docks. Further on it petered out into a path that led eventually to nothing much except the jumble of rocks at the top of Wrecking Point. Berren followed it a little way and then turned down a muddy track, skittering down the steep slope of the ridge and into the stinking backside of Shipwrights. The smell reached out and grabbed him like a hand, shaking him to his senses. He'd forgotten how strong it was here, or perhaps he'd never noticed because he'd never really known anything else. He hopped and skipped down the path, dancing from one uneven step to the next without even looking. This was home, this was, and between that and the smell, he was almost smiling when he reached the bottom. He squeezed through the darkness between the twine-maker's house and the gloomy but familiar half-collapsed bulk of an old compass-maker's workshop. When he came out the other side, he stopped. Loom Street. He sniffed. Over in this part of the city, the air was rich. A heavy base scent of the sea and of rotting fish. A steady mid-tone of manure from the dung heaps. High notes of sweat, of soured milk, of vinegar, of cheap perfume, depending on the time of day. *They don't get air like this up on The Peak. Makes you strong, it does.* When the smell from the fishing wharves got particularly bad, that's what Master Hatchet always said, regular as the tides.

He walked carefully. The cobbles of Loom Street were either uneven and full of holes or worn smooth and slick with a fine slurry of rain and sea-water and dung. The locals here had a saying: You could always tell a Loom Street boy from how clean their hands were. On Loom Street you learned the hard way to wash your hands before you put them in your mouth.

The alley behind the tool-makers' was as dark as it always was in the middle of the night. Berren was used to it. Used to not being able to see his feet or even his hand in front of his face. They used to run down here, even in the pitch black, but today he was more cautious. The alley had a few traps for the unwary. Buckets of slurry, brooms propped up against the wall. Things that would make a noise and give a warning if anyone came. Berren picked his way past them. He reached the little door that led up a tiny flight of steps into the brothel next to Master Hatchet's. It was ajar. A breath of warm air brushed his face, moist and heavy with cheap perfume. A few steps on, the alley ended in one last entrance. Master Hatchet's house. In daylight he could have gone the other way, around into the yard where they kept the dung-carts. The yard had a gate, though, and that was always bolted shut after sunset.

He knocked on the door. Quietly at first, then louder. Hatchet didn't sleep much. Except sometimes when he went out drinking all night and the boys woke up the next morning to the sound of his snores shaking the house.

Berren banged on the door again. This time he heard footsteps, heavy and slow. A glimmer of candlelight seeped through the gaps around the door where it didn't quite fit in its frame.

'Who is it and what do you want?' growled a voice from the other side. Berren's heart jumped inside his chest. A little bit of fear, a little bit of hope, maybe a little bit of despair. Master Hatchet.

'It's me, sir.' His voice had a tremor to it.

'Who's me? And what do you want?'

'It's Berren, sir.'

There was a long silence. 'Berren. Had a boy work here once called Berren. Worthless little shit, he was. Can't be that Berren though. Boy was stupid all right, but not even he was dim enough to come back to Loom Street after he'd taken up with a thief-taker. So you must be a different Berren.'

'Set the dunghill wet so it may rot and be odourless; also set it out of sight; the seed of thorn will decay and die in it. Asses' dung is best to make a garden with; sheep's dung is next; and after that the goat's and also horses' and mares'. Swine's dung is the worst and should be kept apart and thrown into the sea.' All you needed to know to be a city dung-collector. Hatchet made them recite it every day when they went off with their carts. It was the closest thing they had to a password. There was another long silence. The door didn't open.

'Piss off, boy,' he said, at last.

'Master, please ...' No, that was a mistake. Begging and pleading with Hatchet never got anyone anywhere.

'Run away from your new master, did you, little thief-taker boy?'

Berren swallowed hard. 'Yes.'

Now the door did open. Hatchet stood there in a night-gown, clutching a candle-holder. He gave it to Berren. 'Here. Hold this.'

Berren took the candle. Hatchet bent over and reached for something just inside the door. 'Here's your welcome home, boy.' He stood up, holding a bucket, and threw the

81

contents. Berren jumped sideways, but not quickly enough to completely dodge whatever Hatchet had thrown at him. Cold wetness slashed his chest. The candle went out, plunging them back into darkness. Suddenly he couldn't even see Hatchet, even though he knew exactly where he was. He stepped very carefully away, backing silently down the alley, heart pounding in his chest.

'Your new master gives me the ghosts, boy. I want nothing to do with him. I don't want him coming back here and I don't want to see your sorry little face again either. I raised you. Fed you. Sheltered you, and what do you do? So piss off you little ingrate.' He picked up the stick he always kept by the door and banged it on the cobbles. 'You come here again, if I even see you on my patch, I'll give you the thrashing of your life. If you're lucky.'

The door slammed shut. Berren was alone.

12
SHELTER

He stood in the alley, wet and scared. The stink of pig-shit wafted around him. His breathing was ragged. He was trembling. Anger flushed through him. *Sheltered me? You* sold *me!* His fists clenched. He had a mad urge to rush at the door and pound on it until Hatchet came back and then punch and kick all this rage away. But that could only go one way, a bad one. As far as Berren knew, Hatchet had never lost a fight with anyone. He took a deep breath. Loom Street. The arse end of Wrecking Point and Reeper Hill in the middle of the night. Not a good place to be. Not that he had anything much worth taking, but that didn't mean people wouldn't try.

He moved back down the alley to the door of the brothel and gave it a very gentle push. It opened. That was usual enough. Club-Headed Jin would be waiting up the top of the steps if anyone came in. Now there was someone who could have given Master Hatchet a good run when it came to fisticuffs, but as far as Berren knew, the two of them were friends. At least they used to go and get drunk together, which, as far as Berren could tell, made them friends.

The smell of pig-shit followed him through the door. Berren sniffed at his shirt and then recoiled. Jin was good-natured enough. Maybe he'd let Berren stay the night if he kept out of the way, but not with him smelling like a pigsty.

With a sigh he took off his shirt and threw it back into the alley. It was a good shirt. Master Sy had given it to him, and he was fairly sure that Lilissa had brought it. Might even have made it. It was plain and simple and it scratched at his skin, but it was easily the nicest shirt he'd ever had.

Chances were it would still be there in the morning. He could pick it up then, take it out to the sea and wash it clean. Maybe.

'Oi-oi!' Berren jumped. He looked around, back up the steps from the doorway. Dim light framed the shape of Club-Headed Jin. 'Who's that down there?'

'Berren,' said Berren. Jin knew all of Hatchet's boys. He was easy on them most of the time, as long as they didn't mess with his women. The older boys often spent their money here, if they had any.

'Thought you were gone. Heard you'd taken up with a thief-taker. What you doing back here?'

'I don't want to be a thief-taker.' He found he wasn't nearly as sure of that as he was when he'd left Master Sy. He tried to remind himself of the thief-taker's temper. Of the flying ink pot that could have taken his head off. Instead he found himself remembering fresh clean water and meals that were simple but at least not stale or mouldy. Remembering walking with Master Sy through the city streets, gawping at everything, pretending to pay attention to what the thief-taker was saying about who lived where and did what and why. Remembering Lilissa.

Jin made a means-nothing-to-me sort of noise. 'Well you can't stay here and I doubt Hatchet's going to take you back. Running away from your master?' He drew a long breath between his teeth. 'Boys should know better. Now you've run away from two.'

'I said I didn't want to be a thief-taker.' He shouted it up the stairs. 'Hatchet sold me.'

'Oi.' Jin frowned. 'Keep it down.'

Berren sighed and flopped down on the bottom of the steps. 'I don't know where to go.'

'You're not staying here.'

'Where do I go, then?'

'Home. You stupid?'

'Up Reeper Hill and through the back of the docks? In the middle of the night?'

Jin thought about this. 'What's that smell?'

'Master Hatchet threw a bucket of pig-swill at me. He missed,' he added quickly, 'But it's all over the alley.'

'Outside my door?' Jin made a discontented rumbling noise. 'We'll have to have words about that. Who's going to come in through that stink, eh?' He blew out a great lungful of air and then shrugged his shoulders. 'It's late anyway. Not many fellows about this time of night. I won't be sheltering one of Master Hatchet's boys if they've crossed him some, but I suppose if you sat down there all through the night and kept very quiet and very still, I might not even notice you were there. Mmmm.' He shrugged again and then turned and vanished back into his room at the top of the stairs.

'Thank you, Master Jin.'

'Quiet and still,' rumbled a voice.

So he sat on the steps, hugging his knees to his chest to keep warm. At some point he must have nodded off, because when he looked up it was light outside. Not proper daylight, but the grim grey light of dawn. His arms and legs were stiff. The world was quiet. He crept up the steps to look for Master Jin, but the room at the top was empty and he knew better than to go any further; instead he went outside. His shirt was lying in the alley where he'd left it. When he picked it up, the stench almost made him sick. Then he trotted out of the alley and turned right down Loom Street, all the way to the end where it petered out into a shingle beach scattered with ropes and little boats turned upside down, with nets hung up to dry in amongst the broken bones of shattered ships. This was the thin end of the fishing district. South of Wrecking Point and north of The Peak and Deephaven Point was the huge Horseshoe Bay, home of the sea-docks. The waters there were deep and sheltered. North of Wrecking Point, starting here, the waters were shallower and when the winds came in off the sea, they howled straight up the beach and onto the shore. A whole string of small bays and coves were home to the Deephaven fishing fleet; in fact what the city called the fishing district extended for more than twenty miles up the coast and the fishermen who lived in the scattered villages at the far end of that would have been surprised to be told that they lived in Deephaven at all. Deephaven did that. It reached out along its waterways like a greedy prince stretching out to grasp at everything within reach.

Berren felt a pang of anger. Those were Master Sy's words, from one of the rare times he'd been given a break from beating his head against his letters. They'd walked half a dozen miles together along the bank of the River Arr to see how the city never quite came to an end. Past the river-docks, through Sweetwater and past Sweetwater Bend where rich and poor alike collected drinking water from the river before it flowed beside the city proper. Up into the gentle affluence of the River District, where small markets and expensive riverside inns mixed with open farmland.

He shook himself and picked a path down to the sea. The water was cold this morning, the waves gentle and calm. Most of the fishing boats huddled together on the north side of each cove where they'd have shelter from the weather if they needed it. The southern corners like this became something of a wilderness. Debris washed up from storms past lay scattered about, all the pieces too big or too useless to be carried away. They'd stay until winter, when the beach would be picked clean of its wrecks. Anything that would burn and keep people warm at night.

He wasn't alone. The fishermen were already up. Old men mostly, down here. The old, the broken. People who eked out a desperate living as best they could. They'd take their little boats and row out into the water and throw out their nets and take what they could from the bay. None of them paid much attention to Berren as they groaned and dragged their boats into the waves. When he'd finished rinsing and wringing out his shirt, Berren stayed and watched them for a while. A breeze was slowly but steadily picking up, the usual wind blowing from the north-west, trying to push the fishermen back onto the shore. They had no choice but to fight it, labouring through the waves, hauling themselves out through the breakers, fighting against the will of the ocean. Berren shuddered. There was always this. Whatever else the city dangled in front of him and then took away, there was always this. He could spend his life breaking his back against the sea just to make sure he didn't starve.

Of course, if you didn't come from around here, you wouldn't know that the leaky boats that these old fishermen used weren't their own. They paid rent for them, every day, whether they used them or not, to men like Master Hatchet. Most days the rent cost them almost everything they caught.

He shivered again. The wind was chilly and he was already cold. He turned and left the fishermen to their work. He didn't know where he was going to go, only that it was somewhere else. Anywhere but here.

13
OLD FRIENDS

With nothing better to do, he wandered back up Reeper Hill. Outside the rich houses at the top, a few carriages still stood waiting to take the young princes of the city back home after their all-night orgies. Berren gave them a wide berth. Everyone knew about this part of Reeper Hill. Rich young men only a few years older than him, drunk, bleary-eyed from lack of sleep, intoxicated with the most fashionable drugs from across the sea. Tempting targets, but the mentors and the bodyguards, the snuffers who looked after them, knew all about muggers and pickpockets. Most of the men who stood guard up here were old enough to have fought in the war from before Berren had been born. They were Khrozus' soldiers, boys from the countryside. They'd eaten rats and dogs and crabs. They'd stripped the beach of seaweed and made it into soup. In the end, they'd eaten each other as they died. They'd seen an emperor's son crucified alive over the city gates to keep the enemy at bay. And in the end, they'd come through all that and they'd won. A lot of them had stayed.

Each time he came to a carriage, he made sure to walk on the other side of the street. Most of what he knew about the men who stood guard up here he'd learned from Master Sy; but that they wouldn't think twice about gutting him and leaving him to bleed to death was something he'd known for a long time. No one cared what happened to boys like Berren. Even Master Hatchet.

Except Master Sy.

He sighed and stopped in the middle of the street. He couldn't go back to the thief-taker now, could he? Even if he wanted to. Which he didn't, he reminded himself.

'Hoy!' He jumped at the sound of the cry. Someone leaning against one of the carriages was looking straight at him. Someone with a sword. The man made a little gesture, waving him away, and then drew a finger across his throat. Berren gulped and nodded. Standing in the middle of Reeper Hill, bare-chested and barefoot so early in the morning was no place to be; and so he hurried on, down the other side of the hill and into the early morning bustle of the sea-docks. At least there he didn't stand out. The bells from the solar temples were ringing, spewing the devout back onto the wharves after their dawn ceremonies. The temples here did a good trade. Blessings for sailors about to go back out to sea and cures for drunkenness and all-night hangovers. The solar priests did real magic too. Hardly anyone ever saw it but everyone knew, everyone heard stories.

In your civil war, when Khrozus the Butcher rose up against the Sapphire Throne, the Autarch of the Sun in Torpreah denounced him and called upon his priests everywhere to defy the usurper. Yet when Khrozus took Deephaven and Emperor Talsin laid siege to it, the priests of Deephaven very carefully took no sides at all. Why? Why would they do that, Berren?

He'd had no idea. All he knew was that, right here and right now, it didn't matter. Answers to that sort of thing were no good to him now.

Although ...

He grinned and almost jumped for joy. Garrent! He could go to the moon priest. Even if he couldn't think of anything else, he could go there. A sudden energy filled his tired legs and he ran across the wide open space of the docks, weaving in and out of the crowds and the human chains hauling bales and sacks down to waiting ships on the waterfront. Here and there he bumped people in his rush, drawing surly shouts and the odd half-hearted fist which he easily dodged. He was so pleased with himself that he almost didn't see Hatchet's boys until it was too late.

'There he is!'

If they hadn't shouted and pointed and started running, he might even have stopped to talk to them. As it was, they came at him with faces scrunched up for trouble. Two of the older boys, Jerrin One-Thumb and Hair. Berren changed course abruptly, darting for the warehouses and for the alleys that ran behind them. Instinct took him that way; that was where he always ran. The docks were his home and he knew the alleys as well as anyone.

Trouble was, so did Jerrin and Hair. When a fast series of switchbacks didn't throw them off, he careened off a wall and bounced down a passage so narrow that he kept scraping his shoulders on the walls. He hoped it might slow the bigger boys down, but it didn't. He hurdled a few empty wooden crates and catapulted out into a tiny square, launching himself at a gate that led into a warehouse yard. He just about got over it before they were after him, scrambling up. Hair gave Jerrin a leg-up, and suddenly One-Thumb was right behind him. Both boys whooped and shouted as they chased after him, calling ahead to any other boys who were out here.

'Give it up, Mouse,' shouted Jerrin. 'Give it up and I'll go easy on you.' Mouse was what the other boys called him on account of one time when he'd managed to kill three of the mice which plagued their dormitory and ate the old crusts they hid about the place. He'd killed them by snapping a wet shirt at them like a whip. Jerrin, of course, had called him Mouse. They all had names. Jerrin was one of Hatchet's favourites now, but it hadn't always been that way. Hatchet had his name for a reason too, and they'd all found out what it was the day Jerrin had become Jerrin One-Thumb.

Berren ran faster. Hatchet's lesson had stuck to Jerrin like a whore's lips. Mercy was a weakness. Berren didn't waste his breath on an answer but ran harder. His legs were burning now, his lungs working hard, sucking at the air. He didn't even know why they were chasing him.

Except Jerrin wasn't chasing him any more.

His step faltered. Jerrin was walking from the gate, Hair behind him, in no hurry at all. When Berren turned back, he saw why. Two more of Hatchet's boys were already here. Sticks and Waddler. Berren reckoned he could get past Waddler easily enough, but Sticks was another matter. Sticks had long spindly arms and crooked fingers and a knack for grabbing a hold of stuff. And once he had a grip on something, even One-Thumb couldn't pry him loose.

'Always the same place, Mouse,' jeered Jerrin. 'You always come here. Over the gate and round the corner and then through the hole in the wall to Trickle Street.' He was laughing. Berren slowed and stopped. Sticks and Waddler didn't move. They were only there to stop him from getting away. He glanced again at Sticks, who'd always been as close to being a friend as any of them. Sticks looked him in the eye and shook his head. His face was hard. Unforgiving.

'Run off to be a thief-taker, did you?' Jerrin was getting closer but he clearly wasn't in any hurry. Now he'd made his catch, he was going to enjoy himself. 'Rest of us not good enough for you, eh?'

Berren licked his lips. He could try running again, pushing his way past, but there wasn't much chance of that. He could fight. He could do that all right. Fists and feet and teeth, but he was outnumbered four against one and they all fought as dirty as he did. So even less of a chance there.

'You shouldn't have come back here, Mouse. Me and the other new Harbour Men here, we're not happy. Got us up at the crack of dawn, the master did. Made us lose our beauty sleep and all because of you.' He grinned, but Berren was only half listening. The Harbour Men. They'd taken to calling themselves that a few weeks before Berren had gone to the execution. He didn't know why. They were all careful not to use that name in front of Master Hatchet, too. Hatchet never liked his boys forming little gangs. He liked it much better when they were at each others' throats and worked hard to keep it that way. Jerrin must have been on to something for his gang to have lasted this long.

'I'm going to tell Master Hatchet about you and your little gang and what you're up to,' he shouted at them. 'That's what I'm going to do, if you don't leave me alone.' He had no idea what he was talking about, but there had to be *something*.

Clearly there was, too. Jerrin's grin dropped off his face. He snarled and ran at Berren and threw his fist at Berren's face. Berren dodged sideways and ran around him. He glanced at the gate, but Hair was still there. He'd never get past Hair.

'Your ears broke? Hatchet told you to piss off and he sent us all out after to make sure you did just that. Roused us out of our beds.' Jerrin circled, wary. He had the strength but Berren had the speed and they both knew it. 'Oi, Sticks!' he didn't look away. 'Get over here and hold him. Waddler, you make sure no one goes through that hole. Either way.'

Sticks trotted over. Waddler sat down in front of the hole in the wall. Apart from that there was the gate or the locked doors into the warehouse. Those were the ways out. Berren weighed them up. He looked at Sticks again, but Sticks looked like he was mean for a fight.

'Where's your thief-taker master now, little boy?' hissed Jerrin. 'Not going to save you, is he?'

For the first time since he'd run, Berren felt truly frightened. Beatings he'd had aplenty, but something in Jerrin's face, the way he licked his lips, made it seem like this was going to be a whole lot more.

'Scared, Mouse?' Jerrin grinned again. 'Good for you. Because I'm going to kill you.'

Berren was so sure he was going to lunge that he was already dodging out of the way, plotting his path past Jerrin, past Sticks, a quick kick in the privates for Waddler and through the hole. But the blow didn't come. Jerrin was being patient for once. That made it even more frightening.

'Hold him, Sticks.'

That was it. Berren broke and ran. He jumped over Jerrin's outstretched leg and caught a slap around the back of his head. The slap staggered him, but at least he stayed on his feet. He danced around Sticks and was free ...

Sticks caught his wrist. The force of it spun him around, straight into Jerrin's fist. The blow caught him on the cheek, under his eye, and for a moment, the world lost its colour.

'That's from Master Hatchet. He says go away and don't come back.' Jerrin chuckled. 'Now the rest, the rest is from me and the Harbour Men.'

14

A POINT WELL MADE

Berren squirmed and wriggled his fingers, trying to make sure that Sticks didn't get a better hold of him while at the same time trying to pull himself free and dodge Jerrin's fist. He saw the next punch coming. Couldn't get out of the way of it, but managed to lower his head so it caught him square on the skull and probably hurt Jerrin as much as it hurt him. He kicked out at Jerrin's ankle, but One-Thumb jumped out of the way.

'Nice, Mouse. Very nice. If I'd known you could fight like this, I'd have made you one of us.' Jerrin was holding his fist gingerly, rubbing his knuckles. He looked past Berren. 'Hair! Get over here.' Slowly, taking his time, Jerrin took a few steps back. He had a piece of string tied around his waist, and tied to that was a small pouch made of leather, ripped and torn and sewn back together badly. One-Thumb's pouch had an almost religious significance. He'd found it one day a couple of years back, got it fixed up and kept it with him wherever he went. As far as Berren knew, none of the boys had ever seen inside it. Jerrin was opening it now, taking out a wad of cloth and slowly unwrapping something. Awe and anticipation got the better of Berren for a moment and he stopped struggling. He felt the grip on his wrist loosen.

Within the cloth, as Jerrin unwrapped it, something glinted. Something metal with an edge. The magic of the

94

moment passed, replaced by shock and horror. One-Thumb had a knife. Not only did One-Thumb have a knife, but he was going to use it. Berren wanted to scream at him: *That's not how we do it! Hatchet will kill you!* Even the militias and the watch didn't carry blades. City soldiers, the sellswords who looked out for the city's rich – the snuffers – they carried steel, but not the ordinary men. Ordinary men carried sticks or clubs. You needed to settle a matter, you settled it with a beating. Sometimes people didn't get up again after a beating, but usually they did. Usually they learned their lesson and hobbled away. That was the unwritten law of the city.

Blades meant murder. People who carried blades drew attention to themselves. Usually they didn't last very long. If Hatchet knew that One-Thumb had a knife, he'd have thrown them both into the sea. For a second, Berren was frozen to the spot. *He means it. He's going to kill me.*

'Whoa!' The gasp came from Sticks, who was always a bit slower to realise what was going on than the others. Berren felt disorientated. Why? Why would Jerrin do something like this? *What did I do?*

As hard as he could, he wrenched his hand away from Sticks. To his surprise, he broke free. Sticks was still staring at the knife. Jerrin didn't quite have it in his hand yet. It was a little thing, hardly worthy of the name. The sort of thing a rich man might have used for peeling a piece of fruit. There – that was the sort of thing the thief-taker had taught him, and a fat lot of use it was going to be. There wasn't much satisfaction in knowing exactly what kind of knife was about to stab you.

He ran. Sticks made a belated grab for him and missed. Jerrin shouted something, swore and lashed out with the knife. Berren felt it catch the flesh of his arm near the shoulder, felt it rip and sting, and then he was past them both and there was only Waddler in his way. He didn't have time to look at the cut One-Thumb had given him. Didn't hurt much, so he reckoned it couldn't have been that bad.

He was still carrying his stupid shirt, rolled tight, wet with sea water. He gave it a quick shake and spun it around a few times. Everyone knew that trick. In a pinch, a wet shirt rolled up tight was as good a weapon as any if you knew what you were doing, and Berren had had plenty of practice. He tried to think of Waddler as a mouse; he started to scream, whirling the shirt around his head. One-Thumb and Sticks were only a few paces behind him, but at least he was free. If Waddler didn't move out of the way, he'd be able to turn and put up a fight and maybe take out one of Jerrin's eyes before he got stabbed. Jerrin One-Eye. At least he'd remember how he lost it. Berren didn't even feel that scared any more. All he felt was anger.

Waddler took one look at him, squealed and scuttled out of the way. Behind Berren, Jerrin bellowed something. Berren didn't hear what it was, didn't much care either. The hole out into Trickle Street was right there in front of him. He had a way out. He didn't need to fight.

He reached the hole and threw himself onto the ground, half sliding, half pulling himself through it and never mind the scratches and the grazes it cost him. Fingers grabbed at his foot. He kicked them away, heaved himself forward, and suddenly he was free. He jumped straight up and ran a few paces and then stopped. Jerrin was there, head through the hole, pulling himself through. Berren screamed at him, turned back and threw a kick at Jerrin's head that would probably have broken his face if Jerrin hadn't ducked smartly back again.

'Come on then, One-Thumb,' he screamed. 'Come on out! You want a fight! I'm right here, One-Thumb. Come on! Coward! You whore's breakfast! You skag! Sailors' boy! Leper's dressing! Lady's handkerchief!'

'You're dead!' shouted One-Thumb from the other side of the wall. 'You hear me, Mouse? You're dead. I'm putting the word on you. You ever come to the docks again, you ever come near Loom Street, you ever set foot in Shipwrights, you're dead.' His voice dropped low, muttering to the other Harbour Men. Berren couldn't hear what he said, but he heard running feet. Hair and Sticks probably, heading back around. Waddler didn't run that fast.

'Tell you what, Mouse. I'll pass the knife to Waddler here and you let me come on through and we'll see who's the man and who's just a little boy, eh? Because that's what you are, Mouse, a little boy. You think you're so much better than the rest of us, but you're not. You're nothing. Thief-taker threw you out, did he? Because you're street-filth, that's why. Because you're one of Khrozus' boys like Waddler and Hair and no one wants you. You're the one who's going to be a skag, Mouse. A Sailors' boy. Except only for the really ugly sailors.'

The anger was wearing off. Berren started to notice how much his arm hurt. His face too, where Jerrin had hit him. He was having trouble seeing out of that eye now and when he touched his face, the flesh felt puffy and swollen.

He finally stopped to look and see how deep One-Thumb had cut him. Deep, that was the answer. There was blood almost dripping off his fingers. His arm was covered in it. He felt suddenly faint. On the other side of the wall, Jerrin was shouting something at Waddler and Waddler was whining. A moment later, Waddler's face appeared in the hole. He looked up at Berren, frightened half to death.

'P ... Please don't hit me ...'

He jerked forward as if kicked from the other side. Berren clenched his fists and his toes. He was about to kick Waddler in the face, but stopped himself. In the end, he had nothing against Waddler. Like Sticks, they'd been almost friends not all that long ago. Waddler had a knack for finding food and he always shared if one of the other boys was getting into real trouble. So instead of kicking him, he knelt down.

'Maybe I'll come back to settle this and maybe I won't. This is between me and Jerrin, though. If you see me, you just stay out of my way, that's all.'

Waddler looked up at him with wide bulging eyes and nodded vigorously. Then Berren turned away and ran, off into the narrow streets that knitted the back end of the sea-docks into the markets district and the Craftsmen's Quarter behind them. By the time Sticks and Hair came around from the other side, he was long gone.

15

SANCTUARY

In the backstreets of the Craftsmen's Quarter, he managed to get himself lost. The wound in his arm burned. When it stopped bleeding, he put his shirt back on to try and hide it, but it kept breaking open again; soon the upper part of his sleeve was stained red and stuck to his arm. People stared at him in the streets and veered away. Looking like he did, he had to be careful to avoid any of the local militia gangs, which meant keeping away from the main streets and that took even more time. When he reached Weaver's Row and Moon Street the sun was high and the bells from the solar temples were already calling people in to midday prayer. Half the day gone already. And then, somehow, he managed to walk right past the moon-temple doors without seeing them, despite them being as big as a house.

When he found them the second time around he pushed the little side-door open and flopped down onto the floor inside. The door closed slowly, pushing back the light and the heat and the sound from outside. In the dim cool quiet, Berren took a deep breath and sighed. His head lolled. Suddenly the only thing he wanted was to go to sleep.

'Hey! Boy! What do you think you're doing here?'

Out of the gloom and the shadows, someone in pale robes was coming towards him. Much too briskly to be Garrent. Berren tried to focus. His eyes wandered.

'Hey! Get up, boy!' The priest had a long silver staff. He

stopped, standing over Berren and rapped the end of the staff sharply on the ground. 'Get up I said!'

Berren looked blearily up at the priest's face. 'I'm looking … for Teacher Garrent.' Now that he was here, he couldn't think of a single good reason why he'd come. If he found Garrent, what would the old man do? Send him straight back to the thief-taker, that's what. He struggled to get back to his feet. 'It doesn't matter.'

'Teacher Garrent is asleep, so you have me to deal with instead. What is it that you want? Oh.' The priest peered at Berren's arm. 'You're hurt.'

'Yes.' Berren shook himself away. 'Someone … cut me.' He shivered. Jerrin had tried to kill him. It was a terrible truth to face.

'They didn't try very hard. I don't suppose you have any money, boy? Anything of any value at all?'

Berren shook his head. 'Why, sir? Do I need to pay to rest here?' He didn't have the energy to argue or get angry. His arm was hurting quite badly now. All he wanted was to close his eyes and drift away. 'It's all right, I'm going now. Thank you, sir.' *Thank you? Thank you for what?*

'When one comes for healing, it is customary to make an offering of some sort.'

'I don't want healing, sir. I just wanted a place to sit for a while.' Berren almost tripped over his own feet as he headed for the door.

'Teacher, boy. I'm a priest. That means I'm a teacher, not a sir. What's your name?'

'Berren, sir. Uh … teacher.' His eyes kept on closing all by themselves. This was no good. He shook his head, hard, trying to wake himself up. He'd been fine until he'd gone into the temple. The sooner he was back out again the better. He opened the door. And screwed up his face as the brilliance of the daylight outside crashed into him and almost bowled him over.

'Berren?' The priest took a step back and chuckled. 'Berren the thief-taker's boy?' He looked at Berren. Berren peered back, eyes squeezed almost shut against the light, mouth half open. 'If you are, then you have some explaining to do to your master. He came in here last night. He thought you might come by looking for a place to sleep. Looks like you found yourself somewhere less savoury.' The priest smiled. 'Come on boy, I'll see you home. A couple of days' rest and you'll be fine, although I can't promise that'll be true after your master's finished with you. Still, he's not really one for beatings, your master. Is he?' The priest came towards him, one arm reaching out, the other still holding his staff. Berren froze for a second, petrified. Then he turned and bolted out into the street. He ran straight into a clutch of old women, each with a basket full of sheets balanced on their head. Baskets scatted across the street. The women howled curses as Berren bounced off them and away. He dodged between the shouting buyers and sellers who packed out Weaver's Row, and a few seconds later the women and the priest were all out of sight. At least here in the bustle, no one had time to pay him much attention. They might watch him pass and hold tight to their purses, but everyone here had better things to do than call down the street militia ... Gods, he was so tired.

'Berren?' He jumped, ready to run again, then stopped and spun around. The voice was ...

'Lilissa!' He grinned a feeble grin and then, as an afterthought, bowed. The way a gentleman should bow to a lady. She didn't smile or curtsey back, though. Instead, her hands jumped to her mouth and she gasped.

'Look at you. You're bleeding! And look at your face!'

His cheek didn't hurt as much as his arm, but he had to admit that it *did* hurt. 'It's just ...' He was feeling woozy again. 'It's just a little thing.'

'Oh! Look at you! You're about to fall over. Come on!

Let's get you home.' She took hold of his wrist. He pulled away, shaking his head.

'Not back to Master Sy. I don't want to go back to Master Sy.'

'Why not?' She reached out for him again, and again he stepped back.

'I don't,' he snapped. 'I just don't. All right?'

She let her hand fall back to her side and looked him up and down. 'All right. I'll take you to my home then. You can't wander about like this. If any of the city guardsmen find you, they'll think you're one of Khrozus' boys and send you off to sea or even worse, to the mines.'

He almost blurted out that he *was* one of Khrozus' boys, but something stopped him. Maybe he was just too tired to speak. He let her take his hand, which was unexpectedly warm and nice and made him feel safe. She led him past the yard where the thief-taker lived, down another narrow alley that smelled strongly of dogs and to a tiny door. As she opened it, she brushed against him. A shiver ran down his spine. She smelled of the usual city smells, of fish and sweat, but of something else too. Flowers. She led him inside. The whole house smelled of them.

'Lavender,' she said, smiling at him. Sheets of cloth hung everywhere, each one a different colour. They glistened, still damp; on the floor sat half a dozen buckets filled with dark water. Lilissa caught his eye. 'We've been dyeing today. That's why I was in Weaver's Row, to buy some more sheets.'

'You dye sheets?' He caught his arm on a peg set into the wall. Gasped and staggered, and then Lilissa had her arms around him, holding him up, stopping him from falling. He took a deep breath and sighed. She felt good.

'I'm making banners for the wedding festival.' She let him lean on her as she led him through the front room of the house and into a second tiny room at the back. There was one blanket on the floor, a few more rolled up in a corner and space for nothing else. Berren slumped down. He lay back until his head was resting on the floor. He doubted he could have gotten to his feet again even if his life depended on it.

'I'd forgotten about that.'

Lilissa laughed. She sat on the floor beside him. 'How can you have forgotten about *that*? I thought people talked about nothing else!'

'Master Sy didn't like to ...' He choked on the words. 'Don't tell him I'm here, will you?' He turned, managed to focus his eyes on her face. It was a very lovely face, he thought, when you stopped to look at it. Not really beautiful, not like Club-Head's women, but nice. Friendly. Would have been pretty if it wasn't for the freckles, but still ...

She smiled again and looked away for a moment. 'You're so lucky,' she said.

'Am I?'

'To have a master like Master Syannis.'

Berren shrugged. 'I don't feel lucky.' He tried to grin. 'What I feel is a lot of pain, and I reckon I'm tired enough to sleep through a whole solstice celebration.'

She laughed. For a moment, her fingers brushed his hand. 'Master Syannis is probably the most honest, most honourable man in this whole city. Probably the whole empire. He's like a prince.' She squeezed down beside him and whispered in his ear, so close that her lips almost brushed his skin and he felt the wet warmth of her breath. 'I heard once that he really *is* a prince, run out of his home by wicked sorcerers.'

'He's not a prince.' Lying beside him, Lilissa had somehow paralysed him. He'd forgotten about how tired he was; instead, he had a strong urge to turn towards her and kiss her. Except he couldn't move, not even a muscle. *Isn't that what Garrent called him too? The thief-taker prince?*

'Maybe not, but he's a good man. He looked after my ma and now he looks after me. He never asked for anything and he's never lifted a hand against an honest man.' She smiled. 'He's teaching me to be a lady.'

His cheeks were burning. She was so close. He grunted.

'There's other thief-takers in the city,' Lilissa murmured. 'Plenty of them, but you and Master Syannis are different. The rest aren't much different from the thieves they take, but Master Syannis, it makes no difference to him whether his thieves are street urchins or princes, whether they steal a loaf of bread or a kingdom. To him, a thief is just a thief. You're so lucky that he's your master.'

Berren's eyes closed. He felt Lilissa shift beside him, felt her hair brush across his face and then a warm touch of skin on his cheek. And then he was asleep.

16
FORGIVENESS AND BETRAYAL

The daylight outside was gone when he woke up again, turned into grey twilight. The afternoon rains had come and gone – he could smell it in the air. Lilissa was gone too. He could hear her in the next room, though. Two hushed voices arguing about something. He froze, fearing the other voice must be Master Sy, but the voice was that of a woman. When he made out the words, they were talking about banners and dyes and sheets. He sighed and sat up.

'Easy, lad.'

Berren almost jumped out of his skin. Even though he knew the thief-taker was there, he could barely see him. Master Sy sat in the pool of shadows beneath the tiny open window, still as a statue.

'Nasty scratch you got yourself there.'

Berren scrambled to his feet and lunged for the door, but that was like treacle trying to outrun lightning. The thief-taker caught him around the waist and hefted him over one shoulder as though he was a sack of firewood.

'Hope you haven't been making a nuisance of yourself. Mistress Lilissa is someone I call friend, and I'm always good to my friends.'

Yeah? How good? he wanted to ask, but he didn't dare. The thief-taker carried him easily out of the bedroom and deftly picked his way between the hanging sheets outside.

He nodded and smiled at the two women. Berren glared at Lilissa. *I hate you*, he mouthed, but if she saw, she pretended she hadn't. Then they were out, in warm evening air that smelled of damp stone and roasting nuts. Berren's stomach rumbled.

'Not had much to eat while you were out and about, eh lad?' There, right outside the entrance to the yard where Master Sy lived, stood a brazier. An old man shuffled to and fro beside it, roasting nuts. The old man's back was so bent that his head was permanently staring at his feet. He must be daft, Berren decided, to set up here. No one came down this alley in the evenings.

The thief-taker paused. 'Evening, Master Jux.'

The bent-in-half man gave a nod. 'Master thief-taker.'

'I'll have a handful for my supper if you don't mind.'

The old man swept most of the nuts off the fire and into his hand. They must have been scalding hot, but he didn't seem to notice. He tossed them clattering into a pan.

'Keep them for me for a moment, Master Jux.' The thief-taker walked on past, into the yard. He went into his house and up the stairs. Then he dumped Berren into his room and bolted the door.

The last thing Berren smelled before he drifted back to sleep was roasted nuts, wafting up through the gaps in the floor.

He awoke in the morning to find the thief-taker sitting over him again. He had a battered bowl of warm water, some strips of cloth and a needle and thread beside him. Without a word, he set to cleaning the wound on Berren's arm. When he was done washing, he picked up the needle.

'This is really going to hurt quite a lot, lad. My little brother was always much better at this than me, so I'm afraid it's going to be an ugly scar too.' Then he jammed a piece of cloth into Berren's mouth, sat on his chest, wedged

Berren's arm between his knees and set to work. No hesitation, no more warning, straight into Berren's skin with the needle. Berren screamed. The needle had looked almost as big as Jerrin's knife. Now it felt like Master Sy was driving a burning spear-shaft into his flesh. The screaming didn't stop, even as he bit on the cloth; he tried to tear himself free, but the thief-taker had him fast. Wave after wave of agony raged up from his arm. Tears came, forced out of his eyes. He started to think his head was going to explode, even as he kicked and kicked, trying to gain some sort of purchase to lever himself free.

And then, mercifully, the pain started to ease. The needle finished its work. Berren tried to catch his breath. His heart was hammering like a galloping horse and he was breathing like a dying man.

'Oh ... Gods ...'

'Thinking about it, Talon usually used to get his man blind drunk before he set to work.' Master Sy frowned. 'Oh well. Can't be stopping now.' For some reason, Master Sy wasn't letting him get up. It was over, wasn't it? His arm hurt like someone had taken an axe to it, but at least it was going to get better now, right?

The thief-taker grinned at him. 'One stitch done. I reckon another six or seven should do it.'

'Whu ... ?' He didn't get any further before the needle came again. Berren's scream probably reached as far as the sea.

Yes. He was right. It did hurt. It hurt a lot.

When he was done, Master Sy tied a knot in the thread and stood up. 'Thought you'd faint, lad.' He shrugged. 'Later you can tell me how you came to get that. Oh, and when the stitches need to come out, I'm going to ask Lady Lilissa to do it, so you'd best be nice to her when you see her. She did you quite a favour taking you in. Young lady on her own takes a lad back to her house, people start to talk.'

Berren lay shaking on the thief-taker's floor. He was drenched in sweat. For all he knew, his arm had been cut off, because that's how it felt. *No she didn't. She betrayed me. She should never have told you I was there.* Her fault. Her fault he was here, lying in his own blood, dying, probably. Certainly felt like dying.

Master Sy paused at the door and turned back. 'Oh, and Berren, do I have to remind you? About the cutting your hands off and dumping them in the sea if you don't keep them to yourself?' He raised an eyebrow when Berren didn't move. With an effort, Berren shook his head. *Bastard.* 'Good. Don't worry about the blood. Looks like a lot, but you've got plenty. You can clean it up later. When you think you're ready, come down for breakfast. Lilissa's here today so make sure you practise your bows a few times before you show your face. But don't wait around for too long if you like your bread still warm.'

He did like his bread still warm, but moving was beyond him. Finally, when it was too late to do him any good, he must have have passed out, because the next thing he knew, his arm had subsided to merely feeling like it was on fire, and he could smell food, strong in the air. He heard the familiar scrape of the thief-taker's chair, signalling that breakfast was over.

Yes, his arm hurt like buggery but he was hungry. He stumbled straight down as soon as he could make his legs lift him off the floor. Tried not to look at the blood, and yes, there *was* a lot. He gave a surly bow to Lilissa and then pretended she wasn't there. To his surprise, Master Sy let it pass. After they'd broken bread, she quickly left, although not before she'd given Berren a look every bit as dirty as the look he'd got from Jerrin One-Thumb just before Berren had almost kicked him in the face.

The scraps of paper and the quills were gone, Berren noted. For the first part of the morning, Master Sy made a big fuss of bandaging Berren's arm, showing him all the dried leaves and roots he was using to keep the wound from turning bad. The names flew straight past Berren. The one he remembered was the one that came last. Soldier's Blessing, a leaf from somewhere a long way up the river.

'Chew on it. It numbs the pain.' And it did, although not enough. After that, he got on with the rest of his chores in sullen one-armed silence. The thief-taker didn't say a word about letters, and when the chores were done, he went back to trying to teach Berren the manners of a gentleman. Berren hated that almost as much as he'd hated letters, but at least he could do it; and since the alternative was probably more letters again, he applied himself with a furious dedication. By the end of the day, he was exhausted. His arm still burned, even through the constant chewing of Master Sy's leaves, but at least he'd managed to get by without the thief-taker slapping him for doing something wrong.

The next day, Master Sy took him out and bought him a set of clothes that were the finest Berren had ever known. No one mentioned letters again.

Over the weeks that followed, Master Sy took him to each of the city districts in turn and lectured him on what trades happened and who lived there. He told Berren which places to remember and which to avoid, who mattered and who didn't, and a little more of the city's laws. Berren learned to use ropes, how to mend them, how to tie knots that would slip and ones that would hold. He started to learn the care of blades, and of leather, and of bowstrings. He changed his own bandages and dressed his own wound. Best of all, though, was the afternoon when the thief-taker took Berren down to the armouries overlooking the mouth of the river past the end of the Rich Docks. He showed Berren a multitude of weapons and told him their names. Berren had never heard of half of them but he even got to hold a few, to learn how they felt in his hand. He was surprised at how heavy they were, even a short sword like Master Sy's. When the time came to take the stitches out of his arm, Berren did it himself, which was nowhere near as bad as he'd thought. Lilissa hadn't been to visit since that first day.

'Got herself a friend,' said the thief-taker. 'A young man sort of friend, if you catch my drift. A fishmonger's son. A good sort.'

'Is she going to come back?' In one sentence, Berren had gone from hating her to feeling as though he'd been stabbed.

Master Sy shrugged. Then he took Berren down to the sea-docks and they sat by the edge of the water, chewing on another lunch of pickled fish rolls. Berren couldn't stop himself from glancing up and down into the crowds in case he glimpsed Hair or Sticks or Jerrin or one of Hatchet's other boys. Then he realised the thief-taker was smiling at him. So he blurted out everything that had happened and how Hatchet had turned him out and how One-Thumb had tried to kill him. He was shaking by the end.

'I don't know why,' he said. 'You don't stab someone for being on your patch. You give them a kicking, sure, but you don't stab someone. You just don't.'

'Mmm.' The thief-taker swallowed the last of his fish. 'Probably best you avoid the sea-docks for a while then, eh? Lesson for you, though. When you ran from them, you ran like you were running from the watch. From the militia. But they're your friends now. Open spaces. Public spaces. Temples. Crowds. If you need to run from someone, that's where you go, lad. Not into the dark alleys. No one can help you there. You remember that. It's time you started to help me with my work and that means life's going to get danger-ous for you soon.' He paused expectantly. Berren felt a thrill of excitement shiver through him. Lilissa, One-Thumb and his Harbour Men, they were all instantly forgotten. Instead he was imagining himself tearing around the city, chasing after fearful thieves with a sword in each hand.

'Does that mean you'll teach me swords now?'

Master Sy laughed. 'Not yet, lad. I'll teach you swords once you've learned letters, and we'll worry about that again once you've mastered manners. No – we've got a little visit to make tonight, though. Supper with an old friend who might know a thing or two about our pirates. That is, if you can keep a civil tongue about you.' He frowned and stared out across the sea. Berren bit his lip. Letters! Why did he have to learn letters? Worse, why did he have to learn them *first*?

'Master, I'm no good at letters. I'd be really good at swords though, I reckon.'

'Ha!' The thief-taker laughed. 'Then you'll be no good as a thief-taker. If you want to get anywhere, lad, you at least need to read.' He stood up. 'Tell you what. There's things you can start doing so that when I *do* teach you swords, you'll learn faster. You're quick enough on your feet but your arms are weak. Work on your arms. You need to be stronger. Start with that.'

Berren nodded. The prospect of going out somewhere and being a part of whatever plan Master Sy was hatching almost made up for the disappointment. Almost.

'There's always money to be made around the docks for folk like us,' said Master Sy later, as they ambled through the city streets. 'Every year, more ships come and go. There are always people stealing from the merchants who arrive in the city, or, like this, from the ships themselves. Or else they're using the ships to smuggle things past the emperor's tax-collectors. The merchant lords don't mind a bit of smuggling at all, but they don't take well to piracy. They shout and shake their fists at the Overlord and the city officials. When that doesn't work, they come to people like me. It's all grist to our mill, lad. There's plenty of other thief-takers, though. We have to be better then them. Better means we have to know all the things that they don't. We have to keep our fingers to the walls. And I'll tell you something, lad. We'll be back in these docks sooner or later.' He lowered his voice. 'No one knows more about what goes on here than the harbour-masters. Keep your eyes and your ears wide open, lad. The harbour-masters are greedy fellows, the lot of them. They know more about thieving than they let on. I promise you, one of them is up to their eyes in this ...'

It took Berren a second or two to realise that Master Sy had stopped. Not only stopped talking but stopped walking as well. They were on the Avenue of Emperors, a little way up from the docks, and the thief-taker was staring out into the bay. All Berren could see was a torrent of people and carts, moving back and forth, and a forest of masts behind them. Something among those masts had struck his master dumb, but however much Berren peered into them, he couldn't see anything unusual.

'What is it, master?'

Master Sy shook his head. 'Nothing, lad. Nothing. Thought I saw something, but it's gone.' And he went back to talking about the harbour-masters and thefts from ships and how, sometimes, if a ship came in with a particularly rich fellow on board, the men who rowed round the Wrecking Point at night were a lot better armed and a lot better informed. Berren assumed he was supposed to understand that the harbour-masters had something to do with this, although Master Sy never actually said so. Mostly though, what Berren noticed was that Master Sy kept glancing out to sea, looking at something among the ships.

17

THE DISAPPOINTING TRUTH

'If you're going to come with me when I make my rounds, you need to be properly dressed.' They were back in the thief-taker's house. 'Take your shirt off and then wait here.' With that, Master Sy trotted up his creaking stairs into his tiny little bedroom. Berren heard him walk across the floor and stop at the far wall. There was a chest there. He knew that. He'd seen it through the crack when Master Sy had left the door open once.

He looked at his arm. The wound was still scabbed, still bled if he picked at it, but it was healing. Another few weeks and it would be gone. Just an angry red scar in its place. One-Thumb's mark.

The thief-taker came down again, carrying something that jingled. Coins, was Berren's first thought, lots of small coins; but then the thief-taker laid out a piece of metal cloth on the table. Ringmail, Berren realised, after he stared at it for a second. It was a short sleeveless shirt made out of ringmail. It had seen better days, too. Some of the links were rusted and it had a rip where something had punched through it. The sort of hole that an arrow might have made, only bigger.

Berren ran his fingers around the edge of the hole. The metal was sharp and jagged. Definitely too big for an arrow. A spear, maybe.

'Beggars can't be choosers,' snapped the thief-taker. 'It

was hard to find something small enough for a runt like you. You want it or not?'

It wasn't quite what Berren imagined when he saw his future self. Dashing swordsman, yes, blade in hand. Sometimes with a blade in each hand. Inns, taverns, wenches, fights, but always fights won with panache and exquisite skill. Yes, he would kill men, men like Jerrin One-Thumb, but it would be a blur of speed and deadly precision. He would be like Master Sy in the alley.

The ringmail shirt, on the other hand, looked like the sort of thing that let you stagger and crawl away when without it you'd be dead. Except for the hole where someone obviously hadn't done anything much but lie where they were and die anyway. It didn't look very heroic.

'Stupid boy,' snapped Master Sy. 'You think you're too good for this, eh? You might as well come out and say it since it's written all over your face. You think I'm going to teach sword-fighting to someone who can't even be bothered to protect themselves? What a waste that would be.' He sniffed, and then unfastened his own shirt. Berren stared. Master Sy's armoured vest didn't have any holes in it. It looked as though it was made of considerably finer steel too, but it was there nonetheless. When Berren squinted, it seemed to have a sheen of colours to it, a slight shimmer of gold or deep blue depending how the light caught it. 'See. Are you still too good to wear steel?'

Berren was still staring. 'That's amazing. Is it magic?'

The anger in Master Sy's face faded away. 'It's sunsteel, lad. Forged by solar priests and imbued with their blessing. There are some who say that it has sorcerous properties. It's tough, I can tell you that. Best metal there is for weapons and armour except maybe moonsteel, and as far as I know, the only forged piece of that in the entire city is the Overlord's sword.' He blew out his cheeks and sat down. 'You'll need an under-vest before you put that on to stop it chaffing. You might need quite a thick one.' He nodded at Berren's arm. 'I'd wrap your scratch up, too.'

Berren stripped to the waist. He ran up to his room and put on a vest, wrapped a bandage around his arm and then came down and picked up the armour, uncertain, wondering what to do with it.

'There's a hole in the middle for your head. Sling it on and then lace yourself up on either side. Nice and tight. Better to have it tight than too loose and billowing around so everyone knows you're wearing it. Make sure the two halves overlap. Gaps can kill you. Chances are they won't but you never know where a knife might slip in. Most likely, if anyone tries to stab you, they'll try to stab you in the belly. But they won't if they know you've got this on. Then they'll go for the face, the throat, the armpit, the groin. When they do that, armour like this just slows you down. So don't let them know you're wearing it. Let them find out the hard way.'

The ringmail was heavy but it seemed to fit him well enough. Berren set about struggling to lace up the sides. Then he ran his finger over the spear-hole.

'You come with me to do what I do, I need to know you're safe. When you show me you can do something more useful than run away really fast at the first sign of any trouble, I might see about getting that fixed up for you.'

'It's ... it's ...' It wasn't him. Wasn't who he was going to be. No, this wasn't how it would be, this rusty broken mail shirt, but for now he knew better than to complain. Act pleased, that was best. Act pleased and hope for a lesson in swords.

'Yeh, I'm just swimming in your gratitude,' grumbled the thief-taker. 'And no, you don't get a sword to go with it. Not until you learn to use one.'

Berren's heart nearly burst out of his chest. That was as

good as promising to teach him, wasn't it? Master Sy was going to teach him swords!

The thief-taker walked around behind him and undid all the lacing down both sides. 'Tighter, lad. Much tighter. This has to fit you like a second skin. The point is that no one knows you've got it on until they stab you and then instead of falling over dead, you stab them right back. There.' He finished redoing the laces. Berren tried to breathe and found that he couldn't, at least not all the way any more.

'Isn't that ...?'

'No, it's not too tight. The lacing will give a little. By the time we get to where we're going, you'll be fine.' Master Sy grinned and patted himself on the chest. 'When I was forced to run away from my home, this was one of the few things I managed to take with me. I've had it with me ever since. It's turned a blade seven times. Seven times I would have been dead otherwise. You'll learn, lad. The first time it saves you, you'll learn. Come on then. Shirt on, let's go! No dawdling!'

He led the way out into the yard, through the alleys and out into Weaver's Row and then turned left, heading up the hill and then down the other side towards Market Square. The sun had slipped down behind The Peak now and everything was turning to silhouette and shadow. Weaver's Row was wide enough, but all around it, narrow streets and alleys slowly filled with night. *His* streets, Berren reminded himself fiercely. This was *his* time. Deep twilight, when honest men were either back at their homes and in their beds or else revelling and in their cups. This was the time when he and the other boys would run their errands for Master Hatchet. A word here, a threat there, sometimes a purse with a few pennies, sometimes a piece of parchment with a poorly drawn purple blotch on it. Those were Hatchet's warnings. Never went down well, being handed one of those. He'd always hated being the person who had to deliver one.

Almost on cue he heard a shout and then running foot-steps belting away down one of the side-streets. Somewhere nearby a dog started barking. The thief-taker paused for the slightest instant, then kept on going. Fifty yards or so in front of them, a bored-looking gang of street militia ignored the sounds too. You learned quickly enough how it worked in the city. There were the streets that were safe and then there were the streets that weren't. After dark, which ones you used depended entirely on how you and the local militia got on.

The gang was coming up the hill towards them. They looked relaxed, didn't seem too bothered by anything. Berren's stomach clenched. As they passed, Master Sy gave them a short nod and they exchanged greetings. Berren had to bite his lip to stop himself from walking faster. The idea that the street militias were his friends now was going to take some getting used to.

Master Sy was grinning.

'Master, where are we going?'

'We're going to see an old friend of mine who also hap-pens to be a thief.'

Berren frowned, trying to digest this. How could a thief-taker have a friend who was a thief?

'Lad, a thief-taker has to earn his bread. There's no reward in grabbing any old petty pickpocket or cut-purse or robber in off the street. What would you do with them? Take them to Justicar Kol? He doesn't want to know. That sort of thievery is beneath him. Take them to the street militias? You could if you wanted to but they'll not thank you for it and they'll certainly not pay you.' He shook his head. 'If I see a thief cut a purse and I hunt him down and teach him the error of his ways, it's because I hate thieves, that's all. But this thief is a friend.'

'But ...' That still didn't explain *why* Master Sy was friends with a thief.

Abruptly Master Sy stopped. They were close to the edge of Market Square, still well lit with night time braziers and torches. Like the docks, the market never quite went to sleep. It thinned out a lot, but there were always people there trying to sell something and always people willing to buy.

'Look down there.' Master Sy frowned. 'You can't really see it in the dark. I'd heard of this city, you know, long before I ever came here. Even in my far-away little backwater, we'd heard about Deephaven. And do you know what made it so famous to us? That.' He pointed. 'The thing that you can't see down the end of that street. The Upside-Down Temple. I'd heard of that long before everything went wrong and ...' He shook himself. 'When I was younger than you, I always wanted to come here, just to see the Upside-Down Temple. I thought it must be the most amazing thing in the world. And then when I did get here, I had nothing more than the clothes on my back, the sword on my belt and a belly full of revenge. I had other things to do. It was more than a year before I was ready to come and see it. It was like a prize I was going to give myself once I'd started a new life and at least pretended to abandon the one I'd had.'

The thief-taker took a deep breath and sighed. 'And then when I'd done all that and I did come here, it was tiny. After everything I'd thought it would be, it was such a disappointment.' He put a hand on Berren's shoulder. 'Most people are the same, lad,' he said gently. 'Especially at your age. Like thief-takers who turn out to wear a secret skin of armour, maybe. You learn to live with it. Get used to it, even. And then when you meet someone who isn't, it's hard not to like them. Even if they're a thief.' He let out a heavy sigh. 'Of course, when in the end they let you down like everyone else, you'll feel it all the harder.'

18

A NICE BOTTLE OF MALMSEY

aster Sy led him on through Market Square, past the brazier men with their glowing coals, their roasting nuts and their sizzling strips of meat and fish. Leftovers from the day, heavily spiced to hide the smell of them already turning bad, sold for absurd coin to drunks and men who didn't know any better. It was a heady place at night, the market. Women paraded themselves, or else padded softly in the shadows, calling with siren voices to anyone who went past. Bands of players staked out their territories and danced, juggling brands of fire in ever more strident displays. Voices erupted from nowhere, singing songs of faraway places and lost times. Now and then, wagons rolled in through one of the many roads that entered the square. They dropped their sides, shouted their heads off until they had a crowd, hawked their stolen wares and ten minutes later they were gone. Men and women from all parts of the city came to the night market, rich and poor. The market militia did their best, but between the thieves and the cut-purses and the snuffers with their swords come to guard the rich folk, the tension was always there. Having a thief-taker in their midst didn't exactly help, either.

'You might think it would be easier to wear a hood,' said Master Sy, after a gang of boys about Berren's age began following them across the square, hooting obscenities and throwing the odd stone and piece of rotten fruit. His eyes glittered. 'Sometimes it seems that way, but in the end it's always a mistake. Never hide your face, lad. Make sure they always see you coming. Make sure they *know* who's about to happen to them.' He changed direction, striding swiftly towards one of the wagons. The small crowd around it seemed to sense him coming; its raucous shouting fell silent and it parted as the thief-taker approached. The gang of boys dropped back, suddenly uncertain. The three men on the wagon let out a volley of curses, but they were far too late for making a quick escape. They froze. Like startled animals, Berren thought. It made him feel powerful, three big men struck helpless with fear. That's what he wanted. Even more than learning swords, *that* was what he wanted.

Master Sy walked up to the cart and planted his feet. 'Well, well, Lockjaw. You'll have to be a lot quicker than that.'

The middle one of the three men on the wagon shuffled his feet. He was big, almost as big as Master Hatchet, but now he looked like a child caught in the act of doing something he shouldn't.

'Your boys?' Master Sy jerked his head towards the gang that had been following them. Idly he reached into one of the crates on the cart and drew out a handful of something dark and crumbling. He sniffed his hand and then let whatever it was fall back.

'Um. I don't know who they are, Master Syannis, sir.'

Master Sy pulled out a small knife. Around them, the crowed edged and melted away. The thief-taker started poking around in the crate with the blade.

'Dirt, Lockjaw? You selling dirt?'

The man on the cart looked wildly from side to side. 'Er. Yeh.'

'I heard you were in Varr.' The thief-taker reached

into the crate again. This time his hand came out holding something that looked like an onion. Tension poured off the men in the cart like sweat.

'Yeh.'

'Something to do with goods for the emperor's wedding, that's what I heard.'

'Yeh, that's true. Right patriotic, me. Long live his Imperial Graciousness.'

'So how was it?'

'Eh? I don't ...'

'The wedding, Lockjaw. Bells ringing all over the city about a couple of weeks back. Big celebrations. Festival up in Deephaven Square. Even you can't have missed that. They might even have let you in up there for once.'

'Well ...'

'Oh, but you were in Varr, so you'd have missed the bells. Must have been a very fast horse you rode to get back here so quick. Got a fast horse, have you? Suppose you must, since that's the only way you'd be back in Deephaven by now if you'd been in Varr. Must have run the poor animal into the ground.' Master Sy sniffed his hand again, not waiting for an answer. 'So what? Is this what you're selling? Smells good enough to eat.' He started to brush the dirt off. On the cart, one of the men took a sudden step forward and then froze again, just as quick. One look, Berren saw. One little look from the thief-taker was all it took, and the man had stopped in his tracks.

'Yeh,' said the man in the middle again, uncertainly.

'Someone shipped in a wedding present for His Majesty. Flowers for his summer garden. Bulbs. That's what I heard. Right rare and expensive they were. Brought in by a Taki ship, no less. I seem to remember hearing that a crate or two went missing. You wouldn't know anything about that would you, Lockjaw? I mean, with your new interest in selling dirt and unusual vegetables.' Master Sy dropped the thing, whatever it was, back into the crate and carefully covered it in earth.

The man called Lockjaw held up his hands and shook his head vigorously. 'No, no, don't know about anything like that. I'm just an honest trader like anyone else. I don't steal things, Master thief-taker sir, that's not me at all. I bought them in Varr, like you said. Maybe someone else stole them. If they did, I didn't know. That's an honest mistake that is, that's all.'

'Oh, they never got to Varr.' Master Sy shrugged. 'Still, if you say you bought them, then that must be what happened. I'm sure the Takis will be understanding. Come on, lad.' He turned away, took a couple of steps and then turned back. 'Oh, and Lockjaw? Teach your boys some manners, eh?'

'Yes, Master Syannis sir.' The man was nodding so vigorously that Berren thought his head might fall off. Master Sy shook his head and walked away.

'See, lad,' he said, when they were out of earshot. 'That's what I mean. Always show them your face. Make sure they know you. Make sure they fear you. Make sure they know you don't fear them.' Another commotion broke out around the wagon. The three men had jumped down and were laying into the gang of boys, chasing them out across the square, waving sticks and shouting curses.

'So they weren't really thieves then?' Berren frowned in confused disbelief. 'It was like they said? But if they were honest men, why were they wagonning in the market at night?'

'Lockjaw? An honest man?' The thief-taker guffawed. 'No, lad. But Lockjaw's not a pirate either, and at the moment we're looking for pirates.' He smirked. 'Besides, if he stole them from the Takis, I don't think we should be standing between them. Takis have their own way of dealing with things. Right, this way.' He turned into one of the dozen roads that fed into Market Square from the Maze, the warren of narrow streets and alleys that ran between the market, the sea-docks and the Avenue of Emperors. The shadows darkened as the light from the market faded behind them. Only the moon and the stars lit their way now, them and a few dim flickering lights peeping through tiny shuttered windows dotted along the streets. Berren let his hand settle in his pocket, his fingers curl around the familiar feel of Stealer. He knew the Maze as well as anyone. You didn't come here at night without a good reason. Suddenly he was glad to be wearing Master Sy's metal vest.

'Don't worry, lad. It's not far.' Master Sy turned in to an alley so narrow that even the moon couldn't reach the bottom of it. The first you'd know about anyone else coming the other way was when you walked into them. From somewhere up ahead came a dim buzz of noise, the hum of talking, punctuated by staccato laughter. They walked out of the alley and into another street and the noise became louder. Light and drunken chatter spilled into the street from windows and an open door. Berren almost grinned as Master Sy stepped inside and the noise instantly turned deafening. The Barrow of Beer. He'd passed it dozens of times. Hatchet's boys gave the place a wide berth. *No one in there's got anything worth stealing*, Hatchet had told them, *but they might not think the same of you.*

'Stay close, lad,' muttered Master Sy. He sauntered straight to the bar, barging his way through without a care in the world. Berren saw at least one angry snarl start and then die as men saw who the thief-taker was. Slowly, silence fell.

'Kasmin!' shouted Master Sy. From behind the bar, a grizzled old man with an eye-patch and a scar down half his face turned. He stared at the thief-taker and then his face cracked into a grin. Berren saw that Master Sy didn't smile back, though. He looked weary. Sad.

'Syannis! You bastard!' The old man almost ran and embraced the thief-taker as though they were brothers. At once, the noise around them resumed.

'Lad!' Master Sy had to shout to make himself heard now. 'This is Kasmin. Kasmin is a very old friend, even if he's a rogue. Kasmin, this is Berren. He's my apprentice. Stop and take a look at him for a moment.'

Then something strange happened. Kasmin looked at Berren, and then he looked again, and then he stared as though he'd seen a ghost. 'Bloody Kalda,' he whistled. 'Either my memory's gone or he's the spit of ...' He glanced at Master Sy and stopped.

'Isn't he just.'

'Gods blind my one good eye if he's not.' Kasmin threw his arms around the thief-taker again. 'Anyway, it's been a bloody long time.' He looked down at Berren. 'Well boy, I used to serve your master too, once. When we were back in the old country. Long time ago that was now. Bad times, but we still had some fun.' The old man grinned. 'Do you remember in Forgenver when we ...'

'Time enough later for that, old bones.' Syannis spoke softly but his words fell like an axe. He smiled a wan sad smile. 'Serve your prince a drink before he collapses.'

Kasmin forced a laugh. 'Anything you like, your Highness.' A space had formed in the crowd around the pair of them. Berren saw it in the faces of the others in the tavern. No one wanted to stand next to a thief-taker.

'I'd like a bottle of your best Malmsey, old bones. The very best you've got, because I've heard you've got your hands on something very fine indeed.'

For an instant there was a hesitation. For an instant, something wasn't right. Then Kasmin grinned and nodded and jumped back behind his bar as though nothing had happened. It had, though, and if Berren had seen it, so had the thief-taker.

A moment later, two glasses and a bottle were on the bar. 'This what you're looking for?' Kasmin was all smiles. Everywhere except his eyes. His eyes were wide, nervous, ready to run.

Master Sy picked up the bottle, looked it over. Then he put it down. He nodded.

'Exactly what I was looking for. Old friend, we need to talk. I'm afraid you've crossed my path the wrong way this time.'

The old man still grinned, but underneath he looked terrified. Berren knew all about that look; it was the one that he used to see from people who owed money to Master Hatchet. 'Sure. Come round tomorrow though, eh? We'll talk all you like. Chew the fat. Dredge though our memories. Whatever you want.' There was no conviction in the old man's words. Not one bit.

'No.' Master Sy grabbed the tavern-keeper's wrist and held it tight. 'You need to tell me how you came by this and you need to do it right now.'

'I got customers, Syannis.' His voice broke, became pleading. Hopeless.

The thief-taker shook his head. 'Not any more, old bones. Not any more.'

Five minutes and a lot of grumbling and shouting later, the Barrow of Beer was empty and still. Kasmin shut the door and put a bar across it. Then he sat down heavily on a stool. Master Sy settled in front of him. For a long time, neither of them said anything. Berren sat quietly in a corner.

'I'm looking for pirates, Kasmin,' said Master Sy at last.

'I fought some of those a long time ago.' Kasmin sounded immensely sad. Berren picked up an abandoned tankard and helped himself to a few mouthfuls of beer. It was weak and watery stuff next to the beer from the Eight Pillars of Smoke but nowhere near as bad as the stuff he and the other boys had used to sneak out of the Red Loom when Master Hatchet sent them in to cause some trouble.

The thief-taker stood up. He walked to the bar and picked up the bottle again. This time he poured himself a glass. Then he came back and sat down, bottle in one hand, glass in the other.

'I remember. Look me in the eye, Kasmin. Tell me you bought this. Tell me this is honest trade. Look me in the eye and tell me that and I'll be on my way.'

The old man shook with bitter laughter. 'Can't tell you that, old friend. You know I don't have the gold to buy something as fine as that bottle for an honest price.'

'No, old bones, I know that.' He glanced over his shoulder at Berren. 'Lad, get the other glass from the bar. Bring it here. Pour yourself a mug of something and then go wait out the back.'

Berren did as he was asked and wandered through the tavern and out into a little yard, sipping on his mug of beer. Halfway through he wrinkled his nose and tipped the rest onto the dirt. It was starting to make his head fuzzy again and that conjured up all manner of unpleasant memories. And when it came down to it, the beer didn't actually taste particularly nice. He put the mug on the ground and squatted against the wall, waiting for the thief-taker to finish his business. He waited a long time. Eventually he must have dozed off, because the next thing he knew, the sky was lightening with the first touches of dawn and Master Sy was shaking his shoulder.

'Come on, lad,' said the thief-taker gently. 'Let's go.'

He sounded sad. As they walked out of the yard and into a tiny dingy alley that ran up the side of the Barrow of Beer all the way down to the docks, Berren kept sneaking glances at him. There weren't any bloodstains, but that only made him all the more curious. He stopped to peer through a window as they passed the front of the tavern. It was hard to see much through the filth and the way the cheap glass warped the world. He could make out a figure, though, sitting still on his stool, exactly where Berren remembered him.

'Come on, lad.' The thief-taker pulled him away. 'He's got ghosts enough without needing us as well. Leave him be.'

Berren twitched impatiently. 'Master, where are we going?' The whole night looked like it had been an enormous waste of time. Now he was tired and irritable and just wanted to go back to sleep.

'Yes, yes.' Master Sy shook his head. 'We're going home, and then we're going to pack our bags and go down to the river docks and find ourselves passage up the river. Once we're moving you can sleep all you like.'

Berren scowled. 'Where are we going, master?'

'Wherever we're needed, lad. Wherever we're needed.'

PART TWO

AN EXPEDITION
AND A FEW LESSONS
ON TAKING A THIEF

19

DRIFTING ON THE RIVER AND EATING PIE

Berren lay sprawled out in the sun, eyes closed and half asleep. A gentle wind blew across his arms and his face. The midday heat was like a warm blanket wrapped over him. He dozed, on and off, lulled by the sounds of lapping water and creaking wood. Deephaven was an hour down the river behind them, and the quiet was staggering. Sometimes one of the lightermen would call out; a sail would flap, the barge would shift a little, and then it was back to the rhythm of the water and the wood. The sounds were like someone breathing in and out; slow, deep and restful.

And then there was the smell. The sweet, fresh smell of the river. The way the air smelled up past Sweetwater, except even sweeter still. Filled with trees and grass and flowers from the farms and the woods on the city side of the river. Berren had never ventured much further out of the city than the edges of the River District, and even then only the once and with Master Sy as his guide. They were well beyond that now. He stared at the vast openness, at the swathes of green, the huge trees and the forests they made up on the Haven Hills that overlooked the city. Other smells came and went, too. More familiar smells drifting in wisps off the road that ran beside the river, the great wide River Road that ran out of the River Gate, through Sweetwater and right on to the other end of the world, as far as Berren knew. To the City of Spires and the imperial capital of Varr and maybe even further than that. Sometimes, when he wasn't snoozing, Berren watched the road for a bit just to see what he could see. He tried to count the wagons and the carts but quickly lost track. Once he saw a black-clad galloping horseman racing towards the city. An Imperial Messenger! He stared, enraptured, then jumped up and pointed and shouted out, because even Master Sy, surely, must want to see ... But when Berren scampered over to wake him, the thief-taker screamed and stared at Berren wide-eyed, and Berren recoiled as though he'd been stung. The thief-taker stared at him, glassy-eyed and far away. 'You haven't the tools,' he said. Then he blinked and came back from wherever he was and swore and cursed and swatted Berren away, and by then the messenger was gone. The lightermen had laughed and shaken their heads, as though this was something they saw every day.

'Sorry, lad,' said the thief-taker a minute or so later. 'Dreams.' He was looking at Berren hard, though, wearing his sad face, as though he'd dreamed of something bad that had yet to come.

Berren scowled. An Imperial Messenger was what every city boy wanted to be and he'd missed some of seeing one because of Master Sy. Racing with the wind from one side of the world to another, always moving, stopping for nothing except the next change of horse. Some people said they had secret powers, granted to them by the emperor's new sorcerers. That they could freeze a man to the spot simply by looking at him, that they moved so fast that they could vanish in a blink. Berren wasn't sure about that, but they certainly got to learn swords and he was willing to bet they didn't have to learn their letters first. Or have stupid dreams. Bad dreams were for children. Babies. Not for men who carried swords.

Way stations, farms, hamlets and villages dotted the

road, all with their own small jetties out into the water. On the other side of the barge, more little boats pottered up and down the river. Tiny rafts, dozens and hundreds of them, not much more than a few poles lashed together, bobbing about and covered with squawking black fishing birds. Sailing boats, not much bigger than the rafts, wove between them, deft and agile. And then there were the barges like the one where Berren dozed. Big and clumsy, lumbering against the current with a sail barely big enough to keep them moving.

Beyond all those, the far side of the river stretched out towards the horizon. It faded into a maze of mud-islands and channels and creeks and swamps that went on for days. Or so Master Sy had said. The only people who went in there, he said, were the most desperately wanted men with nowhere else to hide, and the thief-takers sent to catch them.

They stopped towards the end of the day at one of the riverside way stations. Master Sy waited while the lighter-men made their boat secure. He bought them a flagon of ale each and then a gammon pie which he cut in half and split with Berren.

'Ever been out of the city before, lad?'

Berren shook his head. The pie was a good one, with thick crusty pastry and big juicy chunks of ham. The sort of thing Master Hatchet would have bought his boys as a treat, except done properly, with soft meat instead of gristly bits and proper thick gravy instead of brown water.

'I don't come out here often,' said the thief-taker. He was picking at his pie as though he didn't really want it. And he was drinking. He finished one flagon and waved for another. 'I'd like to go to Varr one day. Just to see the palace and the Kaveneth and the bridge they built over the river there. Or the City of Spires.' He drummed his fingers on the table, his mind clearly somewhere else. 'Never even got as far as Tarantor.'

'Where we going tomorrow?' asked Berren from behind a faceful of pie.

'Bedlam's Crossing. Kasmin bought his bottle of Malmsey from a trader in Bedlam's Crossing. I know him.'

'Bought his what?'

The start of a smile played around the corner of Master Sy's mouth, but it didn't get very far. 'Wine, lad. The bottle of wine he had. I'll teach you about wine one day. I'm afraid that's something I know rather more about than is useful.' He sighed, picked up his beer and took another deep draft before staring at what was left. 'Malmsey is a strong sweet wine, usually from the vineyards around Helhex. They don't make very much so it's quite rare. One of the first ships to be attacked in the harbour had ten thousand bottles in its hold and they all vanished. I knew they'd start to show up again one day.' He shook his head. He'd still hardly touched his pie. Berren eyed it hungrily while the thief-taker drained his second flagon and waved over a third. Berren had never seen him drunk and had no idea what it would look like. Master Hatchet mostly liked to hit people. The thief-taker, Berren thought, would be one of those morose and moody drunks who got miserable and talked too much about stuff no one else cared about.

'Was that man a friend of yours?' he asked cautiously.

'Which man, lad?'

'The old bloke in the Barrow of Beer. I thought you'd kill him, what with him being a thief.' Belatedly he remembered the look on Master Sy's face as they'd come away from Kasmin's tavern. Too much pie was making him bold. He tried to look shamefaced, ready for the rebuke, but it didn't come. Master Sy simply looked sad again.

'I didn't kill you, did I?' he asked, gently.

Berren bowed his head. 'Sorry, master.'

'Lad, what you saw when we met wasn't something that happens every day. A thief-taker doesn't fight. Not unless he has to, and even then, you don't kill a man without a very good reason.' The thief-taker took a long swallow from beer number three and smacked his lips. His face was starting to glisten. Berren didn't know much about getting drunk himself, except for his one disaster in the Eight, but he'd learned how to spot it in other people. Drunks had always been his first bet for lifting a few pennies. The only trouble being that they often didn't have any.

'When you first met me in that alley, what you saw then is not a thief-taker's life.' Master Sy was starting to slur his words. Only very slightly, but enough to notice. 'You can't win every fight, lad, and you only have to lose one to be dead. No, you don't fight unless you have no choice.' He patted his chest, rattling the ringmail under his shirt. 'Of course, I do try to make sure that any fight I'm in I'm going to win.' He tried grinning again, but it didn't really work.

'I seen people go funny like that,' Berren said. He was treading on dangerous ground and chose his words carefully. 'Like he knew he was in big trouble the moment you came in. Seemed like you knew him pretty well, though. Like you were friends for a real long time.'

Master Sy took a deep breath and sighed. 'Kasmin? Yes. I've known Kasmin since I was a boy, maybe since I was half your age. He was a soldier. He worked …' The thief-taker frowned. 'He helped my father from time to time. He was a brave man once. A strong one, too, and a leader. When the … When I was forced to leave my home, Kasmin came with me. I'd lost most of my family. I was a bit older than you, but not much. I had a younger brother to look after. And another …' He stared at Berren long and hard. Stared right through him, off into some other place and time. 'Yes, another brother, who looked a bit like you do now. We had lots of friends. Or people who said they were our friends. People who should have been. Kasmin came with us. He helped me for a while. When things were at their worst, he was always there.' Master Sy smiled. 'Truth is, he probably saved my life more than once and I never even knew anything about it. He was a good man, but the wandering broke him. He so wanted to go back home, and he could have, too. He had family, but that would have meant leaving us and abandoning his duty. Eventually we heard that they'd been killed, months later. Robbers. He always drank too much, Kasmin. One day he just vanished. Had enough. Walked out into the night and didn't come back. Years later I washed up in Deephaven. I started thief-taking, and then one day there he was, on the wrong end of my sword. I was afraid for a moment, because I knew he knew how to fight. But he didn't. He gave himself up to me; and for all the things he'd done for me and mine before he left us, I let him go. I even helped him a bit to buy the Barrow. It's not the first time he's fallen in with the wrong sort and I don't suppose it's going to be the last.'

Berren decided to try and push his luck one more time. 'He called you a prince,' he said, which wasn't quite true, but close enough.

'No he didn't.'

'Well he called you something like that.' Yes, and it wasn't the first time either.

Behind Master Sy's eyes, the shutters had come down. Berren had gone too far; or else the thief-taker had realised that he'd said too much. Master Sy shook his head and took another swig of beer. 'We've known each other for a long time, lad. We used to call each other all sorts of things.'

Which might have been true, but certainly wasn't the truth he'd been looking for. Something to remember for the next time he ever saw his master drunk, perhaps. But enough for now. Instead, Berren waved his fork at Master Sy's plate.

'Can I have your pie then?' He put on his best grin,

showing off his teeth. Master Sy didn't smile though. He merely pushed the plate across the table.

'Go ahead, lad. I think I should go to sleep. You're in the stables, in the hayloft.'

'Master? When I woke you up on the boat, you said something. I didn't understand. What did you mean?'

'Said something?' Master Sy shook his head, and there came that forced half-smile again. 'No, lad. I didn't say anything. If you really want to know, I was dreaming I was back home again. Some time years from now. And nothing had changed for the good.' He grunted and shrugged. 'Seeing Kasmin, you see. Brings it all back.'

Berren watched him go. The thief-taker walked steadily, no sign that he was half in his cups. For a few seconds, Berren even wondered if it had all been an act, whether Master Sy hadn't been drunk at all. But that was foolish and didn't really make much sense when you came to look at it.

With a happy sigh, he turned back to the remains of the thief-taker's pie. His master might have gone to sleep, but the night was yet young and he had every intention of making the best of it.

20

BEDLAM'S CROSSING

erren yawned and rubbed his eyes. The lightermen worked around him, oblivious. Now and then they threw him a sly glance. He'd spent half the night with them. They hadn't known anything much about Master Sy or thief-taking, but they'd known a lot about Bedlam's Crossing, and about the river, too. And they'd known a lot about how to prize pennies out of Berren's purse. He'd listened to their stories with eager ears and marvelled, paying for each of them with more flagons of pale ale. Stories of the City of Spires with its five curving towers of gleaming white stone, so tall that they scratched the sky. Of Varr and its palaces and temples, all carved from lumps of solid gold as big as a ship. Of swamp-hags who swam across the river from the other side at night and lured men away to a watery grave. Of the river mermaids who sometimes saved them and who were more beautiful even than the emperor's new queen. Of the strange lands further up the river, of three-headed lions and giant snakes with the faces of men and witches who turned sailors to stone. Of sea-monsters that swallowed entire ships.

They were laughing at him now but he didn't mind. After he'd left them, he'd crept back through the way station and found the last few drunks, hopelessly in their cups. He'd quietly cut their purses. Master Sy would probably throw him in the river if he ever found out, but he wouldn't and old habits died hard. No, on the whole the night had gone well.

'There's a thing I've learned,' whispered a voice at his shoulder. Berren jumped a full foot into the air, spun around, lost his balance and almost fell over the side of the barge. When he finally gathered himself together, the thief-taker stood over him. His face looked bleak. Berren's heart raced. The lightermen had left at the crack of dawn, when the way station drunks were still snoring at their tables. He couldn't know what Berren had done. *Can't possibly know.*

Didn't matter what he told himself, though. Believing it was something else.

But the thief-taker's thoughts were somewhere else. He sat down beside Berren and stared at the water, at the rippling waves rolling steadily by.

'Do you know what wisdom is, lad? They say that wisdom is something you get as you age. Improved by the years like a fine wine. Wisdom is spending your effort on the battles that matter and having the grace to smile at defeat in the ones that don't. Trouble is, lad, wisdom comes too late for some. Look at Kasmin. He was a fine swordsman in his time. He was a soldier, a captain in the King's Guard. He had a fine life, filled with everything a young man wants. Wine, women, song, swords.' He smiled. 'I'm sure you can imagine. Everyone loved him. And then he lost it all, and in the end, instead of fighting for what mattered, he gave up. Now look at him. A drunk old man, slipping slowly towards oblivion without even knowing it. Give it another few years and you'll find Kasmin crawling in the gutter, begging from scraps, with everything he ever had, even his dignity, stripped away. Or you'll find him in that same gutter with a knife between his ribs.' The thief-taker shook his head. 'If there's one thing I've learned, lad, one thing that matters more than anything else, one thing I'd like to teach you more than letters or manners or swords, it's not to regret what you can't undo. I'm afraid, though, that that's something you'll have to learn from someone else.'

'Wisdom is knowing what is beyond your power to change,' said Berren, parroting Teacher Garrent. The thief-taker smiled and nodded.

'So you *do* listen. No, there's no shame in making a mistake as long as you can put it right. For the ones you can't, learn what you can learn and then let them go. Go to a priest and find a penance if you have to and then leave it be.'

Berren nodded. 'But master, how will you know that you truly can't change something if you give up trying?'

'You can't bring back the dead, lad.'

'But what if it's something about the living?'

'Then you listen to your heart, lad. Your heart will tell you when it's time to stop.'

'But what if it never does?'

The thief-taker stood up. 'Kasmin's heart told him to give up a long time ago, lad.'

'But what if it didn't?'

The thief-taker shrugged. 'Then don't.' He shuffled away down the deck, back to his stool in the prow. Berren watched him sitting there, staring out across the water, lost in memories. It was only then that he realised the thief-taker hadn't been talking about Kasmin at all. He'd been talking about himself.

He frowned. Did he have any regrets? Did he regret leaving Master Hatchet? Not really. Was he sorry for all the purses he'd cut? He had a good long think about that one. The beatings had hurt, when he'd been caught, but when it came to remorse ... No. Not a trace. Did he wish he'd been born to a rich merchant prince with ships full of gold? Yes, he did, but it was hard to feel particularly resentful that he hadn't. Did he wish that the whore in Club-Headed Jin's brothel had let him touch her? Well yes, he did. A part of him did still smart from that. But he hardly thought about her any more, so maybe that was the sort of thing that Master Sy had been talking about. Maybe that was wisdom, letting that go.

He smiled to himself and stretched out across the top of the deck on his back, squinting at the sky. No, he hardly thought about Jin's women at all any more. A cloud crossed the sun, stealing the heat off his face. What he thought about was Lilissa. Lilissa, who never came around any more. Lilissa who had a special friend who was a fishmonger's son. Lilissa, who lived alone with no one to watch over her and no one to tell her what she couldn't do. Now, could that be something he could change ...?

Abruptly he jerked awake. The sky was grey and filled with cloud. The wind was cool and full of noise and smelled of fish again. The middle of the morning had become the middle of the afternoon. The barge shifted beneath him. He sat up, eyes wide, and looked around. The river had changed; they were right up against the edge, bumping a little wooden jetty. The bank here was covered with hastily made wooden buildings, scrambling over each other to be close to the water. The river itself was full of boats.

The thief-taker jumped onto the roof beside him and slapped him on the back. 'Bedlam's Crossing, lad. Shake a leg. They won't wait, you know. Sleep any more and you'll find yourself in the City of Spires.'

After all the stories he'd heard from the lightermen, Berren wasn't sure that would have been so bad. He rose unsteadily and stumbled along the side of the barge, following in the thief-taker's wake until he scrambled up onto the wooden docks. Almost at once, the barge pulled away, back into the channel of the river.

'I will admit, lad, that I don't take too kindly to being on the water. It feels good to be on dry land again.'

Berren shrugged. The truth was that he'd rather liked

the gentle movements of the barge. They felt restful and sleepy and easy. Master Sy, though ... Well, you could see at a glance how glad he was to be ashore. The darkness that had followed him since the Barrow of Beer had vanished. He was the thief-taker again, the thief-taker who danced through knives and laughed at swords and always knew the answer. Berren definitely liked *this* thief-taker better. If nothing else, you always knew where you stood.

'Bedlam's Crossing,' said the thief-taker again. 'The last river crossing before Deephaven and the sea. Take a boat over to the other side and you can get a coach that will take you to Tarantor, Torpreah, wherever you like. The north road will lead you up to Mirrormere. The river reaches off to the City of Spires and beyond. No one stays in Bedlam's Crossing, but a lot of people come through.' He bared his teeth. 'A lot of goods too. Come on, this way.'

Berren followed. In Deephaven, the river docks were a maze of wooden bridges and platforms. Some of them sat on piles sunk into the river bed, but a lot of them simply bobbed up and down on the water on big wooden floats, held in place by ancient ropes and sheer bloody-mindedness. In a good strong storm, whole strips of the docks were sometimes torn away and blown halfway up the river or else washed out to sea. Both docks were little realms unto themselves, with their own rules and order and Berren knew well enough to keep away. Hatchet always told his boys that the docks had a magic of their own, powerful and old and vindictive. *You go out there, boys, you be sure to make your sacrifices to the old gods of the sea and the river spirits, otherwise that old wood will split apart and close over your head again and they'll take your soul to their inky depths.* The docks at Bedlam's crossing might have been a lot smaller, but they had the same simmering hostility to them. They rocked and swayed under Berren's feet as though trying to tip him over, and he was glad to be off them. Master Sy might not have liked his boat, but to Berren's mind, ground that was supposed to stay where it was but actually shifted under your feet was a thousand times worse.

About a dozen yards further along the cobbled water-front, Master Sy stopped at a door. 'Well, lad,' he said, 'are you ready to meet your first real thieves?'

Berren steadied himself, still on edge. He looked the shop-front up and down. *Barswans' Winery*, it said, on a fancy sign that had clearly been paid for with gold rather than silver. There were windows in the front with dark glass, expensive ones, with good oak shutters reinforced with iron bands. It looked like the sort of shop that belonged on the fringes of The Peak. The sort of place where rich folk went to spend their money on wine shipped in from Brons and Caladir instead of the local hills.

Not like a den of thieves at all. He wrinkled up his nose and scowled.

'Well?'

Berren took a deep breath. Then he sighed and shrugged his shoulders. 'Do I need to have a sword or something?'

'Little tip, lad. If you ever go into a thieves' den looking for a fight, do it with at least a dozen city militiamen at your back. If it comes to fighting in there, what you do is run. But it won't come to that.'

Berren scowled some more. Thieves and watchmen mixed together only ever meant one thing, and that was a fight. It was hard to see why thieves and thief-takers should be any different. But he nodded anyway to show he was ready. If there was one thing he was good at, it was running.

21

ON THE TAKING OF THIEVES

'So.' The thief-taker rubbed his hands together. 'Here we are. Us on the outside, thieves on the inside. What do you suppose we do? Kick down the door and charge through, swords in hand, screaming our heads off?'

Berren made a face. 'Um?'

'In some parts of the city, probably once or twice a year,' said the thief-taker cheerfully, 'what we do when we meet a door is exactly that. There's a little trick about throwing a lantern full of oil inside ahead of you, too. The rest of the time, what we do is this.' He walked up to the front of the shop and rearranged his belt, apparently to make his sword as obvious as possible. Then he waited for a few seconds and banged loudly on the door. Berren tensed, ready to run, but nothing happened. Master Sy didn't move. Out of the corner of his mouth he whispered: 'Give them plenty of time to have a good look at you, lad. If they don't want to talk, come back later with a posse of Justicar Kol's militiamen. But they will. If they don't, that means they're not scared of you. If they're not scared of you, you'll be a very poor thief-taker.'

Almost as if the people inside had been listening, the door swung open. A portly man with grey hair stood on the threshold. He was clutching an elegantly carved staff made of black wood. Behind him was a gloomy room half shrouded in shadow. Beyond that, through another set of rather cheaper windows, Berren could see sunlight and a yard, and some blurry shapes that were probably a few barrels and a wagon. He could see some movement in the shadows behind the man at the door, too. Men, lurking back in the darkness.

The fat man with the staff smiled a sickly smile that barely made it past his lips. His eyes gleamed with anger. 'Thief-taker Syannis.' He leaned on his staff and held out his free hand. 'It's been a long time since you came our way. What can I do for you? Nice case of the Sun-king's red? Or his brandy, perhaps.' The man with the staff made no move to step aside and let the thief-taker in. Master Sy smiled back and peered past him. Berren sidled sideways, trying to look past as well.

'Not inviting me in, Barswan?'

'What is it, thief-taker?'

'Well, since you're inquiring as to my taste in wine ...' Master Sy reached behind him and rested a hand firmly on Berren's head. 'Don't pry, Berren, it's rude. We have no interest in whatever business Master Barswan is engaged in back there. Yet.'

The last word came with the crisp edge of a finely honed blade. Berren saw it wasn't lost on the wine-seller.

'Wine,' smiled Master Sy. 'What's drawn me to your door, Master Barswan, is a fine Helhex Malmsey. A vintage to which I happen to be particularly partial. One I've been looking for for quite some time. Quite rare at the moment, since the only shipment into Deephaven was stolen three months ago. Yet you appear to have some, Barswan.'

The old wine-seller scoffed and shook his head. He took a half-step back into the darkness and began to close the door. 'You're in the wrong place, thief-taker. This isn't Deephaven. You got the wrong wine-seller.'

He got the door halfway closed before it ran into Master

Sy's boot. Berren tensed, ready to run. In the shadows beyond the door, shapes began to move.

Master Sy pulled an empty bottle out of his satchel and thrust it at the wine-seller. 'This is what I'm talking about, Barswan. I know it came from here. I know you're not the one running the pirate gang who stole it. Do I have to come in and have a look around for the rest? Or are you going to tell me where you got it?'

For several seconds, the wine-seller didn't move. Then he growled something under his breath, stepped outside and closed the door behind him. He put a hand in Berren's face and shoved him away. 'Piss off, runt,' he snapped. 'This isn't for you.'

Berren was halfway to whipping out Stealer and jamming it into the fat man's leg, but he caught sight of the thief-taker's face and a slight shake of the head. So he settled for growling and spitting at the fat man's feet, and backed away. As he did, the wine-seller started to talk in a fast, low voice. It lasted a few seconds, that was all, and then the fat man disappeared back into his shop and slammed the door. The thief-taker looked at Berren. Then he beamed and strode away, slapping Berren on the back as he did.

'See how easy that was,' he said. 'That's how it's supposed to be.'

'What did he say?' Berren couldn't help himself, even if a part of him was still steaming, all ready to slip back after dark and burn the place down.

'He said he got it from an old friend in Siltside. Calls himself the Bloody Dag. I've heard of him. He fits. He's a fat mudlark prick who's forgotten that he was born in shit, lives in shit and will die in shit. You know a man's getting too big for his hat when he starts calling himself "the" something.' Master Sy was rubbing his hands together, full of glee. 'I've been half expecting to find out that he had his fingers in this ever since it started. He was always fond of a bit of piracy. Just never thought he'd be clever enough to find a way to do it in the sea-docks.' He started to wander back towards the river. As he did, he threw back his head and laughed. 'That's it, lad. That's our job done. Now we go home, pat ourselves on the back and open up a bottle of something good. In the morning I'll go over to Justicar Kol and give him what he wants.'

'That's it?'

'That's it, lad. Siltside isn't a place for people like us. Not unless we've got a small army at our backs. Goes one of two ways with people who have nothing. People with nothing always want to be people with something, and you can use that. But people with nothing have nothing to lose, either. That's the way it is in Siltside. They're not scared of thief-takers there, never will be.' Master Sy walked on past the docks to a tavern. There were a lot of them, Berren noticed. All called The Boatman's Rest or The Waterman, or A Piece of Dry Land and so forth. It slowly dawned on him what Master Sy had meant about Bedlam's Crossing. Without the boats on the river, the town wouldn't be there. Simply wouldn't exist at all.

The thief-taker chose a place called The Pirate's Head and went inside. He handed over a few pennies for a room and a pie, just as he had at the river way station. Berren waited, fidgeting impatiently, slowly getting more and more wound up as the thief-taker chatted to the barkeep about this and that and nothing much. By the time their pie came out with a pair of plates, he was almost hopping from one foot to the other to contain himself.

'Well?' asked Master Sy as he sat down and cut himself a slice. 'What is it?' The smell was delicious. For a moment, Berren hesitated, torn between his desire for food and his curiosity. Too many years of being hungry meant that the pie won, but as soon as he'd shovelled a few mouthfuls down his throat, he gave the thief-taker an accusing look.

'We haven't *done* anything!' He said angrily. 'How can we have finished? We haven't taken any thieves! We came all the way down the river and for what? For a quick chat with a bloke who sells wine? And that's it?' He shook his head. 'We haven't done anything!' he said again.

Master Sy shrugged. 'We got a name. That's all we need.'

'But what if the fat wine-man was lying?'

'He wasn't.'

Berren banged his knife on the table in frustration. 'But how do you *know*? People lie all the time, and that's just ordinary people. When it comes to thieves, well ...'

For a moment, the thief-taker paused in his eating and glared. 'Manners, boy,' he hissed. Berren bowed his head.

'Sorry, master.'

'Better.'

'But I don't understand. All we did was wander around the city and talk to a few people and now suddenly we're done. Done with what? I don't even know!'

'We've found the thieves we were looking for, that's what we've done.' Then Master Sy made a face. 'No, we've found the thieves that Justicar Kol will *pay* us for. That's more the truth of it. Do you understand the difference?'

Berren grunted, not understanding the difference at all. 'So *we're* looking for someone else?'

Master Sy grinned. The sort of toothy devouring grin that he'd given the wine-seller. 'Yes, *we* most certainly are. Our friend the Justicar is looking for pirates. He wants them to stop, but what he wants even more is to have a gang of men he can put in chains and show off to his lords and masters before he bundles them into a barge and ships them away to the mines. Kol pays in gold, so our first job is to give him what he wants. Now the Bloody Dag is exactly the right sort to put a gang of thugs together and have a go at a bit of piracy, and I don't doubt he's our man. But someone's telling him what ships to raid and we still don't know how he's moving his gang across the city. Justicar Kol doesn't care about those things and he won't pay us to find them out, but a good thief-taker needs to know.' Master Sy smiled. 'It's a long road, lad, and you're right at the start of it. But yes, wandering around the city and talking to people is largely what we do. We ask questions. The skill is asking the right questions in the right places. Every time a ship was attacked, I took a list of what had been taken from one of the harbour-masters. I went through that list and found a few things that would be easy to find if they started showing up in the city markets. Then I looked for them. It's taken the best part of three months, but one of them was bound to show up sooner or later. You might think the city's so large, how could you ever look for anything? Well, the trick there, lad, is that you don't. You tell a few people you know who move wines through the city that you're interested in a certain vintage of Malmsey and you'll pay in silver to know who's got some, and they do the looking for you. Then you wait. You wait and you wait and to pass the time, maybe you take on an apprentice, and then finally one of them comes back to you and says yes, they've found what you're looking for, and your old friend Kasmin has it, of all people. So you give them a shiny silver crown, or maybe a gold emperor, and after that it's easy. You've seen it for yourself.' He shrugged again. 'It's not so hard. You just have to know people. After we've given Justicar Kol what he wants, we'll find out all the other people who've had a part in this. We don't take them though, not when there's no coin in it. We just find out who they are for next time, and make our work just a little bit easier when that next time comes around.' He followed Berren's gaze. 'And no,' he said, 'this time you can't have my pie.' Then he grinned and passed Berren a few coins. 'Go on. Get us another one. We're celebrating, after all.'

22

COURTING DANGER

'No.' The Justicar shook his head. 'My authority stops at the water's edge. I can't do anything with this. You're the thief-taker. You want your money, you go and get him.' They'd been in the Eight Pillars of Smoke for half an hour. The Justicar had listened politely enough to the thief-taker and then for twenty minutes he'd talked about other things, mostly about the penny increase in grain tax recently announced by the Overlord and the likely trouble that would bring. For all that time, he'd pointedly ignored Berren's presence. Now, though, now that he'd finally returned to the subject that had brought them together, his eyes settled on Berren for the first time. 'And I believe I instructed you not to bring your boy into my presence again.'

Master Sy's face didn't change, but Berren heard a rumble of distant angry thunder in his master's voice. 'The boy needs to learn. Where I go, he goes.'

'Well then he must be going to Siltside.' The Justicar smiled and then yawned. 'I'm sure that will be an enlightening experience for him.'

'I don't do my work across the river,' said Master Sy. He still sounded amiable enough, but Berren knew him better. Inside he cringed. Most likely, *he* was the one who was going to feel the worst of Master Sy's wrath, simply because he was there.

'Well neither do I. The difference is that you make a choice, while I am bound by imperial law. I'll have boats and a few dozen good men at the ready first thing in the morning. At dawn, if you like.'

'And who's going to lead your men, Justicar? It had better be someone I know.'

'Oh well, that it most certainly is. You, Syannis. You're going to lead them.'

'I'm a thief-taker, not a soldier.'

The Justicar snorted like a pig. 'And I am simply a trivial functionary voicing the emperor's will, communicated directly into my thoughts by a gang of eunuch mages in Varr who have nothing better to do with their time.' He spat. 'Pull the other one, Syannis. What are you after? More gold?' He reached into his robes and fiddled there for a few seconds. When his hand emerged again, it was holding a small purse. He opened it up and counted out five golden emperors. 'There. In addition to our agreed price. Which you only get if you bring me back this Bloody Dag fellow alive. The guild would like to torture him and then parade him in public up on The Peak. It would help a lot if you could bring back some of their missing merchandise too.' He showed his teeth. 'You know. So that they can be sure you aren't just leading them in circles.'

The thief-taker ran his fingers over the coins. He picked them up and moved them around the palm of his hand. 'Five emperors for a day's work? I suppose that's a reasonable offer.' Then he glanced at Berren. 'Then there's the boy, too.'

The Justicar blinked. For a few seconds, he only stared at Master Sy. Then his jaw dropped. He started to stutter. 'You … You … You must be out of your mind! For …' He glared at Berren. 'You want me to pay for *him*?'

'I believe the entitlement for an apprentice is two coins for every ten to his master. That's the guild's valuation, Kol, not mine. Imperial law, just like you said, and I wouldn't want to cross the guild. Would you?'

By now the top of the Justicar's head was bright red. Shaking, his fingers dipped into his purse and drew out another golden emperor. 'I'll not forget this,' he hissed.

'Oh tosh.' Master Sy snatched up the last coin. 'I could have held out for ten emperors and you'd have paid me. You got a bargain today, Kol, and you know it.' He rose. 'Good day, Justicar.'

Outside, the thief-taker flipped one of the gold coins at Berren. 'There. You earned your first emperor. Go and enjoy yourself, lad. I'll not need you tomorrow.'

'But ...'

Master Sy wagged a finger at Berren. 'No, lad. This is dangerous work now. Siltside isn't Bedlam's Crossing, and I'll wager you your one emperor against all five of mine that Kol will pick the most brutal men he's got for this. Most likely they'll run riot. There's going to be knives and clubs and swords and you don't know the first thing about fighting. Not for real.'

Berren stamped his foot. 'Then teach me, master. Teach me swords! Teach me how to fight so that I can help you!'

'No, boy. I've told you when I'll teach you swords. You listen to me, lad, you hang on to every word you hear and commit it to your heart and then maybe, a couple of years from now, you'll know enough to start being useful to me. Then I might think about teaching you how to fight.' He chuckled to himself. 'If I were you, I'd go and spend some of that gold on learning how to take a drink or two. You might even enjoy yourself. Or take Lilissa down to the docks for the evening. Or go to the market and buy her something nice. Let her know that her fishmonger's son is going to have to strive bloody hard to be good enough for her.'

For a few seconds it worked. Berren's mind wandered.

He thought of Lilissa and how he'd felt when she'd been around him, and how right the thief-taker was, that spending some time alone with her was about as nice a thought as he could think. For a few seconds, until they emerged from behind the courthouse and into Four Winds Square, and he realised that Master Sy was simply trying to get rid of him. Telling him to buy her presents? Telling him to go and spend some time with her? Alone, with no one to watch over them? *Get her out of your head, lad.* That's what the thief-taker used to say. *Got herself a friend. A young man sort of friend, if you catch my drift. A fishmonger's son. A good sort.* And what happened to *keep your hands to yourself with her or I'll cut them off and dump them in the sea and you with them.* Eh?

'Master,' he said, after thinking about this for a few seconds more. Two could play at this game. 'How would I go about courting her? Properly, I mean. Like a gentleman.' There. The thief-taker could hardly complain about a question like that. Berren hid a grin. Master Sy would have to answer, and properly too, or else let him go across the river to Siltside for the fight.

To his surprise, though, the thief-taker stopped. He turned around, put a hand on each of Berren's shoulders and grinned. The most frightening thing was that he seemed truly pleased. 'Now, that, lad, is the first clever question I've heard from you.' He pursed his lips. 'You really want to know?'

Berren nodded.

'You won't be the first to court her, you know. There have been others. This one at the moment trying his luck, I think she likes him.'

'I don't think she likes me, master.'

The thief-taker grunted. 'Don't be so sure.' Then he led Berren out into the middle of the square, to the bronze statue of the late Emperor Khrozus. He leaned back against it and then slid down until he was squatting on the ground. 'Women come in many kinds, as best I can see it, lad. There's those you can win with derring-do. There's those you can win with jewels and gold. There's those you can win with wine and song. There's those you can win simply by being kind. Lilissa's not any of those. How do you court her? With a bit of them all, lad. With a bit of them all. Show her you can look after her. Show her you can take care of her. Show her you won't ever leave her. Show her you can protect her. Show her you can love her. Show her you can take her to places she's never been. Show her wonders. Show her strength. Show her kindness and compassion. Show her she can be anything and so can you. Take her dancing in the sea, take her flying in the sky, take her to the finest table in The Peak, then take her home and take your leave and ask for nothing in return. You can do all those things and you might still not unlock the heart of a lady like Lilissa.' He slapped Berren on the back and jumped to his feet. 'Yes, you can do all of those things and get nothing at all for your trouble; but at least then you can say, in all honesty, that you tried, you really tried as hard as anybody reasonably could, and if she still doesn't love you, well then most probably it's because some half-bastard mage put a spell on her. That or she once fell in the sea and a merman got to her.' He laughed. 'Or maybe she just has a thing for fishmongers.'

The more Berren thought about any of this, the less sense he could make of Master Sy's words. As they walked across the open space of the square towards the Godsway corner and the alley that would take them home, the furrows in his brow grew steadily deeper. The thief-taker strode into his yard. The gang of children were there again; they scattered around him, laughing and chanting, *run while you can, run while you can, run while you can from the thief-taker man,* until Master Sy shooed them away. He unlocked his door and went into the cool gloom of the house.

'Master ...'

The thief-taker didn't even break stride. It was as if he'd been waiting for Berren to open his mouth. 'Take her down to the sea-docks, lad. Buy her a pickled fish in a bun and then take her down to the edge of the water and sit on the wall and watch the sun set. Tell her who you are. You'll get most of your emperor back in crowns and you'll know, by the time you walk her home, whether she wants you to do it again.' He didn't look round, just started to busy himself with tidying the table and cleaning his boots. Berren's chores, on any other day.

Berren hovered in the doorway, uncertain.

'Go on, lad. Sunset won't wait forever and you'll not be doing yourself any favours if you make her run.'

Quietly, Berren closed the door. Outside in the yard, he took a deep breath. His heart was beating quickly, already excited by what he was about to do.

Waiting was only making him even more nervous. Abruptly, he set off, heading for the docks. Not the sea-docks and a sunset, though. No, to the river docks and dawn. To boats filled with swords. To Siltside.

23

CROSSING OVER

Like the harbour on the other side of the city, the river docks were always busy. Berren slunk across them in twilight, feeling his way uneasily along the floating jetties, sticking out like a sore thumb amidst all the boat-boys who ran nimbly back and forth as though they'd been born there. Not that that mattered as long as Master Sy stayed in his house. After a couple of hours' searching he found what he was looking for. Three boats towards the south end of the docks, where the Overlord's barges were kept. He bought a bag of spiced roasted grasshoppers with some of the pennies he'd stolen on the way to Bedlam's Crossing, and then wandered over to the soldiers who stood guard at the Overlord's docks. They eyed him with suspicion.

'I'm Master Syannis' apprentice,' he told them and offered up the bag. 'Are you on the run to Siltside tomorrow?' They weren't, but by the time his bag was empty, he knew which boats would be used. Half an hour later he was in the front one, curled up in the bows under a tarpaulin, with coils of rope piled up around him. The night air was warm and moist, typical for a Deephaven summer. Later in the night, as he dozed, the night-rain came, a light fine mist at first, then fat heavy drops. It drummed against the tarpaulin, trying to get in. Berren wrapped his arms around his head and ignored it. At least the tarpaulin didn't leak. Not like Master Hatchet's roof. Then the next thing he knew the rain had gone, it was dawn, there were voices grumbling and the boat was tossing and rolling as men clambered aboard. Peeping out from under his cover, Berren saw at least a dozen men. They had burning torches and ringmail coats and were loading the boat with heavy crossbows, boasting about how many mudlarks they were going to kill. A part of him couldn't believe it had been so easy. Another part wished it hadn't, but it was too late for turning back.

'There will be no killing unless we have to,' said a sharp voice. Instinctively, Berren ducked down, not even peeping any more but letting his ears do the work. Master Sy was on the same boat! 'And put those torches out. It'll be light enough where we're going.'

'They're not for light, thief-taker. They're for burning mudlarks.'

'No killing!'

There was some more grumbling and muttering about how the mudlarks most likely wouldn't let there be much choice in the matter. Then the motion of the boat changed as they started to row out into the river current.

'How am I supposed to keep a look out when the bloody sun's coming up right in my eyes,' growled a voice just a few feet from where Berren was hiding. 'Can't see a cursed thing.'

The reply came from Master Sy. 'Your Justicar chose the time, not me. They'll see us coming and they'll be forewarned. We'll not be taking them by surprise.'

'Aye, should have come at dusk with the sun behind us for that.'

'The hours they wake and sleep are driven by the tides. They come out when the tide is low to forage for food. The tide is high now. The time is good enough.'

'Better be,' grumbled someone else. 'Otherwise we'll be wading across half a mile of shitty mud.'

'Wading? You'll be sinking with all that ringmail on.'

After that the boat was quiet for a while, silent except for the creaking of the oars and the splash as they dipped into the water. High overhead, seagulls called up the dawn to wake the river.

'Shit!'

'Khrozus' Blood!' The boat rocked violently.

'Shields!'

'What was that? Was that an arrow?'

'I said shields!' The boat rocked again. Somebody roared with rage.

'Holy Kelm! That nearly took my head off!'

'Arrows! Arrows! Raise your shields!' The cry echoed between the boats. Berren shifted, trying to peer out from under his tarpaulin to see what was happening. Except as he lifted up the oiled canvas to peep outside, someone was staring right back at him.

'Gotcha.' Hands grabbed hold of him and pulled him out and then forced him down. In a blink there was a knife at his throat and several angry faces glaring down at him. Justicar Kol's soldiers, when you came to see them up close, were an ugly lot.

'Who the flying beggar's luck are you?'

'Shields, you witless rats!' shouted someone further back.

'I'm with Master Syannis,' Berren squeaked. 'I'm his apprentice.' Most of the soldiers were at the oars, eight of them, four on each side. The others, the ones that held Berren, were haphazardly waving shields in the air. Even as Berren looked up, he saw an arrow streak over the top of the boat, missing them by a few strides.

'Keep rowing, you dolts! And keep your shields up.'

'Let him go!' shouted Master Sy. 'He's mine. He shouldn't be here but he is.' The look he gave Berren was one of sheer fury. 'Boy, if you get stabbed out here today,

158

it'll be bliss next to what's waiting for you when we get back to Deephaven.' His eyes flicked back to the horizon. 'Now row! Row with all your strength! The quicker you get there the less time they'll have shooting arrows at us. Hold your shields up and hold them together and hold your nerve. There's only a few of them.' The thief-taker picked up a crossbow and cranked it back. 'Make yourself useful, boy. Load another one for me.' He stood up and fired, then ducked back behind the shields. 'Swing a touch to the port, lads. Another hundred yards is all.'

'Aye, and then the fun really starts,' growled an oarsman. Berren peeked around the shields. The boat was coming up quickly on a scattering of wooden huts, rising from the water on stilts. Wooden gangways ran around each of the huts and a maze of bridges, some of them made of wood, some of them nothing more than a pair of ropes strung between two posts, linked them together. The huts seemed to go on forever. There must have been hundreds of them. At least on the nearest ones, no one was shooting at them, although he could see a few men gathered there, waving clubs and some sort of harpoon.

'When we get off, we have to be quick, lads,' snapped Master Sy. 'Lightning fast. Else they'll cut the bridges and then it's back to making our way about on the water, except they'll be shooting at us from the sides as well as the front. The Bloody Dag's not far from here if he's at home, and he's not the sort to run. And I want him alive, lads, and so does the Justicar. You hear me? Alive and squealing. Doesn't bother me if he's got one or two bits missing, as long as his tongue can still cluck.' A hand grabbed Berren's head and yanked him back into the middle of the boat. 'Crossbow, boy!'

Berren handed the thief-taker another crossbow and took the one he'd fired. He looked at it, helpless. The handle Master Sy had used to cock it had fallen out somewhere and he had no idea what he was even looking for.

'Here.' Berren assumed it was the crank, but Master Sy was pressing a dagger into his hand. 'Tell me you at least had the sense to wear the mail I gave you.'

Berren looked sheepishly at the bottom of the boat. The truth was that the mail shirt chafed and was uncomfortable, and after the Barrow of Beer he'd only ever put it on once and then taken it off again. It was on the floor of his room, back in Deephaven.

Master Sy rolled his eyes. 'Well it won't protect you from an arrow anyway.' He stood up and then quickly sat down again. 'Twenty yards, lads. Keep those shields up!' He cocked a crossbow himself. 'Hold this,' he said, and then started working on another. 'Once we're ashore, keep out of the way. If any trouble comes after you, run. If you can't run, stick your knife in them. Stick it in good and hard. And listen, lad, listen good. You get into a fight, the most important things are your eyes and your feet. In a fight, people tend to look away at the last second. Don't. When someone takes a swing at you, don't take your eyes off them. When you stick a knife in them, you watch it all the way. Got that?'

Berren nodded. At the front of the boat, one of the men staggered and swore as an arrow hit his shield.

'Five yards,' shouted the thief-taker. 'Ship your oars, lads! Grab your swords! Grapples ready!' There was a scream and a string of shouts from the boat behind. An arrow had found its mark at last. 'Two yards! Grapples!' Two of the soldiers heaved coils of rope and grappling hooks over the wall of shields and began to pull. 'Brace!'

A heavy jolt knocked Berren off his feet as the boat ran into the walkway around the nearest hut. The soldiers staggered, but the thief-taker was already running. 'On, lads! On!'

24

SILTSIDE

Men roared and screamed at each other. The boat shook as though in a storm as the soldiers hurled themselves out and met the first mud-lark defenders. One of the men holding the grappling ropes passed them to Berren. 'Make yourself useful boy! Tie this off!' Then he was gone. By the time Berren had tied the first rope around one of the rowing benches, the commotion of fighting had died down. By the time he'd tied off the second and clambered ashore, the soldiers had already moved on. He could hear where they were from the shouting, and always over the top of it all, Master Sy's voice. 'On, lads! Fast now!'

There were bodies. Fallen off the walkway, lying in the mud under three feet of water, waiting to be rolled away up the river with the rising tide. Berren had to squint and peer at them to see who they were through the lapping waves. Two soldiers, almost lost in a haze of swirling silt. One of them had the harpoon that Berren had seen in him. The spear was buried so deeply that the point poked out the other side. The second one had an arrow in his neck. As Berren watched, a slow string of bubbles popped out of his mouth and climbed their way to the surface. Then a crab scuttled up from out of the murk and started crawling across his face. Berren shuddered. Fifty, maybe sixty yards away, the second boat full of Justicar Kol's soldiers thumped in against another hut. These ones had an easy ride. The mudlarks who'd been waiting to meet it had already run.

Berren glanced into the hut. There was another body there, a mudlark, cut down from behind. Not much else. Nets and fishing lines hung out to dry, that was all.

Something thunked into the wood not more that two feet away from his head, the noise so sharp and sudden that he almost fell into the water in surprise. When he turned to look, he saw an arrow, quivering there. He looked back the way the arrow had come, but all he saw was water and huts and more water and more huts, all jumbled together. Whoever the archer was, they'd ducked into hiding. With a gulp, he ran off, around the walkways, racing for Master Sy and the soldiers.

He caught up with them rampaging through a collection of larger huts. Most of the mudlarks who'd lived there had obviously run away before the soldiers had come, but that wasn't stopping the Justicar's men from smashing everything that would break. Master Sy was in the middle of a shouting match with one of them. In another corner of the hut, one of the soldiers had carefully made a pile of rags and quietly dropped his torch onto it. Master Sy didn't seem to have noticed.

'Master! Master!' Berren waved frantically. The thief-taker dropped whatever argument he had with the solider and ran to try and put the fire out. Except he didn't make it, because one of the soldiers stepped in front of him.

'You get paid for getting your man,' said the soldier. 'We get paid for every hut that burns.'

The thief-taker snapped something back in a language Berren didn't know and strode away again. He grabbed Berren's arm, livid.

'This ...' He snarled and seethed, too furious to speak for a moment. 'You stay here, boy. Stay with these idiots.' He ran outside. Berren took one look and followed. Armoured men setting fire to wooden huts built over the sea didn't seem like such a good idea. When the huts came down and dumped them all into the water and then the mudlarks with the bows showed their heads again, Berren wanted to be somewhere else. He ran after the thief-taker and found him standing outside, hands on hips, teeth gritted.

'See,' he hissed. 'See?'

Berren didn't dare say a word. He had no idea what he was supposed to be looking at.

'There!' Master Sy pointed into the water. A dozen yards away was another hut. The bridge that would have taken them there had been cut at the other end. There was no way across. 'See that hut there, lad? That's where the Bloody Dag hangs his hat. See how close we came?'

As if in answer, a small group of mudlarks emerged from the hut across the water. Several of them had bows, and one of them was carrying a flaming brand.

'Hey, Deepies,' waved one of the bowmen. 'Got a goose and pheasant for you.' With that he touched an arrow to the brand. The arrow caught fire at once. Then he quickly took aim. Master Sy kicked Berren's legs out from under him and they both dropped to the floor as the arrow shot across the water and hit the wooden wall behind them. In a flash, the thief-taker was back on his feet.

'You needn't bother with that, Dag,' he shouted back. 'They're already doing it for you.'

'Aye aye. Well we always knew you Deepies were soft in the head. Hope you can sing a hymn, matey. Going to get mighty wet or mighty hot.' He lit another arrow. Master Sy hastily pulled Berren back inside. The soldiers had moved away. Master Sy stamped the fire out. At least the hut was only burning on the outside now.

'Go back to the boats, lad. Wait there.'

'Master ...'

The thief-taker's face grew dark. Berren winced. 'Boy ...' He stopped. 'Can you swim, lad?'

Berren shook his head.

'Come here.' He jumped to the middle of the hut and kicked away the wreckage that lay there. Underneath was a little door. Master Sy opened it. 'They all have these in Siltside,' he said grimly. 'I hope you learn quickly. Stay here.' Then he ran out of the hut back towards the boat, calling for the Justicar's soldiers. Berren peered cautiously out of the hut back towards the Bloody Dag. He was still there with his gang, arrows at the ready, watching. When they saw Berren they jeered and one of them popped another arrow at him. Berren ducked back inside. He could smell smoke now. The outside wall of the hut was definitely on fire. He opened up the door in the floor. About two feet below, the swell of the estuary water rolled gently up and down.

By the time the thief-taker came back, Berren's hut was burning merrily. Flames were licking through cracks in the walls and the smoke was starting to be choking. Master Sy had three soldiers with him. Without hesitation, he jumped down into the sea, holding on to the edge of the trapdoor with one hand.

'The rest of you, you know what to do. Keep their eyes on you and away from the water.' He looked at Berren. 'Come on, lad, jump in. This won't work without you.'

'What won't ... ?' He didn't get to hear an answer. Master Sy snatched out a hand, grabbed his ankle and pulled and the next thing Berren knew, he was toppling through the trapdoor and into the water. His arms flailed wildly. 'I can't ... !' he started to shriek, and then his head went under.

'Get up!' His head burst into the air again. He took a huge breath, waiting for the next plunge, and clawed at the hut roof, just out of reach.

'Get up!' snapped the thief-taker again. 'Get on my shoulders, boy. Now.'

Once Berren had his arms wrapped around the thief-taker's neck and his legs locked like a vice around his waist, he realised that Master Sy was actually standing on the bottom, with the water rising and falling around his chest. With his chin tipped up, the thief-taker's face stayed mostly out of the water, even when the waves came. Every time he moved, Master Sy swore at him, but other than that and the constant certainty that the thief-taker was about to lose his balance and tip them both into the sea, he felt perfectly safe. Until Master Sy started to walk out from under the hut, wobbling precariously with every step, straight towards the Bloody Dag and his men.

'Right lads,' he roared, 'let them have it!'

He waited, just under the edge of the hut they'd left. Berren could see the men of the Bloody Dag; or rather he could see them from the waist down. The rest of their bodies were still obscured. Then he heard a shout and a scream and one of them fell and toppled into the sea. The others ran for cover.

'Now.' The thief-taker sounded grim. 'Hold on tight, lad.' He waded out, meandering towards the Bloody Dag's cluster of huts. Berren clung on, eyes screwed almost shut, waiting for the moment when one of the mudlark archers would come back and spot them, exposed and helpless in the water right in front of him. Knowing that the thief-taker would die first was little comfort. Yet somehow none of those things happened, and before he even knew it, they were easing under the walkway around the Dag's hut, and into the shadows beyond.

'Keep your voice down now,' whispered the thief-taker. He spat out a mouthful of sea water. 'I can't see too well. There should be another trapdoor. When you see it ...'

'I see it,' hissed Berren. 'It's right here!'

The thief-taker stopped. 'Climb up. Stand on my shoulders if you have to. Then open it.'

Berren did as he was asked. The trapdoor had a big wooden peg running through one edge of it with a catch and a handle. He reached out, touched it, and then paused.

'What if someone's up there?' he whispered.

'Then you'd better hope they don't notice you.'

'But ...'

The thief-taker tensed. 'It's that or be dumped in the water while I try to climb one of the piles, boy. Take your pick!'

As gently as he could, Berren pushed the trapdoor up so that he was taking its weight. He turned the handle. It moved easily, without complaint. He pushed a little more, then stretched up, pushing the door open with his head while steadying himself with his hands. Below him, he heard Master Sy grunt.

The hut, or at least the half of it he could see, was empty. He pushed the door open some more, trying to convince himself that it would make a decent enough shield in case someone was standing right behind him.

They weren't. The rest of the hut was empty too. Berren hauled himself up. He sat on the edge of the hole, dripping and panting, scared witless and tingling with exhilaration. He couldn't remember the last time he'd felt so sure he was going to die. Not even when One-Thumb had had him cornered. But this was what he was here for, wasn't it? This was what thief-taking was all about. This was what he'd come to learn ...

A soggy length of rope landed in his lap. 'Come on, boy, tie that to something and make it snappy. That is, unless you were thinking of taking on the Dag and his men on your own.'

25

THE BLOODY DAG

'The difference,' said Master Sy, 'between a thief and a thief-taker, comes down to two things.' He hauled himself up into the hut, breathing heavily, and took a moment to sit down next to Berren. 'A thief is a coward. A thief-taker is not. A thief will come at you in the dark or from behind, or will hire braver men to do his dirty work. A thief lacks the courage that makes honest men strong. The other thing that a thief lacks is wit, for a man with a sharp wit has no need to be a thief.' He stood up, sea-water running off him in little rivers as he did. 'Justicar Kol's men work for Justicar Kol. It saddens me to see what they're doing, but I'm hardly surprised. Let that be a lesson to you. The Bloody Dag has cut his bridges and answers them with arrows and fire. Any fool could have seen *that* coming. So he thinks himself safe within his walls of water. Whereas I now prefer to think of him as trapped.' Slowly the thief-taker drew his sword. He smiled, more for his own personal pleasure than for Berren. 'I might have used one of Kol's soldiers if you hadn't been here, but in hindsight, they might have been too heavy. So I reckon you've earned that emperor I gave you.'

Even with every nerve twitching, Berren beamed. 'Does that mean I was useful? You said when I was useful you'd teach me swords.'

The thief-taker sighed. 'Is there any chance you'll stay here if I tell you to?'

Berren didn't answer. No, he didn't want to stay here. Partly because he was terrified of being left alone, of being caught and having nowhere to run. And partly because he wanted to be *there,* wherever *there* was. He wanted to see swords flash and blood fly. He wanted to see the three men in the alley again. The speed and elegance of it. He wanted to see it over and over, again and again, until he'd learned to do it himself.

Master Sy shrugged. 'You do what you want, boy. Just keep out of my way and don't get caught. If it comes to it, remember what I told you about using a knife.' He sidled over towards one of the hut's open doors and peeked around the corner. 'Last time around, lad. Here we go. What's in those boxes behind you?'

Berren looked over his shoulder. Half a dozen wooden crates lay piled on top of each other. They looked like the sort of crates he saw constantly being carried back and forth on the sea-docks. They also looked like they'd all been smashed open and looted some time ago. He started to move for a closer look, and then stopped. He hadn't heard the thief-taker leave so much as felt him, felt the pounding of his feet through the boards of the wooden floor. He'd been tricked.

From somewhere outside, someone screamed. Berren forgot about the crates. He raced after the thief-taker and caught up with him in the next hut. One mudlark was already writhing around on the floor next to a smashed bow. An arm, severed at the elbow, lay beside him. Two others were facing Master Sy, but even as Berren raced in, they turned and ran. The thief-taker didn't hesitate and tore after them. 'What does it take to make you stay behind, boy?' he yelled. He sprang across a fragile rope bridge and caught the second of the two mudlarks as they reached the other end together. His sword just seemed to brush the back of the man's neck, but the mudlark still went down as though he'd been kicked by a horse. Master Sy didn't stop. 'If you can't do as you're told, at least stay close!' he bellowed, and then vanished through a curtain into the next hut. 'Don't let them cut you off!'

Berren tore his eyes away from the mudlark groaning on the ground and raced over the bridge. The body at the other end wasn't moving. He was lying on his back, eyes wide open, staring at the sky in surprise. A small pool of red darkened the wood around the back of his neck. Berren stepped over him. The next mudlark he reached was lying inside the hut, just by the doorway. From where he'd fallen, Berren guessed he'd tried to take Master Sy by surprise and failed. His throat and face were a bloody mess. He didn't even have a proper weapon, only a boat-hook. Berren almost felt sorry for him; at the same time, his eyes darted wildly between every shadow and glimmer of movement. He ran on through, back outside onto the walkways where he could at least put his back against a solid piece of wood. Across the water to both left and right, smoke and flames rose from several huts where Justicar Kol's soldiers were finishing their business. Another rope bridge had been cut here, but there was a more solid bridge too. A line of warped wooden planks rested on pilings, suspended a few feet above the water. At the far end was a hut that was bigger than most. The shouting from inside told him it was the right way to go. As he watched, the whole hut shook as something crashed into one of its walls.

He looked again at the line of planks. Walk slowly and carefully and don't get to the other side until it's all over? Or run and pray that none of the planks wobble and tip you off?

A crossbow bolt made the decision for him. It smacked into the wall beside him, inches away from his hip, taking a chunk out of the wood. He stared at it for one horrified moment. Then he ran. He didn't bother to look and see who was shooting at him. As he reached the other end, a body came hurling backwards out of the nearest entrance and almost knocked him flying. He jumped sideways and pressed himself against the wall of the hut as the man landed with a huge splash in the sea. His shirt had a large red stain over the belly. He pawed feebly at the water for a second, and then sank slowly beneath the surface.

'Been raiding ships again, Dag? They know it's you,' came a familiar voice from inside. 'And now they know, they're not going to let it go. It's the mines for you, sooner or later, no getting away from that. No one gives a shit about the rest of your boys though. Don't see why they have to die too. Maybe you'd like to explain it to them.'

Berren didn't hear the answer. There was a flurry of footsteps and the hut shook and then a wet crunching sound, a soft squawk and some whimpering. He crept to the doorway, wary in case any more dead men came flying out of it. The inside of the hut was dark. For a moment, all he could see were shapes.

'Look, lad. The Bloody Dag isn't worth dying for. What have you got there? A carving knife? A piece of cutlery from some rich tosser across the water? Run away. Tell everyone you were there when the jack of thieves fell to the thief-taker king. They'll think you're brave enough.'

Berren's eyes had adjusted to the gloom now. The thief-taker was standing in the middle of the room with his back to Berren. On the other side of him were two men. A big man and a short skinny one who might have been not much older than Berren. The big man had an axe. The short one was shaking. But he hardly noticed those, because there was another mudlark right in front of him, stood frozen halfway between Berren and the thief-taker. He was hold-ing a lump of wood and he was looking right at Berren, pointing a finger straight at his face. Berren could hardly breathe. The mudlark with the club took another silent step towards Master Sy, but his eyes stayed on Berren.

'Thief-taker king, is it?' laughed the Bloody Dag. 'I don't see no ladies' gown on yer head. You cross the dirty daughter with yer thoughts full of slaughter, and all for a pocket full of brewer's mould? Cheap rum, that's what you are.'

The mudlark with the club took another step. One more and he'd be close enough to swing it at Master Sy. No one else was moving. Berren still stood frozen. Paralysed.

'Anyway.' The Bloody Dag shrugged. He wasn't moving either, but then he could see what Master Sy couldn't, could see what was about to happen. 'So what? So maybe it happens you're right. Maybe me and my lads have been slipping across the daughter and helping ourselves to a few trinkets from your rich friends. But it's not like they don't know about it, eh?'

Berren couldn't think. The club-man's eyes burned at him, holding him fast.

'If you're the wedding-ring of thief-takers, you came to the wrong place. I'm the jack right enough. But just the jack.'

As Berren watched, the mudlark with the club drew a finger slowly across his throat. He didn't know what to do. Shout a warning? But what? What should he say? Something, and quickly! But it had to be right ...

'Seems to me you should be looking somewhere else. How would me and my lads know which of your salty dips were ripe for plucking, eh?' The mudlark in front of Berren slowly took the last step he needed. His eyes still didn't flicker. His spare hand slowly went to the club, poised up in the air. The Bloody Dag grinned. He lowered his axe a fraction. 'Tell you what, thief-taker. You turn around and beggars luck back off to yer Deepie friends, and I'll tell you who it is. Everyone wins. How's that sound?'

The thief-taker chuckled. The club lifted a fraction higher. Berren's whole body started to tingle. His mouth opened, but all the words he could think of piled up into each other at the back of his throat and got stuck. The mudlark's fingers tightened. Berren closed his eyes. The tingling stopped. With a scream, he launched himself forward, hurling himself at the man with the club. He had no idea what he was doing. Something. He was doing something. Anything. Anything was better than nothing.

The rest seemed to happen so slowly that he was amazed he couldn't do anything about it. The club swung through the air towards him. He tried to duck out of the way, bending sideways, but the club ducked too. It caught him on the shoulder and clipped the top of his head, and he was flying sideways and not towards the mudlark any more. Except the mudlark's head was suddenly lifting up off the top of his body in a fountain of blood. Behind him, Master Sy was a blur. The Bloody Dag with his axe was on the move too, with a roar of his own. The axe went up and came down, but by then the thief-taker was three steps to the left and it missed. Berren landed; pain crashed in and the world went dark and started to spin. Something heavy fell on top of him. There was more screaming, far, far away, and then all he could hear was his own heart, thumping away, his head throbbing to every beat. For a moment he thought he was dead, but the pain kept on coming and he could still hear the sound of the sea, lapping at the piles under the hut.

He gritted his teeth and pushed up against the weight that held him down, rolling the dead mudlark off his chest. He sat up and opened his eyes and moaned. The only other people left in the hut were the thief-taker and the Bloody Dag. The Dag was lying on the floor, missing his right hand.

'Is he …?' He tried standing up, but his legs didn't seem to belong to him any more. The pain in his head was blinding. When he touched his scalp, his fingers came away bloody.

'He's passed out.' Master Sy came and crouched beside Berren and poked at the wound on his head. Berren flinched away. 'Head wound. Seen a few of those in my time. Not too bad as they go. You're going to have a lump and a headache for a few days.' He shrugged. 'Of course, sometimes people just die for no good reason over a thump on the head. But then if you were worried about that sort of thing you wouldn't have hidden in a boat last night, instead of sitting on the waterfront in the sunset with a pretty young girl beside you.' He pulled Berren to his feet. 'Come on, lad. You did good. We'll get Garrent to take a look at that when we get back. In the meantime, if you think you're going to be sick, try to make sure it's not all over me.'

26

NO REST FOR THE WICKED

Berren barely remembered the return to Deephaven. Master Sy found another boat from somewhere, a tiny little rowing boat barely big enough for the three of them. Justicar Kol's men, it seemed, would be fending for themselves. As far as Berren could see, that wasn't going to be a problem for them.

At some point the Bloody Dag woke up. He screamed and screamed at Master Sy, making threats that Berren could hardly understand. And then later, when the threats didn't work, then came the pleading, the begging, the whining. Nothing made any difference to the thief-taker. Nor much to Berren, who lay curled up in a ball with his eyes tightly shut, moaning and whimpering at the pain in his head. At some point they must have arrived at the docks. There were bumps and jolts and screaming while someone seemed to drive nails into his skull. Then a big black hole of noise swallowed him up. For some reason, his dreams were of the same thing, over and over again. The moon-temple hall, with its column of stone in black and silver and its broken altar to a broken god ...

The next thing he knew, he was lying on the floor, staring at a roof that he knew like his own hands. *His* roof, over his floor, in his room, in the thief-taker's house. Lying still, flat on his back, staring into space. From downstairs, he could hear voices.

He shifted and groaned. The voices stopped. He heard feet running up the stairs and then Master Sy was looking down at him, with Teacher Garrent beside him. Garrent crouched beside him.

'How do you feel?'

Behind the priest, Master Sy only looked impatient. There were still noises from downstairs, too. Someone else. Tentatively, he touched his fingers to his scalp. There was a bruise there all right, a tender lump, a scab but no blood. No open wound. Mostly what he felt was ... hungry.

'The worst is gone, Berren,' said Garrent gently. 'There's a young fellow from the City of Spires. Tigraleff. Been learning our ways and he has a good touch for healing. I managed to get him to have a look at you.'

'You've been asleep for three days,' grumbled the thief-taker. 'If you're well again, we've got work to do.'

'Syannis!'

'What?'

They both stopped and looked guiltily at Berren. 'You rest, young master Berren,' soothed the priest.

Master Sy nodded sharply. 'Don't rest for too long. I'm going to the docks tonight. You can stay here and roll about in your nice warm blankets for another day or so or you can come and be about some thief-taking again.' He leaned closer. 'Lilissa will be there too.'

'Syannis!'

The thief-taker shrugged. He let himself be dragged outside, but closing the flimsy door behind them didn't make either of them less noisy as they argued. Berren couldn't make out all the words, but he could make out some: Something about him and the Justicar and mudlarks and the Bloody Dag and the docks. Something about Lilissa; then something about letters and teaching Berren to read and write and how Teacher Garrent didn't want to do it until Berren was ready and how the thief-taker didn't give two hoots what Teacher Garrent thought, actually, and in fact he'd already paid the solar monastery down in the Armourers' Quarter by Deephaven Fort to take him in for as long as it took. The voices faded as the thief-taker and the priest creaked away down the stairs, until Berren heard them again, through the window now, out in the yard, making their farewells. He shuddered. Letters? Again? The horror!

He lay still for a while. On the other hand, he *was* hungry. *Really* hungry. The sort of hungry he only remembered from the worst days with Master Hatchet. He sat up, checked his head to make sure that the bit with Master Sy and the teacher hadn't been a dream. His head was still there, still in one piece, still hurt like being stabbed when he poked at the lump, but still not bleeding. A healer from the City of Spires? For him?

His arm hurt too. When he took off his shirt to look, he had an enormous bruise. He stared at it and a grin spread across his face. He'd saved Master Sy. He hadn't just helped him, he'd *saved* Master Sy from the mudlark with the club who'd been sneaking up on him, and now Master Sy owed him and owed him big. And owing him big could only mean one thing. Swords!

Voices from downstairs reminded him that, on top of everything else, Lilissa was there. His stomach rumbled. He pulled his shirt back on and slipped out of bed and over to the door. The faint scent of incense mingled with the usual smells of old leather and stale sweat and the ubiquitous city smell, but there was something else. A trace of perfume. He smiled to himself as opened the door. Lilissa. She'd been in his room, and not long before he'd awoken. Quietly, he opened his door and made his way cautiously down the stairs. His legs felt distinctly wobbly from too much sleep, but otherwise he felt absurdly well ...

He froze. His jaw dropped. There was Master Sy,

dressed like a prince. He was in the middle of putting on a fine tunic embroidered all over with tiny gold figures. He already had on big puffy white trousers and a pair of night-black boots that reached his knees, instead of his ordinary loose shirt, grubby trousers and leather overcoat. Sitting with him was the most beautiful woman Berren had ever seen, a real lady, all dressed up like a princess.

Lilissa. It took Berren a moment to recognise her.

'Kelm's Teeth, lad, you took your time. I was beginning to think you weren't going to come.'

Berren hardly heard; he was too busy staring at Lilissa. Lilissa the betrayer. Lilissa who had a friend who was a fishmonger's son. Lilissa the ... Lilissa the ... He finally tore his eyes away and his heart jumped. Lilissa the unbearably beautiful. He took a deep breath and clenched his fists and carefully didn't say a word while he gave her the best bow he knew how to give. There. Treat her like a lady, just like Master Sy had said, and never mind what he was really thinking.

Lilissa returned the faintest of nods and then ignored him.

'Don't stare, lad,' said Master Sy mildly. Even his voice was different, as though he'd dressed that up in princely clothes as well. 'Since you're up, you can come with us. Suppose you've earned that much. You'd better get on and get dressed, though. Best clothes, lad. Chop chop. Time presses.'

Gratefully, Berren ran back up the stairs. He tried his hardest not to look back down at Lilissa, but he simply couldn't help himself. From above, looking down, you could see ... You could see *more*, that was the best way to put it. He shivered and quickly shut himself in his room. Lilissa the betrayer, he reminded himself as he dressed for the second time in as many hours. Lilissa who'd given him shelter and then promptly led Master Sy right to where he was hiding. Lilissa who had a friend who was a fishmonger's son. Lilissa who could have been sitting on the dockside with him a few nights ago, ogling the sunset while he whispered sweet nothings in her ear. Lilissa, who made Siltside and the Bloody Dag and nearly being killed by a swinging lump of wood seem so desperately distant and unimportant ...

No no no. He pinched himself, pulled on his shoes and ran down the stairs.

'Master! Master!' But before he could even speak, the thief-taker was wagging his finger. He threw Berren a crust of bread. Berren tore into it.

'Yes, lad. You did your first bit of real thief-taking.' Master Sy glanced at Lilissa for a moment. 'Turns out to have a bit of wolf in him, this one. We'll have to watch him.' He looked back at Berren and smiled and Berren puffed up with pride. That was it! Surely Master Sy would teach him swords now. He beamed even brighter.

'Master! Why are you all dressed up like that? What's happening? Where are we going?' he asked through a mouth full of crumbs. That got him a sour look. The thief-taker's voice dropped.

'We're going to the docks, lad. We're going to meet Deputy Harbour-Master Regis VenDormen. He is a powerful man, and rich and' – he glanced at Lilissa – 'as many old rich men do, he has a fondness for pretty young women. Lilissa will distract his thoughts, some fine wine will muddy his thinking, and then we shall see what we shall see.'

'Master?' Berren realised that Lilissa was staring at *him*, now. He blushed. 'See what, master?'

'If you believe the Bloody Dag, and I do, then someone in the harbour-master's office is organising piracy against the ships they're supposed to protect. Whoever it is, if I take him, he'll have his head cut off. VenDormen himself won't be having anything to do with something like that, but there's not much happens in the docks that he doesn't know about and so he's probably already raking a cut. If we're lucky, VenDormen might let something slip to tell me who it is.' He took a deep breath. 'Now listen carefully to me, both of you. For this evening, Lilissa is my ward. Do either of you even know what that means? It means that for tonight she's the daughter of some rich merchant from overseas and that I'm responsible for looking after her while she's here.' Berren glared at Lilissa again, trying to remember that he was still angry with her. His heart wasn't in it though, especially when she glared back and stuck her tongue out at him. Her eyes sparkled. Master Sy banged a wooden spoon on the table. 'Are you listening, either of you? You, Master Berren, remain my apprentice, the perpetual thorn in my side. Now you listen to me, both of you! I've known Regis for a long time. If I thought he was dealing with the Dag, I would be going to the Captain's Rest alone. Still, you'd best have a care not to get on the wrong side of him. Be nice, be polite and be quiet. Keep your eyes open, too. Whoever is behind all this is going to be as nervous as a virgin soldier right now and they'll have dangerous friends, too.' He gave Berren a long steady look. 'Much more dangerous than a mudlark with a club.'

Berren forgot about trying to be angry with Lilissa and stared at Master Sy instead, eyes wide. 'Will you have to fight them?' he asked, thinking of the ringmail shirt he wasn't wearing.

The thief-taker frowned and groaned. 'Boy, if there was any chance of that, do you think I'd be taking either of you with me? Do you think I'd bring Lilissa? Gods! No, boy, there'll be no fighting tonight. You sit, you listen, you say nothing, either of you, unless one of us asks you a question. Regis and I have known each other for years. We'll talk about things that sound very dull and then we'll come home again and that's all that's going to happen. Nothing but polite business talk over a very fine meal. Dull as mud. Just keep your mouths shut and your eyes open.' He glared at Berren. 'This is delicate, boy. I want your word. You don't speak unless you're spoken to and you say nothing about our business. Do I have your promise?'

Berren nodded. He couldn't help smiling. Trapped with Lilissa in a tavern, dressed up in all his finery. It was enough to make a lad from Shipwrights wonder whether he'd died and gone to the sun. He rubbed his head. Still sore and starting to ache, but no gaping holes. Good enough.

Master Sy stood up and wrapped a cloak around his shoulders. The cloak was something Berren had never seen before, silver and trimmed with white fur. The thief-taker offered Lilissa his hand to help her to her feet, and then took her by the arm to the door. Berren followed. He felt like he was floating. In the doorway, Master Sy paused. He glanced back.

'Remember, lad, what I said about staring at a lady?'

Berren nodded vigorously.

'You've been doing it ever since you came down the stairs. Time to stop now. And lad?'

'Master?'

'Close your mouth, too.'

He led them out of the yard. For once they didn't go down the alley into Weaver's Row but the other way, the way Master Sy had brought Berren on their first night, out into the Courts District and through to the Avenue of Emperors. A gentle breeze was blowing in across the river tonight, wafting over the top of The Peak, picking up all the scents of early evening fires. Roasting nuts, skewered meats cooked over hot coals, spiced rats baked in clay, a city delicacy ever since the siege. The sour smell of Clothmakers' down the hill, whiffs of smoke from the braziers on the Godsway, fresh wood wafting out of Cabinetmakers'

Cloister across the street. Other parts of the city smelled more mundane, but around The Peak where everyone had money, even the air itself was an adventure. Sometimes a ship or a barge would come in loaded with fruit to bring some new scent to the night air; always, by the next morning, everything would smell of fish again.

As the Avenue of Emperors levelled out and began to open out into the expanse of the sea-docks, the thief-taker turned under an ornate metal arch and into a secluded square, overgrown with trees. There were men here, Berren realised, watching them. The sort of men he usually saw on the top of Reeper's Hill, waiting outside the carriages. Cloaked and hooded, they had a poised, coiled menace to them. These ones had long curved cavalry swords left over from the war, held loose and naked in their hands as they lounged against the walls and in the shadows of the archways. Snuffers. Berren stared with a mixture of envy and admiration. Master Sy wouldn't approve, but they were the way he wanted to be. They looked dangerous.

Master Sy wrinkled his nose. He walked straight through the middle of the square to the other side. Suddenly Berren found himself standing on the threshold of the most magnificent building on the dockside, possibly the whole world, certainly the whole world as far as Berren had seen it. This, he knew, without even having to ask, was the fabled Captains' Rest, the finest tavern in the city, grander even than Teacher Garrent's moon temple. It called itself something different, a loggia, or some other fancy foreign word, but a tavern was what it was and everyone had heard of it.

Master Sy looked him up and down, straightening a fold in his clothes here, brushing away a fleck of dirt there. He spoke sternly: 'Look around you, both of you. Everyone who comes in here has money, a lot more money than us. Watch the way they act, the way they dress. Listen to the

way they talk. See if any of them strike you as unusual.'
He glowered at Berren. 'And whatever you do, don't steal
anything.' Then he smiled at Lilissa, took her arm again
and led them to the door.

27

THE HARBOUR-MASTER

The entrance to the Captains' Rest was a gaping archway that looked more like the portal to a castle or a temple. Two more snuffers stood on guard, these ones in fancy uniforms that matched the arms carved into the arch's crest; they frowned at Berren as he followed his master. Beyond the arch lay another square yard, open to the sky and larger than the first. A wild variety of plants filled the place – scented and flowering bushes scattered around a handful of small trees. Several different ivies competed for domination of the walls. Paths wound around the yard, punctuated by little marble benches, barely large enough for two people to sit on at once. Berren saw at least a dozen colourful birds, perched in the trees and around the walls. A low hum of conversation filled the air. The effect made Berren think he'd walked into the exotic palace garden of some faraway kingdom.

'Copied from the garden at the Watchman's Arms,' whispered Master Sy. 'This is where sea captains and merchants come to make their business.' Lilissa's eyes darted from one thing to the next, wide with wonder.

'It's like a palace!' said Berren.

Master Sy nodded. He pointed to their left. 'Those are the private rooms and lodgings. Only guests are allowed inside there.' He gestured ahead. 'That leads to the grand hall. They won't let us in there either. It's where the Guild of Sea Captains and Traders meets. But over here ...' He turned right down a path, so crowded by greenery that it brushed Berren's legs as he walked. 'Anyone can come here. This is where the food halls are, and the baths, and ... various other diversions.'

From the way he said it, Berren knew that *diversions* meant women. Over the time he'd been Master Sy's apprentice, he'd noticed that the thief-taker became strangely clumsy and fumbling on the few times he spoke on the subject, particular when Lilissa was around. Berren, on the other hand, had grown up with Master Hatchet, near the bottom of Reeper Hill. He'd lived one door away from Club-Headed Jin's whorehouse and he'd already seen about as much as there was to see. He'd begun to suspect that on this one subject, he might actually know more than his master.

He glanced at Lilissa again. Maybe he did know more than Master Sy, but he still didn't know nearly as much as he would have liked.

The thief-taker led them out of the gardens onto a sheltered veranda and then into a wide hall. The delicious scents of food laced the air. Paintings and hangings lined the walls. Berren remembered that he was still ravenous.

'Master? Did it *used* to be a palace?' he asked.

'No. But the Guild of Sea Captains and Traders has a lot of money, and the guild-master likes to think himself something of a king. Now remember what I said, boy, and be quiet. And guard your eyes, *both* of you.'

Berren still stared at everything he saw. Uniformed servants intercepted Master Sy, speaking in hushed whispers. Other men and women wandered through the hall, dressed in silks and satins laced with gold and silver and decked with jewels. Even in his wildest dreams, Berren had never imagined that so much wealth could exist. The ten emperors awarded to Master Sy, such an immense fortune not all that long ago, now seemed paltry. It might have bought a shirt, or perhaps a hat, for people like these. *Might* have.

He stayed close to his master, almost afraid of what would happen if he were to get lost. Everywhere he looked there was a new wonder. Even the air smelled of gold. No hint of rotting fish here, only the damp scents of flowers and incense and the occasional heady waft of Lilissa. She was wearing perfume, something that must have cost her more than a fish-monger's son could ever afford. Maybe she'd bathed, too, in the marble public baths up near Deephaven Square.

He tried not to think about that, but it was impossible. He lost track of where they were. Thoughts raced inside his head, passing through each other, clouding out everything else. Lilissa. Perfume. Baths. Money. Master Sy.

He stopped, frozen for a second. Lilissa and Master Sy? No, it couldn't be. Could it?

The servants led the way through a wide doorway – the handles on the doors were made of gold – and into a cosy dining hall. Perhaps half a dozen small tables stood around the room, all of them occupied. A buzz of voices filled the air. Berren could see at once that this room, and the people in it, were not as rich as the rest. It showed in their clothes. As for the hall, he could tell by the plainness of the wooden tables and chairs and the gaudiness of the curtains and the paintings on the walls. The servants left. Master Sy picked his way across to a table where a man sat on his own. The man was unusually fat, with rolls of flesh hanging from his neck and under his face. Berren disliked him at once. Fat meant rich.

'Harbour-Master.' Master Sy bowed to the man and then introduced Lilissa. 'This is Lilissa. She's ward to my brother Talon, who sailed into the city a few weeks ago on the *Heraclian*.'

The fat man didn't get up. He nodded at Master Sy, but his eyes were all over Lilissa like a bad rash.

'How delightful. And how did you find the *Heraclian*, my sweet?' He didn't even seem to notice that Berren was there. Berren's dislike solidified into a knot of hate and anger and envy.

Lilissa curtseyed. She put on her shy look and stared at her shoes. Then she batted her eyelashes at the harbour-master. Berren clenched his fists. 'She rode surprisingly low in the water, sir. But her cabins were comfortable and she took the seas well enough.'

It was obviously an answer they'd rehearsed. The harbour-master tried to smile, but to Berren it seemed more like a sneer. 'And where is your guardian, pretty one?'

'In Varr by now I hope, sir. He is here to see ...' She stared even harder at the floor. 'I cannot say, sir.'

'No need to explain, little bird. I understand. I know Syannis well, you see.' The harbour-master licked his lips. Berren fidgeted. He had to stop himself from jumping on to the table and screaming: *Fat old man! Keep your eyes off her!* That she'd betrayed him to the thief-taker instead of hiding him and that he was supposed to be hating her for it, all that was long forgotten.

Master Sy pointed to Berren. 'This is my apprentice, Berren. I'm showing him the places of the city that matter most. And of course the people.' He turned to Berren. 'Lady Lilissa, Berren, this is Harbour-Master Regis VenDormen, one of the most powerful men in this city.'

Their introductions complete, Master Sy sat down. Something in his manner made Berren realise that he wasn't the only one who disliked the harbour-master.

The harbour-master immediately set his attention on Lilissa. He spoke to her slowly and carefully and with simple words, so he ended up sounding as though he was talking to a child. All the time he stared fixedly at Lilissa's chest and Berren couldn't do anything except fidget on his chair. He was trying to sound important, but his job didn't sound that difficult. As far as Berren could tell, it came down to deciding where each ship should weigh anchor and when it would be allowed to load or unload its cargo. This sounded straightforward enough, something almost anyone could have done; but just when Berren had felt unable to bite his tongue, Master Sy had elbowed him. When no one else was watching, Lilissa shot Berren a look, stuck out her tongue and made a disgusted face. Berren grinned, sighed with relief, and tried to make himself relax. He nodded and gave a soft gasp and tried to look suitably awed. The harbour-master smiled. Then he promptly seemed to forget that either Berren or Lilissa existed. For the rest of the evening, he and Master Sy talked animatedly about people and places and ships, and Berren was left to pick at his supper. He didn't recognise the food he was eating, and it was far too rich. After a few mouthfuls, his stomach began to rumble. He cleaned his plate nevertheless. He didn't dare not. He smiled at Lilissa and she smiled back, and that somehow made everything else worth it.

At some point, he dozed off. The food had long since ended, but a steady flow of wine came to the table and most of it found its way into the harbour-master. Berren was even given a glass of his own, heavily watered, and that had been around the time he'd fallen asleep. He woke up again with a start, horrified with himself. His head was throbbing again. The harbour-master and Master Sy were getting to their feet. Lilissa was still sitting bolt upright, eyes wide, cheeks flushed. There was a half-empty wine-glass in front of her. She stifled a yawn. When Berren cocked his head, she rolled her eyes.

'It's been a pleasure, as usual,' the harbour-master was saying. His cheeks, which had been pasty white at the start of the evening, were now rosy.

'Yes.' Master Sy helped him up from the table. 'Your company is appreciated, as usual.' He smiled, although

Berren could sense his tension. 'I am, as always, grateful that you find time amid so many arduous responsibilities, for your friends.'

The harbour-master belched loudly.

'There's one other little thing I suppose I might mention,' Master Sy said.

The air changed. The harbour-master's cheery smile fell away. His eyes turned cold and hard. The air seemed to crackle. Unconsciously, Berren sat up straighter and got ready to run. He knew that sort of look. Hatchet got it sometimes. The killing look, his boys had called it. Never mind the hiding you'd take later – when the master got that look, you ran.

'Yes?'

'Those pirates we were talking about a month back.'

'Yes, the fishermen.'

'Well, that's the thing. I don't think it's them. You might cast your eyes over who comes and goes through the Sea Gate in the dead of night.' The Sea Gate was at the bottom of Reeper Hill. In the dead of night, *everyone* came and went through it. 'And who doesn't. I'm fairly sure you won't find any mudlarks using it, you see. And yet they wander your docks. It is a puzzle.'

'I see.' The harbour-master smiled and clasped the thief-taker's shoulder, a gesture of friendship and affection. 'Well, I dare say they come up and down the Avenue of Emperors like most honest folk, but when I see one, I shall ask him. One way or another, this piracy will be stopped. I commend your efforts, sir.' He sounded like he meant it, too, but his eyes didn't change. The killing look never shifted.

Master Sy made his farewells and scooped up Berren and Lilissa, sweeping them towards the doors. As soon as they were back in the gardens outside, he pulled Lilissa close. He whispered into her ear and pressed something into her hand. She stopped, looked shocked, and then Master Sy took her arm and pulled her on again. When they emerged into the Avenue of Emperors, he let go of her and grabbed hold of Berren instead.

'I'm very sorry, Berren, but I've misjudged our friend the harbour-master, and badly so. There are men already following us. Take this.' Now he pressed a small knife into Berren's hand. 'When they come for us, run, do you hear? Run as fast as you can. Look after Lilissa. If I don't come back, tell Kol everything that happened tonight. Don't trust him, just tell him. And then, no matter what he does, leave it be.'

Berren blinked, uncomprehending. 'Wuh?' He could feel the danger, though. He had a sixth sense for that sort of thing. You needed to, in Shipwrights, if you were going to survive. He glanced over his shoulder. Four hooded men had come out into the avenue after them. They were all armed. Snuffers. Master Sy gave Berren a hard shove in the back. He didn't bother whispering any more.

'Now, lad! Run!'

Whys could come later. When someone said run and there were snuffers on the street, Berren ran.

28
SOME LEARNING ABOUT SWORDS

Syannis watched Berren and Lilissa start to run up the Avenue of Emperors. *Not fast enough.* With a sigh, he turned to face the four swordsmen who'd come out of the Captain's Rest. This wasn't what he'd expected, not even half-guessed. VenDormen wasn't supposed to do this, wasn't supposed to be so bold, wasn't supposed to even have any part of this. Gods! The Bloody Dag, in the end, hadn't had a name to give. He'd come here fishing, looking to see what he might catch and he'd accidentally caught a shark.

Oh well. He drew his short sword and raised his guard. *At least now I know who it is. Pity I couldn't have somehow found that out a few hours earlier.*

The Avenue of Emperors, even at night, was about the most public place in the city, short of the docks themselves. People were already stopping to watch – from a careful distance, of course – and the four swordsmen hadn't even reached him yet. Syannis gritted his teeth. *We should charge them. Sell tickets. A penny apiece.* He took a few deep breaths. Four against one. Not good odds. Likely as not he was going to die. Lilissa and Berren would be safe, and that would be his legacy. *Marvellous. Hardly a fitting end for someone who should have been a king.*

There wasn't any subtlety here. The four swordsmen drew their blades and started to spread out as they approached him. Their swords were long and curved. Cavalry swords. Half the snuffers in the city carried those, all left over from Khrozus' army a generation ago. Fenris steel from Neja. The best in the empire. Held an edge like nothing else. Light and long and good for slashing. *Fine weapon if you're on a horse. Not so good on foot. Heh, and I have a nasty surprise waiting for you under my shirt.*

But he couldn't be having them surround him either. They were still half a dozen yards away when he ran at them. It wasn't what they were expecting. *Thought we'd circle each other for a while, eh? So you could come at me from all directions at once? I don't think so.* He launched himself towards the end of their line, at the one furthest out into the street. That one jumped back hastily into a high guard. At the last moment, Syannis ignored him completely and went for the one next to him. They all had their guards up but the switch earned him a moment of surprise. He stepped inside the man's blade and drove his own short sword up into the man's guts. *One gone. Still three left. And I won't fool them with that again.* He kept moving, through them, wrenching his sword free. The man he'd stabbed groaned, fell over and lay still.

No time to think about that. Somehow he'd gone right through the middle of them and no one had been quick enough to land a blow on him. *See. That's what you get for carrying the wrong sword to a street-fight.* His off-hand pulled a knife out of his belt. He spun around to face the three that were left. They were closer together now. Hesitant. Nervous. All good. He didn't wait to see what they'd do next, but threw the knife straight at the one in the middle. It was supposed to take him in the neck, but his aim was a bit high and it caught the man in the head instead, glancing off his temple. The man shrieked and dropped his sword. There was a lot of blood. *Good enough. With a bit of luck that's an eyeball gone.*

Which left two. They had quite a crowd now. *Just as well the Avenue of Emperors is so wide, eh? Wouldn't want to be stopping the traffic.* Still, he took a moment to glance around for places to run. The docks' militiamen could hardly ignore something like this, and the coins in their pockets came from the harbour-masters. There wasn't much doubting which side they'd be on. *Go on you two. You've seen your friends go down and I'm all out of tricks. Run away, damn you!* He could hope. They didn't look old enough to have actually fought in the war. With a bit of luck they'd never actually fought anyone who might kill them. With a bit of luck they were all for show ...

They launched themselves at him, both of them at once. They were good, too, in a schoolyard sort of way. Held their swords just so, good footwork, that sort of thing. Not a clue how a real fight actually worked though; what they ought to have done was danced out of his reach and pricked him to death. Presumably whatever sword-school had spawned them didn't teach that sort of thing. While *he'd* been taught by Shalari, the best swords-woman in the small kingdoms, who'd probably killed pushing a hundred men on the battlefield and whose famous first rule of sword-fighting had always been *don't get stabbed.*

He parried the first sword and deliberately left himself open to the second. The swordsman obligingly lunged and stabbed him in the chest. His sword bent and the impact hurt like a kick from a horse, but the thin ringmail vest under Syannis' coat didn't give. Syannis grinned at him. Time seemed to freeze for a moment.

'Oops,' he said. He could see the dismay in his enemy's eyes. *This* was more like it. *This is what we should have been doing years and years ago. This, not running away.* He drove his own sword into the man's throat and that was that.

Except it wasn't. Blood sprayed straight at his face. He turned his head, screwed his eyes shut, jumped away from where the last swordsman had been, but for a moment he was blind. A moment too long. He felt a horrible stabbing pain in his armpit, just above the line of his mail. He gasped. *That was deep. That was bad.* Not his sword-arm though. *Stabbed. By a cavalry sword. How utterly mortifying.* He spun around, keeping his wounded arm close but not hugging it tight. *Don't let him see how bad it is. Never let them see how bad it is.* He gripped his sword tight and set his face for murder. *Sometimes when they cut you and you don't go down, they run. Go on, run!*

He bared his teeth and stepped slowly towards the last swordsman. 'Go on!' he screamed. 'Stand and fight! I want to play!'

29

ALONE IN THE DARK

Berren ran. Up the Avenue of Emperors towards the square, but that was no good. He grabbed Lilissa's arm and pulled her off towards one side. 'This way!'

'What?'

'*This* way!' He pulled harder and dragged her off the Avenue and down into a pitch black alley that wove its way into The Maze.

'I can't see!'

'Then hold my hand.' Lilissa's fingers slipped into his own without protest or question. He was running for his life, and yet her touch made him feel like the strongest man in the world.

'He gave me a knife! Master Syannis gave me a knife!'

'He gave me one too. Come on!' Berren led her deeper. These streets were his home. Even in the dark, he knew exactly where he was. He knew their twists and turns, he knew their dead ends, he knew which parts were safe and which parts to avoid – although dressed up as they were in their rich clothes, which parts to avoid extended to almost everywhere.

Most of all, though, he knew where the empty houses were. The places they could hide.

Voices. Footsteps. He dived into a doorway and pulled Lilissa close to him.

'Hey!'

He squeezed her hand. 'Shhh!' Even though the moon was up, down here in The Maze he could barely see her. He could feel her, though. Feel the warmth of her right beside him, almost but not quite touching. He could smell her breath, the lingering taste of the glass of wine she'd had while he'd dozed.

The voices came closer. They were round a corner but still coming closer.

'Why are we … ?'

This time he pressed his free hand over her mouth. She was pressed against him now. She grabbed his hand and then froze.

'Shh,' he whispered, quiet as the breeze, straight into her ear.

'I'm going to burn his pig and goat if he don't pay up.' The voices were in the same alley now. Berren counted footfalls. Sticks had taught him to do that, years back. Men. Big men. Three or four of them. Accents, too. Not quite right. Not quite local. Mudlarks, from their rhyming. Not that that meant much. Mudlarks got everywhere. These ones stank, too. A real bad smell of city sewage.

'Yeh? And then what? How's he going get us our three ladies if he can't sail. A good kick in the loaf ought to be enough.' The footsteps stopped. One of them sniffed the air.

'You smell something?'

Laughter. 'I smell you, you rancid oaf.'

'Perfume. Yeh. Khrozus!' Berren tensed. They could always run. No, *he* could run. He'd have to drag Lilissa behind him.

'You're right. Some ground-floor girl been working here I reckon.'

Someone hawked up some phlegm, spat, and then let out a loud belch. Another voice joined in.

'Now everything smells of rotting fish. Thanks, Dree.'

'You're welcome.' The footsteps started again. They walked straight by where Berren and Lilissa were hiding. Close enough that if Berren had reached out an arm, he could have tugged on their coats as they passed. He waited a long time, until he was sure they were gone, before he let himself breathe again.

Lilissa pulled his hand away, gently this time. 'Who were they?'

He shrugged. 'Don't know. Doesn't matter. No one comes in here at night unless they're up to stuff they don't want others to see.' He took a tentative step back out into the alley, then strained his ears and peered up and down. Mostly pointless in the dark, but his instinct was driving him. 'All right. Let's go!' He pulled on Lilissa's hand but she didn't move.

'Berren! What are we doing here?'

He stopped. He hadn't thought too much about what he was doing. Only that The Maze was where he ran whenever he got into trouble.

'We can't go back to Master Sy's house,' he said slowly. 'Not in the dark.'

'Why not?'

'What if they got there first? What if they're waiting for us? What if we got back and then they came?' He didn't even know who *they* were. No, *they* were the harbour-master's men. What he didn't know was what Master Sy had said to make the harbour-master suddenly want to kill them. Not beat them and warn them off, but *kill* them. Straight out and just like that.

Or was it even worse? Had he been planning this even before they'd sat down and broken bread together. He must have, mustn't he?

'I want to go home, Berren.'

'How come those snuffers were so right and ready? They

were going to *kill* us.' He had to keep saying it to believe it. You just didn't do that. Even One-Thumb with his knife probably wouldn't have gone through with it. Would have scared him too much to live with what came with being a killer. But the men who'd come out of the Captain's Rest... He'd seen the way they moved. They'd have gone through with it and then some.

'Berren, I want to go *home!*' Lilissa wasn't whispering this time. Berren huddled back into the doorway next to her, shushing her.

'So do I, but we can't. What if the whole thing was a trap? They could be waiting for us.'

She pushed him away. 'What if it wasn't? Besides, it wasn't about us, was it? It wasn't about me.'

'I saw the way he was looking at you. Looking right at your ... Well, put it this way, if I'd have looked at you like that even when you wouldn't notice, I'd have got a clip round the ear. And he was doing it right in front of all of us.' Somehow the thought of leaving the streets he knew made him quake with fear.

Lilissa snorted. 'Don't be stupid. It's not about me. It's about whatever business Master Syannis has. Something he's found out about that horrible man.'

'Look, I know a place we can hide for the night. Not far. No bother. We'll be left alone. In the morning, when it's light, we'll go up Weaver's Row. It's not far. Then you can go home. We can take a look when the sun's out.' After they'd been to the moon temple and told Teacher Garrent all about what happened. But no need to mention that. 'Look, this place, it's only a few minutes away. Let's get there and be safe. Then we can talk about what we're going to do.' The 'few' was more like ten and he didn't know what he'd do if she still wanted to go home once they got there, but it was all he could think of to say.

Lilissa made a sceptical sound, but she let him lead her

out into the alley again. 'I'm starting to wonder if I should believe any of this. Letting you take me into some dark alley in the middle of the night. Ma would kill all three of us if she could, paths bless her.' There was a tremor in her voice. Anxious, however much she tried to pretend she wasn't. Not as scared as she should have been, though.

'Yeh.' Berren tried a nervous laugh. It helped a bit. 'Well. Like old Master Hatchet said: Dead tomorrow is alive today.'

'Don't think I haven't seen where *your* eyes look either. You're every bit as bad as that horrible VenDerren or whatever his name was.'

'No I'm not. I'm not as ugly for a start.'

'Really? Are you sure?'

'I'm not as fat; I'm sure about that.'

She giggled. 'His bows were better, though.' They were moving. For the moment they had this bit of The Maze to themselves. Berren started to walk more quickly, until they were almost running. 'Dragging me off to a place like this. Bet you've been thinking about it all evening. What would your master say?'

'It was his idea.' Sort of. *His idea I should drag you off.*

'Ah. Tonight was all a big show, was it? All for me?' She giggled again. 'I suppose I'd better go along with it, then, after all that effort. I imagine I should feel flattered.'

You should feel scared and you should be quiet and so should I. That was what Berren wanted to say. Instead he stopped. Paused. Listened. There was still no one about.

'We're here.' He crept into an opening he couldn't even see and listened again. Then he knelt down. Low down in the wall was an old wooden door about three feet high and wider than it was long. His hands traced its shape until he found an awkward hole in the bottom. He lay down and reached through, undid the latch, and the door swung open. Inside was an even deeper darkness than the alley. It was silent, too. Silent as death. He sat on the ground by the doorway and dangled his feet over the drop beyond. There was no way to see how far it was down to the floor.

'What is this?' hissed Lilissa.

'We're round the back of the Sheaf of Arrows.' Berren turned around and carefully lowered himself into the void. The floor was about four feet below him. 'This is the cellar.'

Lilissa didn't move. From where he was now, he could just about see her, silhouetted against the night sky. 'Won't we be caught?'

Berren shook his head and beckoned her down, both gestures lost in the dark. 'Nah. It burned down three years ago. They built it up again, but this bit's full of rubble. No one ever comes down here. That door's the only way in and out.' That's what other boys had told him, anyway.

Lilissa carefully lowered herself to sit on the edge. Berren took her hands, warm and soft in his, and eased her down; but it was only as he closed and barred the door behind her that he realised he had Lilissa to himself in the dark. And that despite everything she'd said, she'd still come with him. The lump on his head thrummed with pain, but with Lilissa beside him he didn't care. What would a fish-monger's son say now, he wondered?

30

WHERE OLD THIEF-TAKERS GO

S yannis screamed: 'Come on!' He couldn't remember that ever actually working. To his amazement, this time it did. He watched the last of the four swordsmen turn and race down the Avenue of Emperors back towards the Captains' Rest. He stayed very still, watching the man go. Then he swayed and staggered. His coat and the darkness probably hid it well enough, but he was bleeding, and badly. Wounds like the one he'd taken killed people. There was a good chance he was dying.

People were staring. *Well if I'm going to die, it's not going to be in the middle of the street surrounded by a hundred gawping onlookers. It's going to be somewhere where no one ever finds the body so no one can be quite sure I'm gone.*

Had to be gone before the watch showed, too. He gritted his teeth and started to jog up the Avenue of Emperors. *Important that VenDormen doesn't know I'm hurt.* Except he really was hurt, and badly, and running was making it a lot worse. He lurched into the next dark alley and stumbled up against the wall. His breathing was much too hard and he could taste iron. *No. Not iron.*

He coughed. Frothy blood filled his mouth. He clenched his fists and screwed up his eyes, furious with himself. *Oh well done, Syannis. Well done. Now you really have gone and got yourself killed. And for what? For a city that isn't even your home? For a gang of greedy merchants who have more in common with the* ... No. He wasn't going to think about that. That was the past.

The urge to sit down was a strong one. Or maybe lie down. Curl up on the cobbles and rest for a while. Maybe that would help him find the energy to walk the rest of the way up the hill. Up into Four Winds Square, across the other side, down the Godsway to the House of Gulls by the River Gate. Yes. That *was* a long way. A little rest first ...

Syannis coughed again and spat out another gobbet of blood. Rest meant death. He didn't have time. He needed to walk, and quickly, and he needed to do it now, and how much it hurt or how hard it seemed really didn't matter. One foot at a time, he compelled himself to move, staring grimly ahead. When the alley emptied him out into the Kingsway, he hardly noticed the people who came the other way. He staggered on up the hill towards Four Winds Square. The River Gate might as well have been in Varr. Maybe he could get as far as the Eight. Someone would be there. Maybe they could send for a priest. Or that Tigraleff fellow. Whoever he was.

No. Kuy. He needed Kuy. He needed a magician. A healer. His old friend. One step at a time, that was all that mattered.

He was almost at the top of the Kingsway when his legs finally failed him. They simply stopped and buckled and pitched him forward and that was that. He managed to roll over, onto his back, pressed up against a wall, away from the middle of the road. Into the thickest of the shadows, where no one would tread on him. That was the least a man could ask wasn't it? To get on and bleed to death quietly in a corner somewhere and not be trodden on?

Syannis, once a prince, now a thief-taker, thought about this for a while. A pair of green eyes stared at him, a stray cat. It stopped beside him and started to lick his face. And then, for a time, the thinking stopped.

31
KNIFE WORK

At some point, Berren fell asleep. When he woke up, he could hear Lilissa's breathing, soft and rhythmic, beside him. He could feel her warmth. For a long time he lay there, still, savouring the moment. He wanted to reach over and touch her, and found himself wondering what her skin would feel like against his fingers. His head, mercifully, was clear.

Light was filtering in through the cellar door. Silently, he rose and crept across to it. Peering through the hole, he could see that there was light in the alley too. Which meant the sun was up in the sky and some hours had already passed since dawn.

'Lilissa?' he whispered. He crouched beside her. In the womb of the cellar, even a whisper sounded loud. 'Lilissa! Wake up!'

She stirred, but didn't wake. In the little light that filtered through the cracks of the door, he could just about make out her face. Very gently, he reached out and touched her cheek.

'Lilissa!'

When she stirred again, his hand jumped away. This time she opened her eyes and sat up.

'I'm cold.' She yawned and stretched. Berren considered saying something about warming her up and then thought better of it. As if in reward, Lilissa wrapped her arms around him and hugged him tight. 'Those men who came after us had swords, didn't they?' She shivered. 'They were city men and they were after us and Master Syannis, weren't they? What are we going to do? Where can we go?'

Having Lilissa with him, he'd made everything seem like a grand adventure, trying to keep the truth of what had happened pushed to the back of his mind. Now he stopped to think about what it really meant. Men with swords. Not city watchmen or district militia, but snuffers. Even Hatchet had had nothing good to say about snuffers. *You keep away from men with swords, my boys. I ain't got no sway with those sort. You cross 'em and they snuff you out like a candle, and all that'll happen next is you'll get swept up and thrown away with the rest of the shit. So just leave 'em be.*

'We need to find Master Sy,' he said. 'He'll know what to do. He'll keep you safe.'

'What if he's dead?' Lilissa shivered again. 'What then? What do we do then?'

Berren shrugged. 'He won't be dead. Master Sy's probably the best swordsman in the whole city. He can fight four men. I bet he could fight forty.' He saw the fight in the alley again, flashing in front of him. Three against one, and the cut-throats hadn't stood a chance. Remembering made him feel powerful. 'Come on. We can go back home now.'

'What if he's not there? Then what?' Lilissa let go of him. Berren went to the doors. He opened them. Daylight flooded in, bright enough to make him flinch away.

'I suppose he might have gone out again. Getting the city soldiers down into the docks to get that VenDormen fellow. Probably need that if he's got snuffers. District militia wouldn't go against snuffers.' He took a deep breath and sighed. 'All right. If he's not there, we can go to your house.'

Lilissa shook her head. Berren offered her a hand and pulled her to her feet, then gave her a leg-up out through the doors and into the alley. Her beautiful dress was torn and dirty. Now he could see her in the light again, she looked scared. But still lovely.

'No,' she said. 'I don't want to go home. Not until I know it's safe. Isn't there somewhere else?'

'There's the temple on Moon Street.' Berren hauled himself out through the doors and carefully shut them behind him. 'We can go there.'

'Oh,' said a new voice from somewhere above them. 'Berren, Berren. I don't think so.'

Berren jumped. He looked up. Sitting on a first floor window ledge, straight above them, was Hair. Berren backed away, keeping Lilissa behind him. Hair? What was Hair doing here? It didn't make any sense, but it certainly wasn't good.

'I'm not on your patch,' growled Berren. 'I got no trouble with you.'

'Really?' Hair leered. His hand kept moving to something he had hidden inside his shirt. 'Not sure One-Thumb thinks the same.'

'Yeh. Well I'm not on his patch, am I. So he knows what he can do, right?'

'This is The Maze, thief-taker's boy. Ain't anyone's patch. And besides, someone's put the word on you, you and your thief-taker master both. Watched you run with your bit of skirt, we did. Been searching The Maze for you all night, and you were right here all the time, eh? Getting some while we was getting rained on. And now it's morning and here you are.' He chuckled to himself. 'Knew this was the right place to keep a look out.'

Being called *boy* by Hair, who was probably exactly the same age and just happened to be a couple of inches taller, made Berren clench his teeth.

'All right then, Hair. You want to carry on where we left off? Bring it on.'

'All right then, I will.' Before Berren could do anything else, Hair put two fingers to his mouth and let out a piercing whistle.

'Run!' Berren snatched Lilissa's hand and bolted down the alley. Hair stayed where he was, laughing like a madman.

'Who was that?' gasped Lilissa behind him. She wasn't running fast enough, but when he pulled on her hand, she almost fell over. 'Hey! I can't go any faster!'

'That was Hair.' What did she think he was going to do? Stop for five minutes and tell her all about Master Hatchet and the dung-cart boys and everything else?

'How did he find us?'

Berren skittered to a halt. Running into the far end of the alley was One-Thumb. There was another boy with him, one that Berren didn't recognise.

'Shit!' He pulled Lilissa off again, this time down a different passageway, one so narrow that the sun barely touched it between its tall walls.

'Get him!'

'He's gone down Wellbottom!'

'*Waddler!*'

He heard another whistle from Hair, two shrill notes. He could see the end of Wellbottom, emptying into the daylight of Bottlemaker Street. A few minutes either way from there and they'd be out of The Maze. He tugged on Lilissa's hand. 'Come *on!*' Fifty yards and they'd be out in the open. Forty yards. What passed for open in The Maze, anyway. Thirty. At least there'd be witnesses. There wouldn't be any stabbings, not with witnesses. Twenty yards ...

A shape stepped into the alley in front of them. Too much in the shadows to be more than an outline, but an outline was enough. Waddler.

'Stop him!' One-Thumb was gaining on them from

behind. Waddler stood at the entrance, hovering uncertainly, but still in the way. 'Get him, you prozzy's hanker!'

Berren let go of Lilissa. He ran at Waddler. 'Out the way!' Waddler was all right. He'd never been one for this sort of trouble.

'Grab him!'

'Move!'

Waddler stayed where he was. He didn't try to grab Berren, he simply didn't move. Berren ploughed into him, bowling him over, bundling them both into the street. He staggered and lost his balance, rolling across the cobbles. He saw Lilissa emerge from the alley and stop.

'Run!' he shouted, scrambling back to his feet, pointing off towards the market end. 'That way! That way!' Waddler snatched at his ankles. Berren kicked him, turned and ran. One-Thumb was right behind them now.

'I'm going to cut you, thief-taker boy. Gut you like a fish!'

He glanced over his shoulder. Jerrin was only about ten yards behind him, but Berren was faster and they both knew it. For a moment, Lilissa was on her own, ahead of them both. 'Catch me if you can, leper-boy!'

A flash of motion caught his eye and then something barrelled into him from the side, sending him flying and knocking him halfway across the street. Then they were on him, Jerrin, the boy Berren didn't know and Sticks. It could only be Sticks, blind-siding him like that.

'Get the girl! Quick!' Sticks ran off. Jerrin and the other boy grabbed hold of Berren. A few dozen yards down the street, an old pedlar watched them. He didn't move, though, and then Berren was being dragged away into another alley. Somewhere quiet. Back behind him, he heard a shriek that could only be Lilissa. He struggled as hard as he could, but the other boys were both stronger. When he started kicking, Jerrin punched him in the face.

'What do you want?' he choked. They were well into the shadows now. Jerrin didn't say anything. They just wrestled Berren to the ground and pinned his arms.

'Get him up,' barked Jerrin.

The new boy pulled Berren to his feet, holding him fast. One-Thumb slipped a knife out of his belt.

'Thought you'd gotten away from us, eh? Thought you were clever.'

'Who's your new friend, One-Thumb? Is he your new arse or are you his? I can't tell.'

Jerrin spat in Berren's face. 'We're the Harbour Men. Told you that before. We got new friends now. What did we do, Mouse? What did we do to make you want to leave, eh?'

'I've never seen him. He's not one of Master Hatchet's is he?' Berren spat back. 'Hatchet don't know what you're doing, does he? He's going to tear your bones out, One-Thumb.'

He'd touched a nerve. He saw that in Jerrin's face, right before One-Thumb punched him real hard in the gut. 'Yeh, we all got our little surprises ain't we, eh? Who'd have thought, Mouse running about with a nice piece of soft skin like that. Who is she, Mouse? She your girl?'

'Leave her out of this!'

'Can't, Mouse. Old Hatchet, he's just a little fish. We're a part of something else now. Something big. Got to do her too. Don't mean I can't have a bit of fun first though, eh? What's she like, Mouse? She a screamer?' He stood back and looked at his knife. Berren tried to lunge at him.

'You touch her and I'll kill you! I'll rip off your head and spit down the hole!'

Jerrin shook his head. 'Really? Maybe she just needs someone a bit better than you to look after her, eh? Mouse hides out in The Maze. You think I don't know where to look? The word's out on you, Mouse, you and your thief-taker. Every gang in the docks is out looking, but I showed you that place, Mouse. Remember? I always know where you go.' He laughed. 'What'd you do, you and your swanky shit-boots master, eh? What'd you do to get the dockside snuffers after you like this?' He shrugged. 'Not as I really care. Pay me for you in silver, they will. Not pennies.'

The boy holding Berren was getting restless. 'Come on! Chop and grill him and be done with it.' He had an accent. Like the men they'd hidden from the night before. Not from the city. Mudlarks again.

Jerrin shrugged his shoulders. 'I'd have done you for the fun of it, Mouse, but now I get some nice shiny crowns for the pleasure. So thanks. Thanks for the money. Thanks for the girl. And now I'm going to rip off *your* head.'

The mudlark boy behind him tensed. Jerrin drew back the knife.

32

FLASHING BEFORE YOU

The River Gate. The Canal. Reeper Hill. As he lay dying, Syannis knew the missing piece of the puzzle. The reason he couldn't work out how the Bloody Dag's men were crossing the city was because they weren't. They were going under it. Bloody long-winded and bizarre way to go about having a revelatory vision, that was, but he supposed there was no logic to that sort of thing. Not much use either, not when you were bleeding to death. A revelatory vision a few days ago about being stabbed in the armpit, now *that* would have been useful.

Something scraped his cheek, then his nose. Bloody stray cat again. He could hear it purring. Didn't have the energy to shoo it away.

'Syannis, Syannis, Syannis,' it seemed to purr. 'Not yet, not yet. This isn't your time or your place.' The cat spoke with a soft voice, sprinkled with a lilting trace of something foreign. He felt its whiskers tickle his face. A paw rested lightly on his lips. He opened his eyes for what he supposed would be the last time. A face stared back at him. A brown face with a hooked nose and a pair of wild lashing eyebrows streaked with white. An old face, from a long time ago. He smiled.

The face smiled back, but there was nothing welcoming in that smile. It was a greedy and hungry smile. Avaricious. Syannis could smell his own blood, thick in the air. The end was seconds away, the last flickerings of life quietly bleeding from him. Strange way to die, he thought. He had no idea where he was. Not lying in a gutter in the Kingsway any more, that was for sure. He didn't remember walking the rest of the way, but maybe he'd made it after all. 'Where the Bloody Khrozus …'

A flash of gold caught the moonlight. Then a flash of steel. A knife, with a strange blade.

'I'm not done with you,' said the voice. 'Not yet.'

✤ PART THREE ✤
JUDGEMENT

33

THE VANITY OF LADY YGALA AND
THE UPSIDE-DOWN TEMPLE

'Bye bye, Mouse.' Jerrin's fingers on the knife clenched tight. He hesitated, though. Perhaps it wasn't so easy to kill someone held helpless in front of you.

The mudlark boy's grip loosened. 'Watch ...!' A shape rose up behind Jerrin and then a large piece of wood crashed down on his head. He dropped the knife and staggered, both hands clutching his scalp, moaning. Blood was pouring down his face. The other boy let go of Berren and ran. Berren stood exactly where he was, too amazed to move. Lilissa lifted her piece of wood again and swung it with all her strength into Jerrin's back. Jerrin screamed and arched and fell over, one hand still plastered to his head, the other now pressing into his ribs.

'Oh gods! Please! Please don't kill me!' He looked up and for a moment his eyes met Berren's. 'Mouse! Please! Please don't let him kill me! I wasn't really going to ...'

He didn't get any further before Berren kicked him in the face.

'You ...! You ...! I ...!' Rage left him incoherent. Dimly, he felt a tugging on his arm.

'Come on! Let's go! Before there's any more of them.' Lilissa pulled him away, dropping her plank of wood. They ran, feet skittering across the cobbles. Back out in Bottlemaker's, Sticks was in the middle of the street, dragging himself towards a wall, knees drawn up into his belly. His face was screwed up in pain. When he saw Lilissa, he flinched away, curled up even tighter. They ran past, on up towards the warm food-smells of Market Square.

'What did you do to him?' Berren couldn't remember ever seeing Sticks go down in a fight. Run away maybe, but never left like this.

'Kicked him.' Lilissa flashed him a grin. Her eyes were wide with an infectious excitement. 'Like Master Syannis showed me.'

Berren glanced back. No one was following them. Apart from Sticks, all he could see was Waddler, lurking in the shadows, trying to keep out of sight.

At the top of the hill, The Maze tipped them out into Market Square, right next to Weaver's Row and the way home. The crowds were suddenly thick. Men and women pushed past each other here, squeezing around the stalls and the rugs spread out on the ground, half of them pointing and shouting. Most people wore plain loose robes in pale brown or off-white, by far the most comfortable clothes for a hot Deephaven summer. Here and there, Berren saw men in breeches, with shirts open to the navel, sweat shining on their pale faces. Men from up the river, from the City of Spires or Varr. There were people painted orange, with black and white stripy hands. Others bald, with hundreds of feathers sticking out of their scalps, tattooed from head to toe. Black-skinned Taiytakei sailors with hair braided down to their knees and tiny blades at the ends. He gasped as half a dozen men wrapped in the robes of the dead walked and laughed across their path, jabbering in some strange language that he thought might be the language of the underworld, until he realised that they were probably just another bunch of foreigners who didn't know that grey was the death-colour and thought the funny looks they kept getting were because of the spiked bands they wore around their necks and wrists. A dozen different languages washed over him, a mish-mash of words from the empire and across the seas, bundled higgledy-piggledy into something new that only existed within the four corners of the biggest marketplace in the world.

Lilissa tugged his sleeve. 'I'm hungry.'

Berren's stomach rumbled in breakfast-less sympathy. A thousand different smells all fought for his attention. Sweet spices, perfumes, scented oils, sizzling skewers of meat, roasting nuts, fruits, all layered on the city's undertones of sweat and fish. He'd been into the market lots of times, but never in the heat of the day, never when it was busy like this. The Market District had its own gangs who gave short shrift to any intruders from the docks or from the wrong side of Pelean's Gate. Hatchet's dung-collectors only got to come and do their work late in the evening, when the crowds were mostly gone and what was left were the wagonners; even then they were watched.

The thought made him uneasy. The market gangs would take it badly if they saw one of Hatchet's boys in the square. He reached into his pocket and pulled out a few pennies.

'Come on then. We'd best get on.' There could be snuffers here too, on the lookout. For all Berren knew, every snuffer in the city was looking for him now. It was a chilling thought. He stopped where a man was baking strips of dough stuffed with shredded fish in a sun-oven. While he waited, Lilissa disappeared into the crowd. When she came back, her face was flushed with excitement.

'Look! Look over here!' When he offered her a piece of fishbread, she hardly seemed to notice. 'Come on! You have to see this.' She pulled him over to a shady corner where the crowd was thinner. Against the pale stone wall stood a single small iron pedestal. In it was a bowl full of earth, from which grew a dark green stalk with a single pure white flower as large as Berren's hand. A man with dark skin and red cloth wrapped around his head stood next to the pedestal, cradling an ornately decorated wooden box. Inside the box were three glass vials. Two burly snuffers with big curved swords stood guard, one on either side. They had red cloth around their heads too. From the way they stood, it seemed to Berren that they were guarding the flower rather than the man. They looked at Berren and Lilissa and sniffed. Berren knew that look. He was used to it. *Not enough money.*

Lilissa didn't seem to notice. She was pointing at the flower. 'Look!'

'What is it?'

'It's a Servin Mountain Lily.'

Berren shrugged. Flowers were for girls. 'It's pretty,' he said.

'Don't you know anything?' Lilissa nudged him hard in the ribs. 'That makes the most beautiful perfume in the world, that does. They say it was that perfume that started the war.'

Berren didn't answer. According to Master Sy, the war stemmed from the greed of Khrozus Falandawn. According to Justicar Kol it had been the mudlarks. Now it was a flower. It had all happened before he was born, and he was fairly sure he didn't care, even if it turned out to have been started by two fishermen having a punch-up outside the whorehouse in Loom Street.

'It's very pretty,' he said again.

'They call it Lady Ygala's Vanity. One day, when I'm the richest seamstress in the city, that's what I'm going to get for my perfume. I'd give anything to smell of that.'

Now *that* was much more interesting to know. 'Really?' asked Berren archly. 'Anything?'

'Maybe.'

Berren stepped forward and pointed at one of the vials in the box. 'How much?' He had an emperor, after all. An emperor ought to buy almost anything.

Disdain met him. Even dressed up as he was in the finest clothes Master Sy could afford, he obviously wasn't good enough. The man holding the box sneered and sniffed and then reached into his belt and pulled out a tiny piece of glass not much bigger than a pea.

'This, sir, is perhaps more where sir's purse lies. A single pure drop of the essence of the lily.'

Berren glanced at Lilissa. She was still staring, wide-eyed and open-mouthed with hope. His heart pounded.

'How much?' he asked.

'Two emperors,' said the perfume-seller, with no trace of a smile. Berren's heart jumped.

'One.'

The perfume-seller stared at him. 'Three.' It took a second for Berren to realise that he wasn't joking. Cheeks burning furious red with shame, he turned away, pulling Lilissa after him.

'Come on.' Two emperors? For what? For a drop of something smaller than a fingernail? How ridiculous was that? It was absurd. It was criminal for anything to be so expensive. For a moment, he wondered about slipping back and somehow stealing a bottle, one of the proper bottles. One of *them* must cost about as much as the ship that had brought it to Deephaven in the first place. But no. The perfume-seller had snuffers with him, and he'd had enough of those for one day. And besides, he had to think of Lilissa.

Except that was the trouble. He *was* thinking of Lilissa. He was thinking of how happy he could make her, and for that, two emperors seemed nothing short of a bargain. Right here was something that no fishmonger's son could ever give her. He could have shown her ...

Shown her what? That he was better than whoever this other boy was? Was that it? He growled and surged forward, forcing his way to the edge of the market where it emptied out into Weaver's Row. Lilissa had to scurry to keep up.

'Hey! Berren!' he couldn't get her face out of his head. The look of hope when she'd thought, for that one instant, that he was somehow rich enough to buy her perfume that was named after an empress. 'Berren! It doesn't matter. I really like it that you asked. It's very sweet.'

Sweet. That cut deeper than One-Thumb's knife.

'Is that what you call your fishmonger? Sweet?'

The words came out, bitter and envious. Envious because he'd seen something more in that look of hope she'd worn. For an instant, he'd seen love; and now that he'd seen it, he knew he'd give anything to see it again. And bitter because, even as he spoke, he knew that in speaking those words, he'd drive her away. As soon as they were out, he would have given anything to take them back.

For a long time she didn't answer. Finally he stopped, turned around, ready to get it over with.

Except she wasn't there. She was twenty yards back up the street, standing still. She wasn't even looking at him at all. Dragging his feet across the cobbles, he walked slowly back to join her.

'Look!' She pointed down a street that led back into The Maze. 'It's the upside-down temple!'

She hadn't heard him.

Berren stood beside her and looked. It was true. At the end of the street was what looked exactly like a very small temple, turned upside down so that it was standing on the tops of its dome and its towers. As he looked, Lilissa slipped her arm into his and pulled him close; later, if Berren had been asked, he wouldn't have been able to say a thing about what he'd seen as he stood in the middle of Weaver's Row and stared at Deephaven's most unlikely monument, but he could have talked for hours about how absurdly lucky he had felt.

34

THE GOLDEN KNIFE AND THE
SECRETS OF THE WATERFRONT

They walked back in silence, hand in hand, until they reached the thief-taker's yard. As soon as he opened the door to the house, Berren could smell that someone else had been there. The air carried the taint of rotting fish, much stronger than the yard outside, and of something else. Something cold and dead. Upstairs, a board creaked.

'Master?' Berren had Stealer in his pocket and now he gripped it tight. Snuffers? Could there be snuffers here, lurking in wait? Most likely it was Master Sy, but better safe than sorry. He crept up the stairs, quiet as a ghost, and pressed his ear to Master Sy's door.

Lilissa watched him from the open door to the yard. Berren pressed a finger to his lips. 'Master?' he whispered again. From inside he heard the knocking of a window shutter against the wall. Caught in a breath of breeze perhaps.

'Master?' he said again, louder this time. There was no answer. The shutter fell silent. Berren's fingers settled on the handle of the door and then paused. He'd never been into the thief-taker's room. The door had no lock; sometimes it was even ajar, and he'd sneaked a peek. But he'd never gone in. Never dared.

He took a deep breath. Quiet as he could, he eased the door open.

The inside of the thief-taker's room was plain enough. An empty bed, a wooden rack for hanging clothes, and beside them, a table. In another room the table would have seemed perfectly ordinary. Here, though, it looked almost like an altar. Short squat candles were arranged around three sides in a semi-circle. There was a quill and a pile of papers and a bundle of letters, tied in ribbon. And there was a closed box. A plain wooden thing almost as long as his arm.

That was all. No chests, no closets, no space under the bed, nowhere for someone to hide. There was no one here.

He stepped across the threshold, still poised to run. A purse hung from one end of the wooden clothes-rack – he couldn't help but notice that. The shutters of the window that looked out over the yard were open. A faint wind drifted in through the room and down the stairs, carrying the smell of the city. He went to the window and peered outside into the yard, but it was empty.

'Berren?' Lilissa's voice came at him from the window and the door, both at once. 'Are you all right?'

He frowned and scratched his head. He was sure he'd heard someone in the room when he'd come in, but where were they now? He peered down out of the window. It was a long drop. You couldn't simply jump out and expect to just run away. And Lilissa would surely have seen …

'Yeh,' he called. His eyes moved restlessly about. Maybe he was imagining things. Maybe the creak of the floor had been nothing. Old houses did that sometimes; yet he couldn't shake the sensation that he wasn't alone, even now. He shivered.

He was about to leave when his gaze stopped again on the table and its temptations. He paused. The box was open. Berren stared. He was certain, as certain as he could be, that the box had been shut when he'd come in. Yet now it wasn't. Inside it was a knife. A strange thing; the blade was an unusual shape, more like a cleaver than a knife.

For some reason he couldn't fathom, his hand reached out and he picked it up. When he took the knife out of its sheath, the blade shone like polished silver. Strange curling patterns marked it. Berren noticed all these things, but most of all, he noticed that the hilt was made of pure, carved gold. He weighed the knife in his hand. It was heavy, much heavier than it looked.

It was solid.

He tried to think about how much it must be worth. Then he tried not to. Next to this, ten emperors was nothing. And yet here it was, in Master Sy's room, next to his bed. Unguarded.

'Berren!' Lilissa again. Her voice had an urgent ring to it.

He wanted to put the knife back but his hands wouldn't move.

'Berren!'

Berren ... whispered the air. He stared at the blade, his eyes wide. It seemed that the patterns in the steel had begun to shift and swirl ...

'Berren! Please!'

With a shudder he threw down the knife. It clattered on the floor, loud and accusing. Biting his lip, half closing his eyes, he picked it up again and quickly put it away. As an afterthought, he closed the box. Just in case. Just in case of what, he wasn't sure, but he did it anyway. Then he snatched the thief-taker's purse and ran down the stairs.

Lilissa looked at him, eyes wide. 'What's up? You look pale as a ghost!'

'He's not here.'

She put a hand on his shoulder. 'Let's just wait. I'm sure he'll be back.' She smiled, but Berren barely noticed. He needed space, that's what he needed. Space and to be away from the thief-taker's house for a bit.

'I'm going out,' he said. 'Ought to get some bread. Need some clean water too. You want to come? Or do you want to wait? In case he comes back?'

'One of us should stay.' Lilissa let out a deep sigh. 'You come back quick, all right? Please?'

Berren nodded vigorously. 'Yeh. Back as quick as I can.' On impulse he stopped and turned, pulled her to him with one hand and cupped her face with the other. He kissed her, sharply aware of the warmth of her against him from his chest down to his thighs. For a moment, all he wanted was to pick her up and run, somewhere far far away. He kissed her again, looking for a sign, the slightest sign that she felt the same.

No sign came. He let go. He couldn't read her expression at all. Amused, maybe. A little surprised, perhaps? Definitely not overwhelmed with desire, that much was for sure. He scowled and then nodded.

'I'll bring you back a spice cake,' he said, and hurried out the door before either of them could say anything more. That was it. His head was full now. Completely full. Between Master Sy and Lilissa and One-Thumb and being chased by snuffers and now some weird knife, there was a good chance it was going to burst, or at least that was how it seemed. He got as far as the Godsway before he even noticed where he was. He paused there and bought spice cakes like he'd promised. He treated himself to one there and then. After the night they'd had, they deserved it, he thought. Both of them. Then he tried to think, tried to work out what he should do, but it was all too difficult, all too complicated. Wait, that's what he ought to do. Probably go to teacher Garrent and stay there until Master Sy came back, which he surely would. And if he didn't …

For some reason he couldn't make himself think about that.

He sighed. Water, then. Whatever happened to the

thief-taker, he was going to need fresh clean water when he came back. And that, at least, was something Berren could get. As soon as he'd finished gobbling down his spice cake, he ran on down to the river docks, to the Rich Docks, to the sprawl of wooden jetties that reached out into the water like the remains of some nest of monsters. The usual Tower-Day market was set out on the cobbles along the riverside. The combination of the market and the frantic loading and unloading of boats gave a crushing weight of people, all trying to move in different directions. When he'd been living with Master Hatchet, the Rich Docks had been one of his favourite haunts. Even when someone caught him picking their pocket or snatching their purse, they could never catch him. He'd simply slip away. It was a comfortable place. Felt like home.

For all the same reasons, it was a terrible place to try and carry something like, say, four large buckets full of water. On the way back he'd have to leave the dockside by the House of Gulls and go straight up the Godsway.

Yeh. The House of Gulls, the one Teacher Garrent had shown him from the top of the moon temple. He knew more now than he had then. A witch-doctor lived there, or at least that's what the lightermen had said. A potion-maker and a healer who dealt in curses and wishes and could speak with the dead if you brought him some token. Berren wasn't sure how much of that was true and how much was the usual tales you got from lightermen.

The crowds thinned. The smell he was used to from Shipwrights, the stink of fish, filled the air again. All there was at the end of the Rich Docks were large wooden ware-houses. Lots of them and all the same. Past the pillared arch into Godsway, before the River Gate itself, there were a few more. These ones were old and empty.

Almost empty. As he got closer to the River Gate, the smell got worse and worse. At the gate itself it was almost overpowering. He looked up. Gulls circled overhead. He had no idea which house belonged to the witch-doctor, only that it was somewhere here. The ground was slippery between the cobbles, coated in a filthy slime. Something cold in the air made his skin prickle. The smell, the horrible smell ... It made him gag. It reminded him of Master Sy's room, of the stink he'd sniffed when he'd first opened the door to the thief-taker's house. The soldiers at the gate wore scarves over their faces, covering their mouth and nose. As he passed them, Berren smelled perfume. He hurried on, glad to be away.

Past the River Gate and the Grand Canal bridge then, because only an idiot drew their water from the docks. He quickly skirted around the back of the Poor Docks and reached the edge of the city. Here, past the last of the boats, the river water was clear and didn't smell overly bad. Further on into Sweetwater, a cluster of little jetties had been built so that the city-folk could take their water without getting covered in mud. Anyone with any sense, or at least any sense of taste or smell, came at least as far as here to take water from the river. Master Hatchet had once told him that the villages in the River District further upstream were forbidden, by order of the Overlord, from throwing their waste into the water, just so that it stayed clean for the rich city-folk. Berren waited patiently, queuing to get onto one of the jetties. There didn't seem to be many rich city-folk dipping their buckets in the river today. Never were. Rich folk had servants to do that for them.

Or apprentices, he thought, as he filled up his own. It was almost a ritual now, coming out here with Master Sy's buckets, filling them up and reminding himself that he was the thief-taker's servant. He'd come to take pride in it.

When he was done, he paused for a while by the river bank. Took a drink, washed his face, tipped a little over the lump on his head to soothe its throbbing. Then he set off back the way he'd come. Usually he went the long way home, working his way through the slums of Talsin's Forest by the walls until he reached Pelean's Gate. Then across Market Square and back down Weaver's Row. It was half as long again as following the river from the docks and there was always a chance of being set upon by one of the gangs that roamed the slums, but it was cheap. The quick way cost money, a penny to go back into the city through the River Gate. On most days, that was a penny saved. But not today. Today he just wanted to get back.

And then what? What if Master Sy was dead? He couldn't go back to Master Hatchet, that was clear enough. Couldn't even imagine ever wanting to, either. Cleaning dung off the city streets? Cutting purses, begging, stealing, never knowing whether today was the day they caught you and cut off a finger or maybe worse? No. Not any more.

Tailoring? Weaving? Cloth-making? Leather-working? All good solid trades. Not something to ever make a man rich, but certainly good enough that a man could be sure of having food on the table each night. Not the sort of trades where a man had to worry about snuffers and mudlarks and thieves and pirates and being cursed or poisoned.

Fishmongering?

No, not that either. The thief-taker had opened his eyes. He was Berren, and one day he was going to be great. One day people were going to know his name and they'd shift on their feet and make the sign of the sun and the moon and hope he never came their way. He was going to learn swords, be the greatest swordsman ever. And the best thief-taker too, but that would just be the start. He'd sail away with a band of men and they'd conquer some place somewhere and he'd come back a king. *Those* were the dreams the thief-taker had given him.

The thoughts made him laugh at himself. Fool's talk. Anyway, Master Sy wasn't going to be dead. Most likely he'd be waiting long before Berren got back, angry and impatient as ever.

At the Grand Canal Bridge, he put down the pails of water for a quick rest. As he did, the first drops of rain started spattering around him. He snarled and raised his fist at the sky. That was the city mocking him, that was. Waiting for him to walk all that way and then starting to rain, far earlier than usual. Mocking him for his daft thoughts of sailing away from it.

Around him, people slowed and smiled at the sky. Summer rain that came this early in the afternoon was a treasure, an hour or two of unexpected relief from the heat. And then the rain would go and the clouds would part and the sun would shine and the streets would sweat and swelter like everyone else, right into the evening; and then at night every wall in the city would drip with damp and it would probably rain again.

A waft of stinking air rose up from the waters of the canal. A reeking smell of sewage that made him screw up his face in disgust. Like the mudlarks from The Maze the night before, only a lot worse. He left his buckets where they were and pushed his way to the other side of the bridge, over to where the stagnant canal waters festered their way into the outskirts of Talsin's Forest and vanished under a web of bridges. Some were stone, some were wooden, most of them were just massive tree-trunks levered across the waters during Talsin's siege of the city and left there ever since. According to Master Hatchet, every now and then one of them rotted and collapsed, taking half a row of slums with it. The people who lived in Talsin's Forest just went on and filled in the hole and built on top of it again. Probably the only bits of the old canal that weren't completely filled in with rubble by now were the bits out in the open; the bit that ran under Berren's feet to the river, and the bit out by Pelean's Gate. He shuddered and went back to his buckets. Some of the men who went to Club-Headed Jin's brothel reckoned there were tunnels or caves that went all the way from Pelean's Gate to the sea; old tunnels that supposedly got dug under Reeper Hill during the war or even before. No one went down there. Filled with monsters, that's what they said. Evil flesh-eating man-fish things. That was what made the place stink so. Fish-men who crawled out at night and took people back down to the tunnels and ate them. That's why people vanished sometimes. Fish-men kept the canal clear too, so they could roam right across Talsin's Forest and across to the docks if they wanted. Berren wasn't so sure about any of that, and he was pretty certain the thief-taker would just laugh. No one he knew had ever actually seen a fish-man, after all. But then again, people *did* disappear, and the canal *did* stink something rotten, and the bits you could actually see never did seem to dry up.

He picked up his pails, crossed over the bridge to the River Gate again and handed over his penny to the soldiers who took the toll there. Time for a different bad smell. If there was one thing Deephaven had in abundance, it was bad smells.

'Which one's the witch-doctor then?' he asked nervously, sheltering for a moment from the rain. Talking to city guards was something he'd spent years learning not to do. In the world he was used to they meant nothing but trouble.

The soldiers looked at him. One of them wrinkled his nose and pointed, straight at a narrow alley between two of the warehouses. Berren thanked him and hurried on. Fish-men. That was just silly stories told by men too far in their cups to know what they were saying. Probably the witch-doctor was the same. Being scared was silly. So he stood, just inside the gate, and stared at the alley where the guardsman had pointed. He could see a doorway right enough. In the doorway, little things were squirming in the shadows. Cats. Lots of cats, hiding from the downpour. At least the rain washed away some of the smell.

The door opened and the cats vanished inside. Berren quickly looked away. A few seconds later, a figure appeared. For a moment it paused, shrouded in the shadows of the house. The witch-doctor. Berren was certain of it. His heart jumped. The witch-doctor, come to take him for his insolence!

No, that was stupid. Hundreds and hundreds of people walked in and out of the River Gate every day. It was hard to imagine that even a very busy witch-doctor could curse more than a handful of them. Even so, with every step towards the Godsway arch, he half-expected to feel a heavy hand on his shoulder.

No hand came. As he reached the arch, he risked another glance back towards the door. What he saw was a man, hurrying quickly away, heading towards him, face bowed against the rain. The man ran right past him, without seeing him, without even noticing that he was there. Berren stood absolutely still, and watched him go.

It was Master Sy.

35
SYANNIS

There were children playing in the yard again, the same scruffy half-a-dozen ragamuffins who came in every few days and sang songs and chased each other with sticks until someone else in turn chased them away. As Berren came into the yard, soaked to the skin, they were dancing. The rain didn't seem to trouble them at all.

'Man with no shadow that nobody knows
Comes to harvest that which he sows
Great white tower made of stone that grows
Home to the makers of all of man's woes

Four great wizards come out of the sky
Lay to rest the dead that rise
Two born low and two born high
Touched by silver, three will die

Dragon-king and dark lord's bane
Each will wax and then will wane
The Bloody Judge lifts his hand
All is razed to ash and sand

Black moon comes, round and round
Black moon comes, all fall down.'

Today Berren ignored them, hurrying past and into the thief-taker's house. The door was open, and when he got inside, there was Master Sy, sitting at the table, bright and awake. There was food on the table. Fruit and bread, but no sign of Lilissa. Berren stood in the doorway, and stared.

'Are you ...' He didn't know what to say.

'Am I what, boy?' The thief-taker's face was clouded. He looked angry and troubled. Carefully, Berren put down the buckets of river water just inside the door. Outside, the children had stopped their game. He could feel their eyes on his back.

'We ran away into The Maze and there were mudlarks and everything. We hid in this place I know. And then we came back and you weren't here.' He wondered whether he should say anything about One-Thumb and the Harbour Men.

Master Sy looked at him. Looked through him, as though looking at something that was inside Berren that neither of them had ever seen before. 'I was careless, lad. I got cut. I should never have fought four at once. That's always too many, no matter how many tricks you know. Best you know that.'

Berren nodded. This was more like it. Four men! Four men with swords! He'd fought them and he'd nearly won. *Had* won. Like in the alley but even better. 'I went to get water. When I was coming back, I saw you. You came out of the house on the river docks. The one where Garrent said not to go. That why you were there? Where's Lilissa?'

'The House of Cats and Gulls.' The thief-taker laughed, but his face was cold and unfriendly. 'Funny place to wake up. But if I hadn't then I would have gone there anyway to find out why I wasn't dead.' He lifted his shirt. In the hollow of his arm was a livid scar, as long and as thick as a finger. 'They didn't just cut me, boy. They good as killed me. And Lilissa's gone home, boy. Where she should be, back with her fishmonger's son and well away from the likes of us.'

Berren stared at the scar. *That* was from last night?

'Well? Do you like the rain so much, boy, or are you coming in?'

'The witch-doctor did that?'

Master Sy rolled his eyes. 'Witch-doctor? Is that what they've told you he is?' He shook his head. 'I'll take you to him someday. But no, a snuffer did that. One of them touched me, and badly. Saffran healed a wound that would likely have killed me.' He straightened his shirt, sat down at the table and gestured to the seat next to him. 'You want to know about me and the witch-doctor on the docks? Then come in and break some bread with me. I'll tell you about where we come from. And after that we have work to do.'

Berren looked at his feet. 'I took your purse to go and buy some food.' He showed Master Sy the purse, and then the little bag of spice cakes he'd bought on Godsway for him and Lilissa to eat.

'Well now you can give it back to me. Besides, as you see, I have another. So that being the case, come here and sit down. Do it now.' He had steel in his voice this time.

Berren walked in, closed the door behind him and sat at the table with Master Sy.

'Do you remember, when I first brought you back here, I told you that someone had stolen something from me a long time ago? You asked me what had happened to them, and I said that nothing had happened. Nothing at all. Do you remember that?'

Berren nodded. Behind him, someone shouted something out of a window. The children in the yard yelled and cursed back and then ran away. Everything went quiet.

'They stole my family from me, Berren. They stole my family and my kingdom.'

Berren stared in disbelief. 'They stole a kingdom?' That seemed impossible. How could a ...

'How could a poor thief-taker in a city like Deephaven have once been a king? Is that what you're thinking?' Master Sy laughed, bitterly. 'Yes, indeed. How could he? Well I was never a king, Berren. But I *was* the eldest bastard son of one.' The thief-taker picked up a knife and cut a strange-looking fruit in two. Red juice ran down his fingers and then his chin as he bit into one half. The other half he put on a wooden plate and pushed it along the table. 'Dragonfruit. Don't suppose you've ever had one of these before?'

'No.'

'Well you'd best have one now. You might not get another chance and they're not to be missed. They grow them in the south and ship them up the coast. They don't reach the markets in Deephaven all that often. Usually they go straight to the tables up on The Peak, or else they go down the river to Varr.' He shrugged. 'There must have been a good harvest this year. Food for princes, this. It's bruised and past its best, but still.' He took another bite. 'What do you want, lad? Had enough of thief-taking now you've seen the nasty side of it? You want to go back to your Master Hatchet?'

'No.' Berren shook his head. 'I can't. They'd kill me. And ...' he took a deep breath and let it out slowly. 'Even if I could, I thought about it and I don't want to.' The three men in the alley, the Bloody Dag's mudlarks, now the snuffers on the Avenue of Emperors. That's what he wanted. To be like that. Deadly.

'No, I didn't think so.' Master Sy stabbed the knife into the wooden table. For a moment, Berren felt a tremor of doubt, a little voice that told him to run, run away now, that that was the best thing to do. But it was only a little voice, half lost in a crowd. Swords. He wanted to learn swords. A hundred other things, too, but mostly swords. He wanted to be someone who could face down four men in a street and be the one who walked away. And the only person who could ever give him that was sitting down in front of him, offering him the fruit of princes. The thief-taker pushed the plate to him. Berren eyed it hungrily. He could smell its juices, sweet and sharp both at once.

'I was born in a city called Tethis. You won't have heard of it.' Master Sy chuckled. 'Kasmin and your witch-doctor Saffran Kuy are probably the only others in Deephaven who have. Tethis had a king. Still does, I suppose. We and the other Small Kingdoms were vassals of the sun-king, but we were so small and so far away that no one much cared about us. I doubt he even knew we existed.' He laughed again, sad, lost in memories. 'We used to fight each other a lot. Mercenary armies, since none of us could afford one of our own. And only in the summer months, between plant-ing and harvest. We were all so gods-damned poor. Must seem strange to you, living in this empire of yours, with an emperor grand enough to rival the sun-king himself, and this his second greatest city. Look across the river, over at the mudlarks. That was our world. We didn't even have any temples, any priests, not any worth speaking of. But still, it was *my* kingdom, and I was a prince and I lived in a palace, even if it wasn't a grand one.' He looked at Berren and then looked at the dragonfruit. 'I've never had one of these before either, but I'm told the air does something to them. After a few minutes they go bland and sour. It's like eating mulched paper. So are you going to eat that or not?'

Berren picked up the fruit and sniffed it. It was the best thing he'd ever smelled.

Which made him think of the perfume seller on Market Square, and his look of disdain as Berren had asked how much a vial of his Servin Lily scent would cost. He bit into the red flesh of the fruit and couldn't help smile as the

233

flavours of spring and flowers and all the passions he'd ever known blossomed inside his mouth. Deadly. Deadly and rich. *That's* what he wanted.

'Good, eh?'

He nodded.

'Saffran Kuy and his brothers came to Tethis when I was about your age, give or take a year or two. Garrent doesn't much like him. I suppose you might have noticed that.' Master Sy paused, watched the blank shrug in Berren's face, and nodded in satisfaction. 'That's just the edge of it. The sun-priests hate him. They've tried to drive him away from here more than once. They call him a necromancer and say that he raises the dead. Rubbish, all of it, but that sort of persecution was why they came to Tethis. It was a place where they could work in peace. Or so they thought.' His voice trailed away. Berren took another mouthful of fruit. The juices made his head buzz.

'What work?' he asked, without really thinking.

'Oh, I don't really know.' The thief-taker's brow furrowed. 'Whatever magi do. If there's a dark side to them then I certainly never saw it. I never really asked too many questions. Saffran saved my life once and now he's done it again. That's all I need to know. When a man saves your life, that's a debt that goes far beyond anything else.' He winced. 'I paid that debt once. Now I suppose I shall have to pay it all over again.' He sighed and shook his head. 'Where was I? Oh, Tethis. Yes. I did a terrible thing, back in Tethis. Or rather, Saffran did a terrible thing because I'd asked him to. Such a mistake. And we never had a chance to put it right, either, because they hadn't been with us for a year before ...'

The thief-taker abruptly got up and walked across the room. 'I think you know the rest. Soldiers came. Mercenaries hired by the merchantmen of Kalda. The kingdom was taken. Stolen. Come on, lad. Eat your fill and then let's go.'

'You were really a prince?' First Garrent and then Kasmin, but he'd never quite believed it. Couldn't. Not Master Sy the thief-taker.

'I was.' The thief-taker shrugged. 'That was along ago, lad. A past best forgotten.' The way his eyes flashed told Berren it was anything but. 'Kasmin, Saffran Kuy, me, plenty of others – fate picked us up and scattered us. Some of us fell here in Deephaven. And that's all there is; nothing more to know.'

'Master ...' He wanted to ask about the knife up in Master Sy's room. Was that some king's treasure he'd stolen as he fled? But the thief-taker was getting ready to leave and Berren knew better than to press his luck. Another time, perhaps. When they'd had their next little victory and the thief-taker let his guard down for a moment. 'Master, where are we going?'

'I know where the last of our pirates are hiding. Time to put them in irons.'

'You do?'

He smiled. 'Yes. Kol's going to be there, and his soldiers too. It'll be messy. Worse than Siltside. But I know where they keep their boats now. I know where they come from and how they move through the city, and I know who's been helping them do it. I didn't understand before, but now I do, and so now we finish our work. You want to learn about how to be a thief-taker? You want to see it happen, the real truth of it? Then now is the time. You can come, at least for a part of it.'

Berren stuffed the rest of the fruit into his mouth and grabbed a hunk of bread and a slab of cheese. Master Sy smiled.

'Good lad. I'll keep you safe this time, I promise you. And I promise you I'll never take Lilissa a-thief-taking again. That was stupid. I never thought Regis was a part of this, but it was stupid anyway. I could have seen you both killed and then where would I be?'

The thief-taker picked up his belt and his sword and buckled them around his waist. He moved with a smooth, quick purpose, like the Master Sy that Berren had always known. Berren grinned and jumped to his feet.

'Where are we going?'

Master Sy paused for a breath at the door. 'To Talsin's Forest, lad. To the canal. Don't forget your ringmail.'

36

THE GRAND CANAL

They went back the way Berren had come, back out along Weaver's Row and Moon Street, straight down the Godsway to the River Gate. By the time they got there, the rain had stopped and the clouds had split apart. The cobbles along the waterfront steamed, baked under the summer sun once more. The smell was back too, although muted and dull, as if the worst had been washed away into the river. Berren's pace picked up as they passed the witch-doctor's door. He couldn't help but stare.

'That's the one, lad. Never you mind what Teacher Garrent tells you, there's nothing wrong with Saffran Kuy. Maybe there's no such thing as a mage who's pure, maybe all wizards have a darkness to them, but then Saffran's no worse than any other. Go to Kol or the Eight Pillars of Smoke if you ever need some help, but when even that's not enough, you come here. Wizards, lad, can do most anything they set their mind to.'

Berren wasn't so sure of that. There had to be plenty of things that wizards couldn't do, otherwise the emperor would be a wizard too, right? 'If wizards can do whatever they like, why does he live here? Why live in a crumbling old warehouse on the stinking riverfront of a city that's not even his own?' Or why didn't he do something when soldiers had come with swords and spears to Master Sy's home. *That* was more the question Berren wanted to ask, except he didn't dare.

'Go and ask him if you like.' Master Sy must have seen the look of horror on Berren's face. He laughed out loud. 'Maybe gold and silks and women and wine bore him, eh lad? He lives here because that's what he chooses, just like you and me, and that's all there is to it. Do you still have that knife I gave you?'

Berren shook his head. He didn't remember losing it, but it was gone. Maybe in the fight with Jerrin and the mudlark boy. Still had Stealer, though.

'No matter.' When they reached the gate, Master Sy stopped to talk to one of the guardsmen. They spoke like old friends for a minute or two while Berren fidgeted and cast glances back at the witch-doctor's house. Then the soldier opened a door into one of the gate towers and went inside. Berren hurried through the gate and out the other side, eager to be going on, but Master Sy didn't move. A few seconds later, the guardsman came back and gave something to the thief-taker. A crossbow. A big one. They exchanged a few more words and then Master Sy carried the crossbow over to Berren. Up close it looked huge.

'Don't suppose you've ever held one of these before, have you?'

Berren shook his head.

'Going to learn now, then. This is a military crossbow issued to soldiers in the service of the emperor. Apparently the old emperors preferred their longbowmen from somewhere down south and stationed them everywhere. Your new one doesn't seem so bothered. When we return through the gate, remember to give it back. Right.' The thief-taker hoisted the crossbow over his shoulder and sauntered away down the street towards the Grand Canal Bridge, oblivious to the stares he was getting. Walking down the street with a sword on your hip was one thing. A crossbow over your shoulder was quite another. Once they reached the bridge, Master Sy headed for the riverside. He lifted the crossbow off his shoulder and leaned nonchalantly against the parapet wall. He cocked his head across the river.

Berren looked. Siltside sat straight across the water from where he was standing. The tides were low now. Between Berren and the nearest stilted huts, there were a few hundred yards of sluggish water, and then maybe a quarter of a mile of dead flat mud, gleaming like white gold in the afternoon sun. Berren squinted. The reflections of the sunlight were so bright that he could barely see the ramshackle scatter of houses out there. If he looked hard, though, he could see the holes that the Justicar's soldiers had burned. The black scars they'd left behind.

'Have you ever seen a piece of wood that's just started to rot, Berren? Tiny white-capped shoots grow out of the deep brown of the wood. If you catch the rot then, scratch it away, cut out the roots and treat it with tar, the wood can be saved. But if you don't, then the rot quickly spreads. You might still only see a few shoots on the outside, but the roots will run everywhere. Then your wood is only good for burning.' Master Sy glared out over the glittering water. 'That's what they are, boy. They're this city's rot, but they're just the bit you see, and Justicar Kol, for all his talk, is too scared to cut out the root. Well if that's what he wants ...' The thief-taker clenched his teeth. He had a mad look in his eye and he was grinning. Berren wasn't at all sure he liked the look of that. He was quite certain that if he was a mudlark, now would be the time to be scared and run away. Right now, while the thief-taker was still stoking up his fire. 'They come from there,' he said. 'Our pirates. They come from over there in the middle of the night. Right beneath us.' He pointed at the bridge under their feet. 'Then they go up there.' The other side of the bridge and Talsin's Forest. 'And then they vanish under the stinking streets beside the old wall. I reckon they must go all the way along the wall in their little boats, all the way under the roads and the houses, but I reckon they can't go all the way to Pelean's Gate, because that means coming through the Shipwright District and out into the open again. No, they must hide their little boats down there and then they scuttle through the streets and back into the tunnels under Reeper Hill. Must have other boats there. Then they muffle their oars, row out a couple of hours before dawn, rob whatever they can rob and slip back again before it gets light. But they'd have to stay there, that's the thing. They'd have to spend the day in the tunnels and then come out when it's dark again.' The thief-taker frowned furiously. 'How do I know all this? Because the Bloody Dag told me back in Siltside after I cut off his hand and threatened to take the other one. Now Kol's got him and claims he won't say a word. Strange. I wish he'd told me how they were getting through Shipwrights without anyone seeing them, even in the middle of the night, but it doesn't really matter.' He gave another savage grin. 'We'll find that out the easy way. By asking. Do you want to know why I'm the best thief-taker in this city? It's because I wait and I wait and I wait.' He took the crossbow and unhooked a metal bar from underneath it. Then he stuck the metal bar into another part, braced the crossbow with his feet and cranked the string back. 'Are you watching? Yes. I wait until I know everything, and then I strike. I cut out the rot, root and all. I burn the wound and seal it with tar.' He picked up the crossbow and squinted at it. 'Our friend the Justicar knows a lot more than he's telling, and something's got him rattled. I reckon he's known our friend Regis is up to his neck in it for some time and wants to leave him be. Well I can't be doing with that. Here.' He passed the crossbow to Berren. 'Point it out over the water. They attacked another ship last night. I knew they would, Bloody

Dag or no Bloody Dag. Too obvious a prize to miss. I've been waiting for this one for more than a month. *That's* why we went to the Captains' Rest last night, why it had to be exactly last night. I didn't think it was Regis, and I certainly didn't think he'd be quite as mad and bold and arrogant as to have us cut down in the street outside, but I knew it was someone. My mistake. It won't happen again. Now we have to finish it the bloody, messy way. Did you see any mudlarks in The Maze last night?'

Berren nodded. 'Stank of the canal they did, too.'

'Well there you go. Might even have been our pirates then.' He stood behind Berren and showed him where to put his hands on the weapon, how to hold it, how to stroke it with his fingers and press it against his cheek. 'Hold it steady but not tight. The emperor's crossbows aren't the best in the world by any means but they're made well enough. Right. Got it steady?'

There was a moment of stillness and then Master Sy carefully fitted a bolt in front of the crossbow string. 'What you're holding, lad, is the most powerful weapon in the world, in its way. It takes a man about a year of constant practice to become any good with a blade and another ten to truly master it. The same goes for a longbow. Now I'll admit that either is a better weapon than what you've got, once it's mastered, but that's not the point. The point is, lad, that with a crossbow, all you have to do is hold it steady, find your target, point it and then a little click on the trigger and if you hit a man out to fifty paces or even more, it doesn't much matter what armour he's wearing, down he goes. A vulgar weapon for thugs if you ask me, but no one did. Go on. Point it at something and pull the trigger.'

Berren picked a seagull, sitting on the water about a hundred feet away. He pointed the crossbow as carefully as he could and pulled the trigger. He felt the crossbow jerk, sideways and upwards. The seagull cawed and flapped up into the air. Berren reckoned he must have missed by a good three feet.

'Much more gentle. I've got four more bolts and that's it. You can practice with one more and then we go. Come on, come on! You missed! Get cranking!'

'Go where?'

'Never mind that! I want you to pretend your enemy is running at you with an enormous axe!'

'Then I want to pretend I'm running away!' Berren struggled to re-arm the crossbow. Master Sy had made it seem simple enough, but in Berren's hands the bow almost had a life of its own. Every time he tried to pull the metal crank, the bow slipped out of his hands.

'Harder, lad! Much harder! Ach! Give it here.' A moment later the crossbow was armed again. Master Sy handed Berren a bolt. Berren loaded it, picked another seagull, pulled the trigger and missed a second time. Master Sy shrugged. 'Around about now, Justicar Kol and his solders are going down into the tunnels under Reeper Hill. By the end of tomorrow, half these pirates will be dead and if I don't get to them first, so will the other half. If that happens, I've got no one to point a finger at the harbour-master. Kol will sit on his hands and a month from now it'll be like we never did any of this.' The thief-taker snorted. 'Enjoy your crossbow. It's the sort of weapon for a day like this. Me, if I had one, I'd have brought a big axe. Come on then. Time to cause trouble for some bad people.'

The thief-taker finished crossing the bridge and turned sharply left to walk along the bank of the stinking Grand Canal, past the row of battered grain silos that marked the start of the Poor Docks. The path was narrow, overgrown and littered with a sprinkling of dead rats, killed by the poison lures around the silos. Berren knew about the silos. There was good eating on a dead rat, but not if it came from here. Even the cats and the birds, it seemed, had learned. Nothing had picked at the bodies. Fifty yards on, past the end of the silos, a massive tree-trunk spanned the canal, the first of hundreds. The water turned black and vanished beneath a chaos of rickety huts and washing-lines, of mongrel dogs and shouting. Talsin's Forest.

'During the siege, Talsin had the biggest trees he could find felled right up the river, past Varr even. They took the branches for arrows and spears and floated the trunks down the river to span the canal. He'd pretty much finished the job by the time Khrozus seized Varr and made the whole siege a waste of time. So here it is. Talsin's Forest.' The canal path simply vanished, blocked by a wall of wood. Even sideways, the first of Talsin's trees was still taller than Berren. All the bark had been stripped away. For kindling, he supposed. There were footholds cut into the wood.

'Right.' Master Sy started to climb up. 'Remember one thing, lad. Around Talsin's Forest, no one likes a thief-taker.'

37
BREAKING DOORS AND TAKING NAMES

'In other parts of the city,' said the thief-taker cheerfully, 'what we do when we meet a door is knock, and then wait patiently for an answer. Around here, however, what we do is this.' He walked up to the front door of a little shack, span on his heel and slammed one leg out sideways, heel first straight into the weathered wood. He didn't so much kick it down as kick it right into the gloom beyond. The walls shook and dust rattled out of the roof. If he'd kicked much harder, Berren reckoned the whole place would have come down. Before the door even landed, Master Sy marched on in, bare steel in his hand. 'Now you'll notice that it's a bit gloomy in here and it might take your eyes a moment to adjust. That can be the moment someone sticks a knife into you, so that's why we do this.' In his other hand he was holding a lantern, one that he'd lit two streets away. Now he smashed it into the floor in the middle of the room. Greasy burning oil spread around it. A few burning streaks spattered his boots, but the thief-taker didn't seem to mind. The edge of a straw mattress started to take flame. Berren stayed where he was, in the doorway. The whole shack was made of flimsy bits of wood. With a bit of luck the afternoon rains they'd had might stop the whole place from going up. Or maybe not.

Out the back another door hung open, swinging back and forth on its hinges. Master Sy grunted. 'Of course, usually we just get on with throwing the lantern on the floor instead of talking about it first.' Ignoring the fire, he ran for the other open door. Berren had little choice but to follow.

'But you can't just ...' You couldn't just go around setting places on fire! Even Berren knew that. Even Master Hatchet had known that. One house goes and next thing you know it's the whole street and half the district. Maybe up on the other side of the city walls where almost everything was made of stone it didn't matter, but out here ... He crashed out of the back of the shack, hard on the thief-taker's heels.

'Oh, they've got buckets, they've got a canal. It's right there.' Master Sy's words came between breaths as they raced along a maze of alleys. The man they were chasing was only half a dozen yards ahead, not quite far enough to dive out of sight, even here. He tried throwing a couple of startled early drunks and a pile of broken chicken cages in their path, but Master Sy barged right through, knocking them all flying as though they weren't even there. 'Besides, most people would thank you for burning down the Forest. I'm sure Justicar Kol will happily tell you that it's every bit as bad as Siltside. Just closer.'

The thief-taker wasn't going as fast as he could, Berren realised with a sudden jolt. He was *letting* the man from the shack, whoever he was, stay just ahead of them. Why would he do that?

'I'd get a bolt ready if I were you,' he called. 'Here we go.'

It was almost as if Master Sy had known in advance everything that would happen. The man from the shack ducked around a corner and dived into an open doorway. Master Sy raced in right behind him, jinking sideways as he went through. A flash of sunlight glinted off metal as a dark shape lunged at the thief-taker. Shouts erupted from the gloom inside. Berren froze. He'd been too busy running to pay much attention to anything more than keeping up, but now he felt acutely aware of his surroundings. The streets in Talsin's Forest were little more than narrow pathways between ragged rows of shacks and huts, all piled on top of each other in whatever space their builders had been able to find. The sun was still high enough to touch the ground, but half of the street was in shadow. Ragged children with wide wild eyes stared at him from doorways. When he met their gaze, some of them scuttled away only to return as he looked elsewhere. Others simply stared back, silent and unblinking. There were no men or women on the street at all, but that didn't mean they weren't near, only that they were hiding. The place had been full enough when he and the thief-taker had first appeared. He could feel them, watching him like the children were but hidden away in the shadows, peering out of gaps between the ill-fitting walls, out from behind curtains. He could feel them waiting, cautious but eager for the spoils of whatever was happening. Like vultures. Their hostility wrapped him up with hungry arms, eager to devour him. They could sense his hesitation, he was sure of it. His doubt.

Nervously he fumbled one of Master Sy's bolts into the crossbow. The other choice, of course, was to follow into the dark hole of the doorway. Several loud voices were swearing and cursing, and he heard the crash of a piece of heavy wood against a wall, hard enough to shake the whole house. Apart from the sounds of the fight, the world had fallen eerily silent.

'Come on, lad.' Master Sy's voice woke him up and unfroze his legs. 'It's done now. You can come in.'

Grateful, Berren scurried off the street and into the twilight inside the house. Three men were sitting against the far wall. Two were frowning and groaning and nursing their bruises. The third simply sat very still, glassy-eyed, breathing fast. It took Berren's eyes a moment to adjust; when they did, he saw that one side of the last man's shirt was covered in blood.

'Careful.'

Berren looked to his feet. He was about to tread on a fourth man, lying face down in the straw. He jumped away.

'He won't bite you, that one,' snorted the thief-taker. 'He's dead.' There was blood on Master Sy's sword, still oozing down the blade and then falling off at the hilt in thick heavy drops. Berren held his crossbow up high, pointing it at the three men sat against the wall. His hands were shaking.

'Hey!' The middle of the three men pushed himself even further back. The thief-taker put a hand on Berren's shoulder.

'It's fine, lad. The fight's done. These gentlemen won't be giving us any more trouble.'

The one on the end who wasn't slowly bleeding to death tipped his head sideways and spat. 'Oh look,' he said, sneering at Berren. 'One of the emperor's new soldiers? Out to make a name for yourself? See your kind every day.'

It was a jibe Berren was used to. Anyone of his age got used to it. *Khrozus' boy* ... Conceived and then left fatherless during the siege of Deephaven in the civil war.

Master Sy tutted and shook his head. 'Careful there, Threehands. I might think you meant that as an insult.'

The man turned to the thief-taker. 'Really? You must be a stranger here then, otherwise you'd know how the common folk in these parts are filled with love for their emperor.' He sneered and spat at Berren again. 'You, you're nothing. Stale bread by winter, you'll be. Stuck in some alley.'

'So rude.' Master Sy's eyes didn't move from the three men. 'Berren, would you like to shoot him? I shan't mind if you do.'

Berren shivered. He didn't know what to do. He half lifted the crossbow and then hesitated. The man was a mudlark, he realised. Probably they all were. Not that it made much difference.

'Berren, is it.' The man called Threehands narrowed his eyes and stared at him. 'I'll be remembering that name. Berren, Berren, Berren. Berren the dead. Berren the headless. It'd make a rhyme for you. Red Heron, how about that?' Then he spat. 'How about this. Stale bread. That's you. Know what that means?' He drew a finger across his throat.

'Doesn't seem right, does it?' Master Sy's voice dropped almost to a whisper. 'Killing a man after he's been beaten. He means it, though. It's you or him.'

'Berren the meat. Berren food-for-rats.' Threehands half grinned, half sneered, showing off a row of rotten teeth.

Master Sy sniffed. 'Another thing that doesn't seem right is a man who's showing such little respect. Go on, lad. Put a bolt into him. Show him who's the boss. You're the master, he's the slave. He should be fawning at your feet, licking your boots, begging for his life. No respect at all, lad. You have to kill him, don't you? You've got to show the others, right? Got to show me, too. I need you to be a man, now, not a boy. Show them you're a man. Kill him.'

For a second time, Berren lifted the crossbow. He pushed it against his shoulder and aimed down the arrow at Threehands; first his head, then his heart, then back at his face. He was shaking. It made him want to howl with frustration but he couldn't stop himself.

'Come on then, *boy*,' sneered Threehands. 'You know why I'm not quivering and quaking? Because I know what you're like, you Khrozus' boys. All fury and spit and no bite. You're not going to bone-hill me. You're not man enough.'

Berren swallowed hard. The shaking was worse. Slowly

and carefully, he lowered the crossbow. 'No,' he choked. 'Can't. 'S not right.' There was a lump in his throat so big he could hardly breathe. He could feel his face burning. He bit his lip and clenched his toes inside his boots.

'Aw, look. Ickle boy going to cry now, is he?' Threehands put both palms across his crotch and thrust it once in Berren's direction. A gesture of utter contempt.

'Good lad,' said Master Sy. 'Right choice. Tomorrow I'll tell you why.' In one sudden movement he jumped forward and kicked Threehands solidly in the face. Before anyone could move, he jumped back again. 'Now then. Who wants to tell me about their mudlark friends who row across the river and up the canal to rob ships in the harbour? Anyone?'

The man next to Threehands shifted uneasily, but Threehands himself didn't seem bothered at all. He spat out a couple of teeth. 'Who wants to know?'

'So you can come after me and gut me in an alley?' Master Sy laughed.

'Think I won't?'

'I'm Syannis.' A flash of something crossed Threehands' face. Fear? Alarm? Recognition, at least. 'Yes, that's right. *That* Syannis. The thief-taker. And you're in my way.'

38

THE ART OF ASKING QUESTIONS

'What d'you want, thief-taker?' Threehands sounded sullen now. The one at the end who'd been bleeding had slumped sideways. He wasn't breathing any more.

'Mudlarks,' said Master Sy with infinite patience. 'You know, people like you. They come across the river. They go up the canal. They steal from ships in the harbour. They come back again. You must know something about that. You're not shifting what they steal, but nothing comes through Talsin's Forest without you knowing about it. And these are your friends. So you must know something.'

Threehands wrinkled his nose and shrugged. 'You're fishing for turds, thief-taker. Nothing goes up and down the canal any more. Not even the shit that used to float down from Pelean's Gate.' He glanced at Berren and sneered. 'There's always a few of the emperor's new soldiers floating face-down in the water, but they ain't got anything and they don't go anywhere. Mudlarks, though?' He shrugged again and stuck out his bottom lip. 'Plenty of us about. Don't know nothing about any coming across the daughter. So now you've had your fun and wasted your time, why don't you take your pet house-boy out of here and stick your sword up his stained glass where it'll be all warm and comfortable instead of waving it in my face.'

For the first time, the man in the middle looked up and

250

spoke. 'We got friends, Undertaker. We cross the right palms with silver. You'll never work again after this.'

'That so, Blacksword?'

'No, thief-taker.' Threehands was shaking his head. 'You won't get the chance. You'll be saying hello to steel before the night's done.'

'Really, Threehands? And who's going to do that? I know it's not going to be you because when you were born someone took out your spine and put an eel in its place. Slippery and twisting and hard to break maybe, but you've not got the balls to face me in some alley, not tonight, not ever.'

Threehands glanced at the man beside him, the one Master Sy had called Blacksword. Berren took a step away, still holding the crossbow ready. He wasn't sure which one of them bothered him the most. Threehands with his swearing and his cursing, who obviously meant every word of it. Or the other one who didn't say anything, but whose eyes spoke of too many dead men at his feet.

'Lad, you don't know these folks, so let me tell you something about them. Threehands here gets his name because even when you can see the two hands on the ends of his arms, he's got another one in your pocket. Blacksword, you might think he got his name from some piece of wicked-looking steel, but actually he got it from a whore. Bits rotted off, didn't they, eh Blacksword?'

'You want to lick them, thief-taker?' Blacksword yawned. When he looked up at all, mostly he looked at Berren rather than at Master Sy. Every time it made Berren shiver. *Yes, boy, I'm looking at you. Remembering you. Remembering who you are.*

Master Sy shook his head. 'See, lad. These are a pair of thieves who think they own the world. Little men who all started like you. Remember that, lad. Once upon a time they walked the streets clearing dung for a penny a week.

Now Threehands here thinks he matters. He's got men like your Master Hatchet wrapped around his finger. He pays money to the city so that people like me leave him alone. Don't you, Threehands?'

Threehands blew a snort and shook his head. 'You don't know the half of it, thief-taker. Piss off now and maybe I'll give you until nightfall to get out of the city.'

'He runs his gangs and he buys men like Blacksword here to keep men like me away from him.' Master Sy grinned. 'How's that working out for you, Threehands? Anyway, lad. He thinks he's important, too important for us to touch him. He really does. Well, lad, here's your first real lesson. You ain't worth a brown bit as a thief-taker if the thieves don't soil their trousers when they see you coming.' He lunged forward and took a back-handed swing with his sword so fast that Berren wasn't sure whether he'd seen it right. No one moved. Then Blacksword spasmed, gurgled, and half his face fell off. He rolled over onto the floor, twitching and arching his back. Master Sy's sword had caved in his temple on one side and come out of his cheek on the other, splitting him neatly in two along a line that ran just under his nose. Berren gulped. The thief-taker rounded on Threehands. Threehands backed away into a corner.

'You … You … You can't! I'm going to mess you up, thief-taker. I'm going to carve you so bad that your mother won't recognise you.' The sneering disdain was all gone now, though. Berren could see Threehands for what he really was. A coward.

'My mother's dead,' said Master Sy shortly. 'My father too, before you go there. Thank you for bringing back those painful memories. You make what I have to do now so much easier.' He sheathed his sword and jumped onto Threehands, dragging him to his feet. Berren skittered away. Madness! Threehands was beaten and broken, but he was also a lot bigger than Master Sy. He wasn't about to miss out on his opportunity, either. He went for the thief-taker with everything he had, fists and feet. Berren stumbled back to the door, ready to run. The two men were too close and moving around each other too fast for him to dare the crossbow. And yet, as he watched, something strange happened. For all that Threehands looked bigger and stronger, he never seemed to land a punch on Master Sy. He lunged, and every time the thief-taker somehow wasn't there. Master Sy, on the other hand, landed blow after blow. Not like Threehands' great swinging fists, but short punches that seemed to find their mark every time, mostly into the ribs and kidneys. Punch after punch after punch, and then Threehands gave a roar and hurled himself at Master Sy and somehow ended up face-down on the floor. The thief-taker landed on his back with a tiny knife in his hand. He put it straight to Threehands' throat. Berren watched, heart pounding. Half of him wanted to run, but a macabre curiosity held him fast.

'Mudlarks,' the thief-taker said, and with a flick of his wrist cut off an ear. Threehands screamed. 'Canal.' He stabbed the knife into Threehands' shoulder and twisted. Threehands shrieked again. The knife moved back to Threehands' throat. 'Everything you know. Right now.'

'Khrozus' blood!' Threehands squirmed like and eel but Master Sy had him fast. 'Kelm's Teeth! Pelean's screaming ghost!'

'That's the feel of a blade inside your flesh. I'm just going to keep on going deeper and deeper until I hear what I want to hear. Yes, yes, keep wriggling and squirming. It's a good test for me. I'll do my best not to cut into anything important until I decide *I want to*.' Master Sy leaned forward to shout the last three words into Threehands' ear.

Berren's skin prickled. Half of him still wanted to run,

but now he wasn't sure which one of the two men scared him the most.

'Yes, yes, yes. Don't kill me, thief-taker. Your promise. Your word.'

'Tell me what I want to hear and I'll leave you alive, Threehands. My word as a gentleman.'

'Yeh. Right. Whatever you think that is. Ahhhh!' Three-hands screwed up his face as Master Sy tightened his grip. 'Yeh, yeh. There are mudlarks who go up the canal now and then. Something to do with the docks. I don't know what they do there.'

'How do they get into the inner city, Threehands?'

'How should I know? Find out for yourself, thief-taker. Maybe they fly. Maybe they turn invisible. Maybe they're snow-faeries in disguise.'

'Not helpful, Threehands, not helpful. No, that's not enough to keep you alive. Where do they leave their boats?'

'The usual place, thief-taker. We look after them until they come back.'

'For a price.'

'Do I look like a bleeding philosopher?' He squealed as Master Sy twisted the knife.

'Philanthropist. What about once they get into the city?'

'Not my patch and you know it, thief-taker. Could be anything. Don't much care as long as they pays their dues to pass up the canal. Stuff in the docks, is what I heard. Like you said.'

'What stuff in the docks?' Master Sy shifted his weight, digging a knee harder into Threehands' back. Threehands groaned.

'*I don't know!* They're just hands, I know that much. They don't even know what they're heading over to do. Someone inside the city tells them. Something to do with ships. That's all I know!'

'Yes, yes.' Master Sy sighed. 'Sad thing is, that's probably true. Well let's suppose I have a fair idea who it is. You still haven't told me enough for me to have bothered coming out here. I could have guessed all this from the comfort of my rocking chair. What about coming back? How do they come back? That's what I really want to know.'

'Same way. They come back the next night, right late and always soaking wet and stinking. Straight out of the canal. Out from under the water like they're fish-men or something.'

'*Are* they fish-men?'

'Don't be a half-wit, thief-taker. There's no such thing. That's just stories for frightening the likes of your soldier-boy.'

Master Sy smiled. 'Do they have poles with them, Threehands. Short bamboo poles?'

'Yeh.' Through the pain, Threehands managed to sound puzzled. 'How'd you know?'

The smile grew wider. Master Sy withdrew his knife. 'They walk under the water, Threehands, breathing through tubes. That's how they get through Shipwrights. People would notice boats, but the tip of a pole? In the dark? That would work. Thank you, Threehands. That's the last piece of the puzzle.' For a moment, the thief-taker relaxed. Straight away, Threehands convulsed, kicking his legs up and twisting, trying to free himself. He almost managed it, but after a few seconds of furious grunting, the thief-taker had him pinned again.

'Now now, Threehands.'

'You got what you want and you've killed three of mine already. Now piss off before you become the most important thing in the rest of my life.'

'Oh, I mean to be.' Master Sy turned and slashed his knife across the back of Threehand's left knee. Threehands screamed.

'You *bastard!*' He must have seen the knife come up a second time. The scream turned into a begging whimper. 'No! No! Please, not ...'

The knife slashed the back of the other knee. Berren had no illusions about what Master Sy had just done. Threehands had been hamstrung. He'd never walk again. For someone who lived the way Threehands lived, Master Sy might as well have killed him. It would have shown more mercy.

'Respect, Threehands.' Master Sy got up. 'No respect.' He looked at Berren. 'There's two things that thieves have to know about you. The first is that you keep your word. If you say you'll let them go, you let them go. If you promise not to kill them, you let them live. The second thing is that their life is yours. That you are the be-all and the end-all of their existence. That no one owns them more than you do. They have to know that, they have to know, from the moment they see you, that there is only one thing they can do, and that is to tell you everything you want to know and then pray that it's enough. They need to fear you as though you're the gods themselves manifest before them. Don't you, Threehands?'

'Every penny I have is on your head,' Threehands slurred. 'Every penny.'

'Nowhere near enough, Threehands. Come on lad.' He put his arm around Berren's shoulder and turned him away, pushing him firmly but gently out into the bright evening light of the street. As they left, he glanced back into the shadows. 'Hey, Threehands. Anyone I should send your way to help you out?'

A strangled scream tore out of the gloom. 'I'll see you dead, thief-taker. I'll get a priest. I'll get something. I'll be waiting for you, you and your puppy. Some dark night, some dark alley, you'll never know ... You royal *hunt!*'

Master Sy froze. He patted Berren on the shoulder.

'Excuse me, lad. I won't be having language like that.'

He turned and went back. Berren didn't look. It was better that way. Better not to know. There was some incoherent screaming and then a sort of gargling sound and then nothing. A moment later, Master Sy came back out.

'Did you kill him?'

Master Sy shook his head. 'Of course not. I promised I'd let him live and that's what I've done.' In his hand he had a ragged piece of bloody flesh. It looked, Berren thought, uncomfortably like a tongue. Master Sy glanced at it and then carelessly tossed it down the street. 'I can't promise he won't bleed to death, of course. Sometimes that happens. But most probably he'll live. For a bit.'

With the satisfied smile of a job well done, the thief-taker strode off down the street. 'Home now, lad. This last bit's not for you. Not quite sure where we stand with Kol, and messing with him isn't like messing with the Dag across the river. Best you stay out of it. Too dangerous. You should get yourself some sleep. Big day tomorrow, if all goes well. Actually, you know what? Maybe you should find another place to bed down, just for tonight. Just in case. Ask Lilissa if she'll lend you her floor. I'm sure she'll understand. You never know. There are some crazy dangerous people in this city.'

Shaking, a little bemused and certainly glad to be away, Berren hurried alone back to the River Gate and up the Godsway. After what he'd just seen, he could only agree.

39

TO HAVE AND TO HOLD

Some time with Lilissa. So much had happened. It was hard to remember that it was only last night that they'd spent the night together hiding in The Maze. Hard to remember that only this morning she'd saved him from One-Thumb. Since then, he'd seen Master Sy kill a man in cold blood and mutilate another. He shuddered. The thief-taker had had Threehands' blood all over him. He looked the part. A butcher. Was that right, doing that to a man, even to a thief? Then again, Threehands had been clear about what was going on in *his* mind. Berren supposed he ought to be glad.

Whenever he stopped to think, his head filled up with Threehands and Lilissa. Listening to Lilissa breathe in the dark. Master Sy clutching Threehands' tongue. Running away from Jerrin. Blacksword's face, split in half. The man beside him, quietly dying while they talked. Holding Lilissa's hand outside the upside-down temple. Kissing her. There was a lot that hadn't been said. Somewhere he still had half a bag of spice cakes back at Master Sy's house. They might be crushed to crumbs by now, but cake was still cake. Cake would help. They'd talk. He'd tell her what he'd seen today.

Except when Berren reached her house, someone had been there before him. Her tiny door hung open, flapping feebly back and forth in the evening breeze. As he came closer he caught a smell of her in the air. The smell of flowers. Lavender.

Cautiously, he went inside. Behind the door, everything had been turned upside down. Every piece of furniture was smashed, every piece of cloth ripped and slashed. On the opposite wall, someone had scratched a symbol. He'd had a good enough idea who'd done this even before, but now he knew. One-Thumb; the sign made that plain as the sun in the sky. One-Thumb, and he was waiting for him round the back of Trickle Street with his Harbour Men. They'd taken Lilissa and now they were taunting him. *Come and get her if you can.*

He clenched his fists. What he ought to do was wait. Wait until Master Sy came back from wherever he was under Reeper Hill, and show him what they'd done. They'd be dead. No doubts about that. One-Thumb, Sticks, Waddler, Hair, the mudlark boy, whoever he was. Probably Hatchet and every one of his dung-boys. The thief-taker had shown what he could do today, what was lurking behind his manners and his quiet talk. He was a murderer, a snuffer, the best and the worst of them. For a moment, as Berren thought of Master Sy's fury, he almost laughed. Jerrin hadn't the first idea what he'd done.

Or maybe he did. Berren's laughter faded. Jerrin in The Maze last night had been no accident. Maybe he knew where the thief-taker was. Or maybe he thought Master Sy was dead. Maybe, maybe, maybe ...

He stood up. He understood well enough what he had to do. The sign scratched into the wall was for him, for him and no one else. That was Jerrin's challenge. *Come on, thief-taker boy. I've got your girl. Take her back if you think you're a man.* A bitter laugh escaped him, because Lilissa wasn't his at all. Until yesterday she'd belonged to some fishmonger's son he couldn't even name. And even that didn't make the slightest bit of difference. He had to do what he had to do. He wasn't a boy any more. Not now.

He scurried back to Master Sy's house and let himself in through the back. There he took one of the thief-taker's coats from the peg by the door and wrapped it around him. It didn't fit, was much too big, but it hid the crossbow. That was what mattered. Bad enough walking up the Godsway carrying it, but around the docks ... Around the docks, that would mark him as a snuffer, and the worst sort at that.

He thought about waiting until hours after nightfall, but what would Jerrin do if he thought no one was coming? What would he do to Lilissa if he got bored of waiting? What if something happened to her because he didn't come? So he didn't wait; instead he ran, out of the house, up the long straight climb to the top of the hill and down the other side into Market Square. The flower-seller and his bodyguards were still there; Berren barely noticed. He ran on, across the square, oblivious to the twilight crowds still teeming there. Braziers were lighting up and with them the first night-time smells of smoke and coal and burned fish, but all Berren could smell was lavender. In the edges of The Maze, he ran straight past the Barrow of Beer.

No, wait! He stopped. Out of breath, he walked slowly back up to the Barrow and peered inside. The tavern was full, its tiny shutters open wide, flooding the street around it with the noise of talk and the smell of stale beer and a whiff of Moongrass. Cautiously, Berren left the crossbow in the shadows and pushed his way inside. Men stopped what they were saying and watched; they didn't stare, but they followed him with their eyes nonetheless. This time Berren didn't care. He pushed his way to where Kasmin was standing with some of his customers, chuckling at some joke one of them had made. They stopped when they saw Berren. The old man's eyes narrowed and his lips drew back to show his teeth. Kasmin made more sense now. He, too, knew what the thief-taker could do. That was why he'd been so scared.

Berren bowed. A perfect bow, exactly as Master Sy had taught him. 'Sir. I need your help.'

'If Syannis wants something more, tell him to come and ask for it himself.' He glanced left and right at the men beside him. 'At another time.'

'My master didn't send me, sir. I am asking your help for me, sir.'

'You?' Kasmin sneered half-heartedly. It was a show, Berren realised. For the men who were with him. He set himself firm.

'I need a blade, sir. A sword.'

The men around Kasmin roared with laughter. Kasmin didn't even blink. 'I have no swords here, boy, and even if I did they wouldn't be for you.'

'I need—!' he started to shout, but a cuff round the face knocked him to the floor.

'What you need is manners,' snarled Kasmin. He grabbed Berren by the shirt and hauled him to his feet; then lifted him up into the air and carried him through the bar and threw him out the door. He stared as Berren shakily got back to his feet.

'Sir …' However much it hurt, he couldn't give up. He couldn't face Jerrin and his gang alone. Not if he hoped to win.

'Now piss off!' Kasmin roared, and he turned and strode back into his tavern to a chorus of raucous shouting. Berren made a series of angry gestures at the men staring at him through the windows and hurried away. A minute later he was back, though, this time in the yard behind the tavern, skulking in the shadows. Kasmin had to have a sword in there somewhere, he just had to, and one way or another, Berren needed it. He watched the door to the back of the tavern. He'd been this way already once.

The door opened. Kasmin rolled out an empty barrel into the yard. Then he looked straight at where Berren was hiding. He stood still, then let out a long breath. 'Whoever you are, I can smell you. So who's there?'

Other times Berren might have run, but not tonight. If it came to that then he was closer to the gate than Kasmin. He stepped out into the evening gloom.

'Sir, I need a sword.'

Kasmin shook his head and laughed. 'You're one persistent stable-mucker, aren't you? Khrozus!' he shrugged. 'I meant what I said. I don't have a sword and I wouldn't give it to you if I did. And no matter what Syannis and I used to be, if you come into my tavern again like that, I'll do more than throw you out onto the street. You're a thief-taker, boy. Whatever was once between your master and me, you're not welcome here.'

'I need ...'

Kasmin rolled his eyes to the sky. 'What bit of *no* don't you understand?'

'Then will you at least hold a message for me, for Master Sy?'

'Fine. Make it quick.'

'If I don't come back, tell him I went looking for Lilissa. She's a friend to Master Sy.'

'Well her mother was at least,' muttered Kasmin. 'Heard that much.'

'Tell him Jerrin One-Thumb took her and I went after him. Tell him ...' And then it all came out, about what he'd found when he'd gone looking for her, about One-Thumb and the Harbour Men and The Maze and the harbour-master's snuffers. Kasmin just stood there. Didn't move, didn't blink. Just stood.

'Bit long,' he said, when Berren finally finished. 'Don't know if I'll remember all that. But I suppose I got the bits that matter.' He took a long look at Berren and sighed. 'How many of these "Harbour Men" are there?'

Berren shrugged. 'At least five. Probably seven or eight.' Yeh. Might even be that, he mused to himself. Jerrin had had friends outside Master Hatchet's gang.

'Then a sword won't help you, boy, not when you don't know how to use it and I ain't got one anyway. Go home. Wait for Syannis.'

'I know Jerrin. He'll ...' He couldn't bring himself to say it. 'He might hurt her.'

'He might just hurt her anyway. After he's done with killing you.'

Berren said nothing, just stuck out his jaw. He was going. Right now. No matter what. If Stealer and a crossbow with one bolt were all he had, then Stealer and a crossbow with one bolt would just have to do.

Kasmin tipped his head back and swore loudly at the sky. 'Ah, for the love of ...' He sighed and threw up his hands in despair. 'Look, boy. If I pass your message on to Syannis, he's going to know you were here. And then he's going to ask me why I didn't stop you.'

Berren took a step towards the street. 'Because you couldn't catch me.'

'Fine. Reckon that might even be true. Wait there.' Without pausing for an answer, Kasmin turned and strode into his tavern. When he came out again, he was holding a long knife in a sheath. He tossed it at Berren's feet. 'Better for you than a sword. Anyone ever tell you anything about how to fight? At all?'

Master Sy's words were there in his head, just as the thief-taker had spoken them. 'Run. If you can't run, stick them good and hard and watch it all the way.'

'Good advice as any.' The old man shook his head. 'You know you're fighting too many, don't you? You know you're going to get yourself killed, right?'

Berren shrugged. He hadn't really given it much thought, truth be told. It was a thing that needed to be done and that was all there was.

'Going to do it anyway, eh? Well you bring me my knife back, boy. My lucky blade, that is. Saved my life twice since I gave up soldiering and came to this godsforsaken hole of a city. Hold it close, boy. Pick them off one by one. Don't play fair. Don't let them see you coming. Kill 'em from a distance with that crossbow. Ach,' he waved Berren away. 'Why am I wasting my breath on you. You'll be dumb and you'll get yourself killed or else you'll get lucky and learn something. That's pretty much how it goes. I could feel that mail you've got on under your shirt. Make the most of it. Now piss off. I got customers.' He turned and stamped back inside. Berren watched him go.

'Thank you,' he called. He tucked the knife and its sheath into his trousers. Picking up his crossbow and wrapping Master Sy's coat around him, he set off once more for Trickle Street. Strange thing was, even though he knew Kasmin was probably right, he didn't feel scared at all.

40

ONE-THUMB

Berren reached Trickle Street as the sun was setting, sinking into the sea beyond the docks at the end of the street. Trickle Street didn't go anywhere much, just crept down from The Maze to the sea-docks like a thief, hoping no one would notice. No one had much use for Trickle Street either, and now Berren found it empty. He took off Master Sy's coat, folded it carefully and left it. Thing only got in the way. Then he went to the hole in the fence. One-Thumb was right. Whenever he'd had to run, he always came here, to the derelict arse-end of the sugar traders' warehouse. This was *his* place, not One-Thumb's. He knew it inside and out, better than anyone. One-Thumb had come here to make a point.

No, he told himself with grim determination. He'd come here to *try* and make a point. He was going to regret it.

He reached the hole in the fence and crouched down beside it, peering inside. Sure enough, there was Hair, sitting across the yard, picking his fingernails when he was supposed to be keeping watch, bored as anything. Jerrin would have Waddler round the other side. Waddler and Hair always got the shitty jobs.

Berren fingered his crossbow. It was a big and heavy and clumsy thing, but it was sure to put a scare on anyone on the other end of it. Jerrin would probably wet himself. Or else he could just shoot Hair and be rid of the thing.

That would be easy. Hair wouldn't even see it coming. He was just sitting there. Shoot Hair, and then creep up on Waddler round the other side with Stealer. Take his face off with Kasmin's knife just like Master Sy had done to that Blacksword bloke. Then into the tumbled-down shacks where One-Thumb would have Lilissa. That's what the old tavern-keeper would have told him to do. Probably Master Sy as well, judging by what he'd seen today ...

He moved aside to where Hair couldn't see him even if he bothered looking, and fingered the crossbow again. He'd known Hair for years. As far as it ever went with Hatchet's boys, they'd almost been friends until Hair had fallen in with One-Thumb. Hair hadn't ever done him any wrong, not even any mischief until now. He was probably only here because he couldn't think of anything better and because One-Thumb wanted his gang to be as big as possible so he could feel strong.

No, he couldn't shoot Hair. He'd probably miss anyway if the seagulls were anything to go by. Cut him up, like Master Sy had done to the mudlarks? No. Couldn't do that either.

He put the crossbow down and went back to the hole in the fence. As quietly as he could, he started to slip through. He was almost out the other side before Hair happened to look up and see him.

'Crap!' He scrambled to his feet as Berren got up. 'Mouse!' He glanced over his shoulder, looking to where he was going to run. 'Don't ...' Berren grinned to himself. Hair was *scared* of him. Hair had never been scared of him. No one had ever been scared of him.

'I'm waiting out here for One-Thumb. You tell me something, Hair. The lady he's got with him. Did you touch her?' He pulled Kasmin's knife slowly out of its sheath. In the fiery light of the setting sun, the blade gleamed. It was beautiful. He leered at Hair. 'Did you?'

Hair was still backing away, shaking his head. 'Not me, Mouse.' He couldn't take his eyes off the knife. It was a long blade, a good foot of steel, lovingly sharp. A real butcher's knife. Not something a tavern-keeper would have much use for, Berren thought.

'Well that's good, Hair, because that means you and I ain't got nothing to quarrel about. Not unless you think different.' Berren started to walk slowly towards Hair. Inside, he was shaking, even though he had the knife and Hair had nothing. *What if he doesn't run? What then?* He steeled himself and kept his eyes locked onto Hair's face, watching his every glance. When it came down to it, Hair wasn't a fighter. Hair would shout and threaten, but in the end he always ran. 'You could just go,' he offered, circling away from the hole in the fence back to Trickle Street. 'You never saw me, and I never saw you. Don't have to be anything more.' He nodded towards the hole. 'You want to leave, I won't stop you. Like I said, there's no quarrel between us. Not yet, anyhow.'

Hair swore loudly and turned and ran back into the ramshackle huts at the back of the sugar-merchant's stores. Berren watched him go. It was done, then. In a few seconds, he'd be telling One-Thumb that Berren was here and calling him out. One-Thumb would come out because he was the boss and that meant he didn't have any choice. He'd come out in front of all his Harbour Men and he'd strut and taunt and jeer. That was what he did, what made him seem strong to people who didn't know any better. And then, when it came down to it, he'd fight, because if he didn't then everyone in his gang would know he was spineless. By the end of the next day the whole docks would know, and after that even Waddler would laugh in his face. Berren ran it all through his mind, playing it out as he waited. A good part of him still wanted to run. He could do that. Didn't matter, did it, if Hair and the rest of

Hatchet's boys knew he was a coward? It wasn't like he was ever coming back here. Master Sy would tell him that he'd done the wise thing. He'd make out like Berren had been brave *not* to stay. Lilissa, well, she'd probably say the same as Master Sy anyway. She'd probably think he was an idiot for coming at all.

He'd seen the real thief-taker today, though. Seen what it took to be feared the way he was, and there was one person he couldn't run away from, one person who would always know and always be there to remind him of what he chose. There was Berren, the thief-taker's apprentice, the boy who wanted to learn swords more than anything in the world. The boy who wanted to learn how to be deadly, a whirlwind of steel. A killer. And what was the use in all that learning if you were always too afraid to use it?

Berren gripped Kasmin's knife. One-Thumb was a prick, anyway. He had it coming. He forced himself to see the mudlarks in Talsin's Forest again, how ruthless Master Sy had been. He told himself Jerrin was the same. Whatever happened, he deserved it.

And by the time he'd thought all of that, it was too late anyway, because there was One-Thumb, leading his Harbour Men out of the back of the sugar-merchant's warehouse. Sticks came behind him, and then Hair and three other boys. One was a stranger. The other two were more of Hatchet's dung-cart gang. Weasel, who was a couple of years younger than Berren but had the makings of being a nastier piece of work than even One-Thumb. And Slipper, who wasn't much of anything as far as Berren knew, but had a way of getting out of places. Last of all came the mudlark boy. He had Lilissa with him, and the sight of her made Berren's blood burn. She looked ragged and broken. Her clothes were torn in places. When the mudlark boy pushed her out, she stumbled and almost fell.

She didn't bother trying to run; and then Berren saw why. The mudlark boy had a leash around her neck, as though she was some sort of dog.

'I didn't think you'd be this dim, Mouse,' sneered Jerrin, taking up a stance in front of his gang. 'What you going to do? Fight us all? All eight of us? All on your own?'

Berren didn't move. His legs were shaking. He hoped, in the half-light, none of them could see. But he held his ground. He lifted up Kasmin's knife and pointed it straight at Jerrin, forcing the rest of him to be still. *Never take your eyes off him.* 'Just you, One-Thumb. You and me.' There, and now he bit his tongue hard enough to bring tears to his eyes. That was all. That's what Master Sy would say. You and me, and then he'd stand and watch and wouldn't say another word, while Jerrin's mouth worked the rest of him into a stupor.

Jerrin's lip curled. He started to pace up and down in front of his boys. 'You and me, Mouse? You think I can be bothered with a flea like you?' He walked stiffly, though, like he was still hurting from the thump in the back he'd taken from Lilissa. Berren said nothing. He tracked Jerrin with his eyes and the point of his knife and the rest of him didn't move. With a jolt he remembered again that it was still the same day. They'd fought One-Thumb once already. Beaten him, too.

Jerrin stopped. His hand went to the back of his head. Did the other Harbour Men know what had happened that morning? The mudlark boy had been there and seen it all and he'd run away. Sticks had taken a kicking too. They probably all knew, then. Gods! Berren felt a surge of glee. He bit his tongue harder. It was hard not to crow about One-Thumb taking a beating from a girl. And it was clear enough that Jerrin was still hurting.

Yeh, except he'd be hurting on the inside too and itching for some revenge. And he was big. Berren had forgotten, somehow, how big Jerrin was. He probably stood taller even than Master Sy.

'Too scared to say anything, Mouse? Too terrified to move? It's too late to run away now, isn't it? Here, look, you were one of us not all that long ago. You could have been a Harbour Man. You still can. Jack it in with that master of yours and pitch in with us. I'll let you live. All you have to do is grovel in the mud on your belly, like the crappy little worm that you are. That's all. Five minutes of shit, Mouse, and then you're one of us.' He sniffed and touched the back of his head again. 'After that you can watch while I help myself to this ground-floor girl of yours. But no need to get all jealous on me, Mouse. We're a gang. Everyone gets their share of the spoils. You can have her too. You'd have to go last, but you can have her. I think I'd have to insist, in fact. And let's face it, Mouse, she's a ripe piece and far too pretty for you to ever get her any other way.'

Goading. That's all it was, but still, if Berren bit his tongue any harder, he wouldn't have one any more. He could already taste blood. His silence was working, though. He could see that. Jerrin's foot started to tap. Behind him, some of the other boys were getting restless. They weren't liking the way this was going and their unease was infectious. Jerrin ran his hand through his hair and started to pace again.

'You know what? Maybe I think you're an ungrateful little turd. Maybe I'll just cut open your belly and she can watch you dying in a corner. Yeh, you know what? I think that sounds a lot better. So yeh. That's what's going to happen. Last chance to run, Mouse.' He stopped pacing and came a couple of steps closer, still keeping a dozen yards between them. He pulled his own knife out of his belt. It wasn't much more than a long finger of steel, and Jerrin's size made it seem smaller still. Berren smirked.

'She's a ground-floor girl, Mouse. You didn't know that? Truth is, we started without you.'

Berren didn't flinch. Inside he wanted to scream, but on

the outside, he was as steady as a rock. Lies. They had to be. He had to believe that.

'Oh what?' Jerrin shouted, his voice breaking slightly. 'Teeth! What's wrong with you, Mouse? You have an accident in bed and piss your wits out? *Say* something!'

That was it. Jerrin had run himself into a corner. He didn't have any more choices to make. There was nothing left for him now except to come running, screaming, waving his arms and his knife, and one of them would die. And Berren had a strange warm certainly that it wouldn't be him.

They didn't find out, though, because that was exactly when Kasmin and three other men came bursting out of the doors behind the Harbour Men, shouting their heads off and waving sticks around their heads, and everything fell into chaos.

41

THE THIEF-TAKER'S APPRENTICE

Sticks went down first, thumped around the back of the head before he could even turn round. The rest of Jerrin's Harbour Men wilted and ran. Kasmin pelted after the mudlark boy and dragged him down, then punched and kicked him until he stopped trying to get up again. The others swung their sticks and looked at Jerrin and then at Berren and then back at One-Thumb again. They grinned and licked their lips. Jerrin's eyes darted between them, looking for a place to run, but they kept back, content to wait. Berren watched as Kasmin got up from the mudlark boy and walked back to where Lilissa stood, her mouth still open in surprise. Kasmin whispered something in her ear and then turned her face so she was looking at him. Berren couldn't hear what either of them said; after a moment, Kasmin left her. He walked back to the mudlark boy, lifted his stick up high and brought it down on the boy's legs with all his strength. Bones cracked; the boy screamed and Lilissa sank to the ground, burying her face in her hands. Berren's skin went cold and numb. Could easily have been the boy's head.

He looked at One-Thumb again, this time with a coldness in his heart. He hissed softly and started to walk, very slowly, towards where One-Thumb was still standing.

'Tell me again, Jerrin,' he whispered. 'Tell me again what you just said about her. Started *what* without me?'

One-Thumb turned to look at him. He was shaking. Kasmin and the other men stood still and watched. Lilissa still had her face in her hands.

'Tell me, Jerrin!' said Berren, louder this time. 'I want to know.' He started to walk faster. One-Thumb stared back at him in disbelief. He was afraid. It was written all over him. He was scared and he didn't know what to do, while Berren felt himself getting stronger with every step.

'Come on, Jerrin,' he said for the third time, almost shouting. 'Let's hear it! Started *what*, exactly? Come on! Tell me!'

Jerrin stared right back at him, too petrified to move. He started to shake his head. 'I ...' And that was as far as he got before Berren was standing right in front of him. Without any hesitation at all, almost with a will of its own, Jerrin's hand snapped back and then thrust forwards again, stabbing his knife into Berren's midriff. He didn't even look to see what he was doing, just kept staring right back up into Berren's face, a look of utter disbelief on his face. Berren didn't move, didn't even think to defend himself, only grunted and staggered back a step. He hadn't expected than. Hurt a lot less than he'd thought. He put a hand to his belly, but when he looked, there was no blood. Under his shirt, he was wearing Master Sy's ringmail. For a moment, he'd forgotten.

Berren raised his knife and pointed it at Jerrin's face. 'You cowardly little shit.' He took a step forward. Jerrin had tried to kill him. No question this time. Now there would be blood.

'I didn't touch her!' Jerrin gasped and took a step back. 'Never did. I swear.' As Berren advanced, Jerrin backed away. 'Please! Please, Mouse ...' Blood dribbled out from the corner of his mouth where he'd bitten his own lip. He dropped his little knife. 'Mouse ...' Any moment. Any moment now, Berren knew, he would strike.

Abruptly Jerrin's legs gave way and he fell over. He managed to get onto his knees, then fell over a second time as Berren loomed over him and raised Kasmin's knife.

'Please! Mouse! Please!'

For a second, Berren clenched the knife. For a second he did nothing. He saw Master Sy and the mudlarks from Talsin's Forest and he knew what he had to do, but his hand wouldn't move.

'You going to do it or not?' growled a deep voice behind him. Kasmin.

For another second he stayed stock still. Then slowly he stepped away and lowered the knife. No. Not to a man grovelling on the ground. Couldn't do it. Not even to One-Thumb.

Kasmin pushed past and brought his stick down on One-Thumb's head as hard as he could. Quick and sharp and no messing about. Jerrin's startled look stayed on his face for a moment, and then blood ran down over his face and he toppled backwards. Kasmin looked Berren up and down.

'Boys from Shipwrights should stay in Shipwrights,' he growled. The men behind him murmured agreement and nodded. 'Harbour Men?' He spat on One-Thumb's corpse. 'Not any more.' He wandered back to Sticks, who was on his hands and knees, throwing up and moaning on the floor. Berren almost couldn't bear to watch, but Kasmin's cudgel didn't come down a third time. Instead, Sticks merely got another kicking. 'Boys from Shipwrights should stay in Shipwrights,' roared Kasmin. 'Do you hear me?' He swung back to where One-Thumb lay, glared as though he'd never seen Berren before. 'What about you, boy? You call yourself a Harbour Man?'

Berren took a step back. He shook his head, not quite sure what to say.

'Your girl?'

This time Berren nodded.

'I like the look of your knife, boy. You leave that here and I'll let you go. Both of you. You hear?'

Berren nodded again, more quickly this time. He dropped Kasmin's knife on the ground and then the sheath as well. Glad to be rid of it.

'You'll not be telling no thief-takers about us, now will you, boy? If I were you I'd keep my mouth tight shut. You got that?'

Berren nodded again.

'Go on then. Piss off. Both of you.'

There was blood on his hand. Someone's. Not his. Jerrin's, maybe, from when Kasmin had cracked his skull. He wiped it on the leg of his trousers then ran to Lilissa, still squatting on the ground and sobbing into her hands. He tugged her to her feet and looked at her. One eye was red with tears, the other purple from a huge bruise on one side of her face. Her hair was a tangled mess. She was still wearing the dress that had made her look like a princess, the one she'd worn to the Captain's Rest, except now it was ripped and ruined.

He touched her swollen cheek. She was beautiful. Then he looked around him. Kasmin had his knife back now; he and whoever the men were he had with him were already turning to go. Sticks was staggering off as fast his legs would carry him; Hair and Waddler and the rest of Jerrin's boys were long gone. There was the mudlark boy, pulling himself on his arms to get away, wailing and moaning. And then there was One-Thumb, flat on his back and dead as a rat. Berren felt sick. *This* was thief-taking?

He turned away. His head was spinning, his throat was as dry as parchment. His skin tingled, his arms and legs felt as though they didn't really belong to him any more; the rest of him seemed so light that he might lift right off the ground and fly in the first gust of wind. Nothing seemed quite real any more.

Except Lilissa.

He took her hand. 'Come on,' he said. 'Let's go home.'

42

THE ONE THAT GOT AWAY

They sat at a table together in the Golden Hart, the closest tavern to The Peak that Master Sy was prepared to afford. It was a place where rich people went, not thief-takers, and certainly not a dung-boy cut-purse from Shipwrights. It was the middle of the day, the sort of time when a place like this was quiet and empty, but the few people there still stared at them both, muttering under their breath as Berren and Master Sy passed their tables. The tavern-keeper, on the other hand, didn't seem bothered in the least. He gave the thief-taker a nod as if they were old friends. Almost before Master Sy was in his seat, a whole roasted duck was set down on the table in front of them. Then bread, still warm from the oven, two glasses, and a bottle of something dark and red. Master Sy picked up the bottle and turned it over in his hand. He was smiling.

'Now that's something you don't get to see every day.' He sighed a happy sigh. He was limping, Berren had noticed. Not badly, but enough that Berren could see. 'You drink much wine in Shipwrights, lad?'

Berren nodded vigorously. Watery stuff that Hatchet's boys stole from Club-Headed Jin when they got the chance, which wasn't very often. And then they'd wait for Hatchet to be asleep or drunk, and they'd get it out and pass it from one to another in the dark. Times like that they'd all been a gang together.

Times like that. Yeh. He'd spent most of the night lying awake, thinking of One-Thumb lying dead in the dirt. Thinking of the horror on Lilissa's face when she'd seen the blood on his hands. He'd gone to Trickle Street to save her, to win her, and somehow, in the saving, he'd lost her. He'd seen it in her eyes even as they were leaving. It left a bitter taste, one that jarred with the thief-taker's good humour.

Times like that. Yeh. Times like that hadn't come around too often. Mostly they'd been at each others' throats, like cats in a cage.

'Well not like this you haven't.' Master Sy broke the wax seal around the bottle's neck and levered the cork out with a knife. 'This is from my home, lad. It's come halfway around the world to be here. Just like me.' He poured one for himself and then tipped a thimbleful into Berren's glass. 'Mind, though. Remember the beer in the Eight Pillars of Smoke. This is stronger stuff. Try not to make an idiot of yourself. Sip it. If you gulp it, it'll knock you flat. Like all the best things in life.'

Berren took a sip. Even as the wine touched his lips, it seemed to steal into his mouth, setting his tongue on fire. He recoiled and coughed and the thief-taker laughed. Then Master Sy tore a wing off the duck and waved at Berren to eat.

'What happened to your leg, master?'

'Oh, I landed badly chasing one of the Dag's pirates in the tunnels under Reeper Hill.' He shrugged.

'Did you get them?'

'They were there right enough. Hiding away with their loot. Caught them red-handed. Unfortunately Justicar Kol and his soldiers got there first. Kol himself.' He shook his head. 'I forget, sometimes, that our Justicar used to swing a sword with the best of them. No.' He sighed. 'Our pirates are all done now. We did what Kol wanted us to do. We got the Bloody Dag out of Siltside and then we rounded up his men and now they're all dead or on their way to the mines and that's the end of it.' Master Sy's lips twitched, as though he'd tasted something sour. Berren paused between stuffing strips of juicy meat into his mouth.

'What about ...?'

'And where were you last night?' This time the thief-taker raised a knowing eyebrow. Berren flushed and looked away.

'I went to Mistress Lilissa, like you said. Just in case.'

'Hmmm.' Master Sy nodded. 'Didn't do anything you shouldn't, I hope.'

Berren shook his head. What was he supposed to say? Master Sy always knew everything, always. 'I kept her safe,' he said, which was at least true. 'I didn't touch her. I just kept her safe.'

'Then you did good.' The thief-taker sniffed and gave Berren a look that cut like glass. 'Kasmin came by in the small hours. Seems there was some trouble in the Barrow of Beer last night.' His eyes didn't flinch and Berren felt like they'd nailed him to his chair. 'He didn't say much as to what it was about. Mentioned something about you having a run-in with a gang from the docks.'

Berren opened his mouth, but at the sight of the thief-taker, everything he could think of to say dived straight back down his throat. The thief-taker raised a hand. 'I don't think I want to know anything about it. Kasmin said you did good, and he doesn't say that about much. I half expected to pay a visit to Mistress Lilissa and find you a bloody mess on the floor again, but no, the next thing I know you're on my doorstep. And not even a scratch. Although you do look as though you were up for most of the night.'

'Talking.' Berren gave a non-committal shrug. Yeh, they'd talked. Not for long, though. He'd spent most of the night roaming the city. Lilissa's face when she'd looked at him had been too hard to bear. You could hardly blame her for wanting a nice safe fishmonger's son. Not after what she'd seen. But still, looks cut worse than blades sometimes. After that, he couldn't have slept even if he hadn't kept on seeing Kasmin crack One-Thumb's head open. 'Did he ... ?' Ah, what to say that wouldn't make things worse? But that was the thing about Master Sy, the thing that made him the thief-taker he was. You never knew how much he knew. And the only way to deal with that was to say nothing at all.

'Did he what?'

'Did he say anything else?'

At last Master Sy's eyes wandered elsewhere and let him go. The thief-taker chuckled. 'He said I ought to get on and teach you swords before someone else does. I imagine he meant him.'

Berren almost jumped out of his seat. For a moment, Jerrin's dead face stopped staring at him. For a moment, the memory of Lilissa closing her door was gone. 'Did he ... ? And ... ?'

'Patience, lad.' Very slowly, Master Sy nodded. 'Yes, I'll teach you how to fight with a sword, lad. You have my solemn promise to that. But letters first. I'll get the priests at the solar temple to do it. You'll do your letters with them by day, and in the evenings, once you're started, I'll show you how to hold a sword.'

'Priests?' Berren's faced scrunched up in despair.

'Yes, priests. You want to learn swords, you learn letters. That's the price.'

Berren slumped and rolled his eyes.

'Be good to keep you out the way for a few months.' Master Sy gave him a sharp look. 'Strange thing. Kol's men didn't manage to take a single one of those pirates alive. That's why I was doing a stupid thing like chasing after one of them in the pitch black and ended up buggering my foot.' He snorted. 'We can't take a man like Regis down without having someone to stand up and point a finger, and there's no one left who can do that. Kol doesn't want to know. We have to let him go. For now. So best you're out of the way.'

'But what about the Dag?'

'Already on his way to the mines, nice and quiet. A few weeks from now he'll be a thousand miles away where no one gives a fig what he says. And no one comes back from the mines. He'll most likely be dead before the winter.'

'But won't he ... ?' Berren shivered. He had visions of snuffers, creeping after him everywhere he went. 'Master, won't the harbour-master ... Isn't he going to try to ...'

'He'll watch us, lad, and we'll watch him, and sooner or later he'll be doing something he shouldn't and I'll be there waiting for him.'

'Yeh.' Berren grinned. 'In a dark alley.' Except every time he thought of that, of the day he'd met the thief-taker, now he saw Jerrin too.

The thief-taker shook his head. 'No, lad. Not like that. That's not how it works. That makes us no better than the thieves we catch. Don't you worry. You apply yourself to learning your letters and leave our friend the harbour-master to me. Once I'm done with him, I promise you: swords.' Master Sy reached under the table. His hand came back holding another golden emperor and he slid it across the table. 'You still got the last one?'

Berren nodded. 'Most of it.'

'You remember what I told you to do with it?'

He nodded again.

'Well here's another one, lad. For your part. Now go and get it right this time.' He laughed and touched Berren lightly on the back of the hand. 'Probably best to avoid the sea-docks, though. I'd try the Point if I were you.'

The thief-taker pushed back his chair and stretched. 'Now if you'll excuse me, lad, I was up all night and I haven't had any sleep and even thief-takers have to rest. So I'm going home. And you, lad, for the rest of today you can do whatever you like. Have some fun.'

Berren watched his master hobble away. From behind, the limp looked worse. And then, once the thief-taker was gone, he sat back in his chair and picked the duck-carcass clean while he stared out of the window. The summer sun was high and sunset was still hours away. He smiled the happy smile of a full belly. He walked outside and stared down the hillside towards the sea-docks and the dozens and dozens of ships from every corner of the world, all sitting there in the gleaming shimmering water. He had two emperors in his pocket. For a day, the world was his.

He saw One-Thumb again, for a moment, shouting and cursing and pleading and whimpering, and this time he smiled at that too. He thumbed his nose at his ghost and slowly walked down to the sea. Somehow, he knew the thief-taker was right. Even if he didn't quite know what it was yet, he could be anything.

Whatever. I. Like.